BOOK II
THE
PANTHEON

CARRY YOUR DEBT

E.J. CAMPBELL

MEL
ÞOM
ENE

PRESS

Carry Your Debt

The Pantheon: Book Two

Copyright © 2025 E.J. Campbell

ejcampbellauthor.com

Published by Melpomene Press.

This is a work of fiction. Names, characters, places, brands, media, and incidents are either the product of the authors imagination or are used fictitiously.

To Cass, Ash,
Chaos & Spice,
Tash, Bel
& men in corsets.

AUTHOR'S NOTE

The Pantheon series is a dark reverse harem, set primarily in a contemporary fictionalized version of the United States, and is part of the over-arching criminal underworld universe of *Imperium in Imperio*. While care has been taken to keep the writing authentic, the author is Australian, so if you find any inconsistencies or errors of any kind, please send her an email!

Contact information is in the back of the book.

Our heroine is sexually adventurous, and will have more than one love interest #whychoose. Books in this series will contain topics/tropes that some readers may potentially find distressing.

Please be mindful of your triggers before reading.

The Pantheon series as a whole will depict or reference the following (those that appear in Book II are *italicized*):

- *graphic violence*
- *criminal activity*
- *traumatic brain injury, MVA*
- *addiction, risk-seeking behavior (including drugs, unsafe sex)*
- forced sterilization
- sexual assault, sexual assault of a minor
- *death*, loss of a loved one
- *profanity*
- *MF, MM, MMF, MFM & other group sexual scenarios (all 18+)*
- primal play & CNC, *dub-con*
- breath play
- *voyeurism*
- DP
- *mild D/s*, bondage/restraints, toys
- *gentle femdom*, pegging

PLAYLIST

CRYBABY · *VOILA, phem*

INTO IT · *Chase Atlantic*

SECRETS · *PLVTINUM, NEFFEX*

WRONG WITH ME · *Traceless*

FEEL NOTHING · *The Plot In You*

FOR HER · *Xavier Mayne, ELIO, Chase Atlantic*

WISH I COULD FORGET · *SLANDER, blackbear, BMTH*

I'M A SUCKER FOR A LIAR IN A RED DRESS · *Adam Jensen*

NEW ADDICTION · *The Haunt*

BODIES · *Bryce Fox*

DRIVE YOU INSANE · *Daniel Di Angelo*

STILL HERE · *Nick Alexandr*

STARPHUCKER · *Beauty School Dropout, Royal & the Serpent*

HABIT · *Nino Lucarelli, NEEN*

LOOK WHAT YOU'VE DONE · *ROMES*

OXYTOCIN · *Chandler Leighton*

ONE NIGHT STAND YOU · *Beauty School Dropout*

DADDY ISSUES · *The Neighbourhood*

HOLDING ME DOWN · *Picturesque*

STRANGERS · *Bring Me The Horizon*

DEVILISH · *Chase Atlantic*

MY WORLD · *KILLBOY*

HURRICANE · *44phantom*

SLEEPLESS · *Dutch Melrose*

CHEMICAL · *The Devil Wears Prada*

KING OF DISAPPOINTMENT · *Echos*

CHASING HIGHS · *Too Close To Touch*

I WASN'T MADE TO FALL IN LOVE · *Miko*

DOOMED · *Bring Me The Horizon*

MAN IS BORN FREE, AND HE IS EVERYWHERE IN CHAINS.

— *THE SOCIAL CONTRACT*, JEAN-JACQUES ROUSSEAU

THE PANTHEON

Sabine • *The Librarian* • Winters

Jackson 'Jax' • *Zeus* • Grayson

Rhett • *Dionysus* • Orbison

Tristan • *Apollo* • Sinclair

Lake • *Hermes* • Miller

Callum • *Ares* • Jameson

Atlas • *Hades* • Rhodes

IMPERIUM IN IMPERIO
CRIMINAL UNDERWORLD

CONCORDIA
Neutral

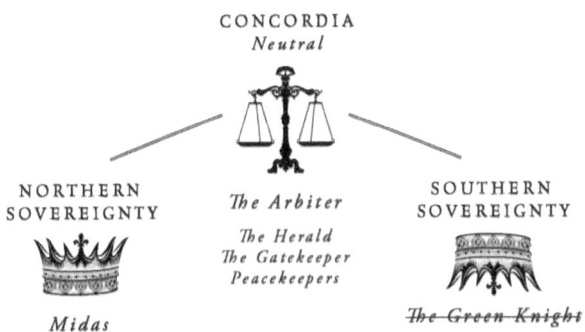

NORTHERN
SOVEREIGNTY

The Arbiter

The Herald
The Gatekeeper
Peacekeepers

SOUTHERN
SOVEREIGNTY

Midas

~~The Green Knights~~

SOUTHERN FACTIONS
TWELVE LABORS : LEADERSHIP TRIALS

GRAY MEN (SUITS)
The Gray Man
2 HEIRS COMPETING

IRISH MOB
Smiley O'Sullivan & Cashel Reilly
2 HEIRS COMPETING

STRANGE ACES MC
Trick Mahoney
1 HEIR COMPETING

ESCONDIDO CARTEL
Carlos De León
3 HEIRS COMPETING

OTHER NOTABLE FACTIONS

THE GORDIAN KNOT
Midas
NORTHERN

ALESSI MAFIA
Sandro Alessi
NORTHERN

ASANO YAKUZA
Asano Kento
NORTHERN

ORDO AB CHAO
Four Horsemen
NEUTRAL

WHITECHAPEL FOUR
Scalpel, Ghost, Ferryman, Muse
NEUTRAL

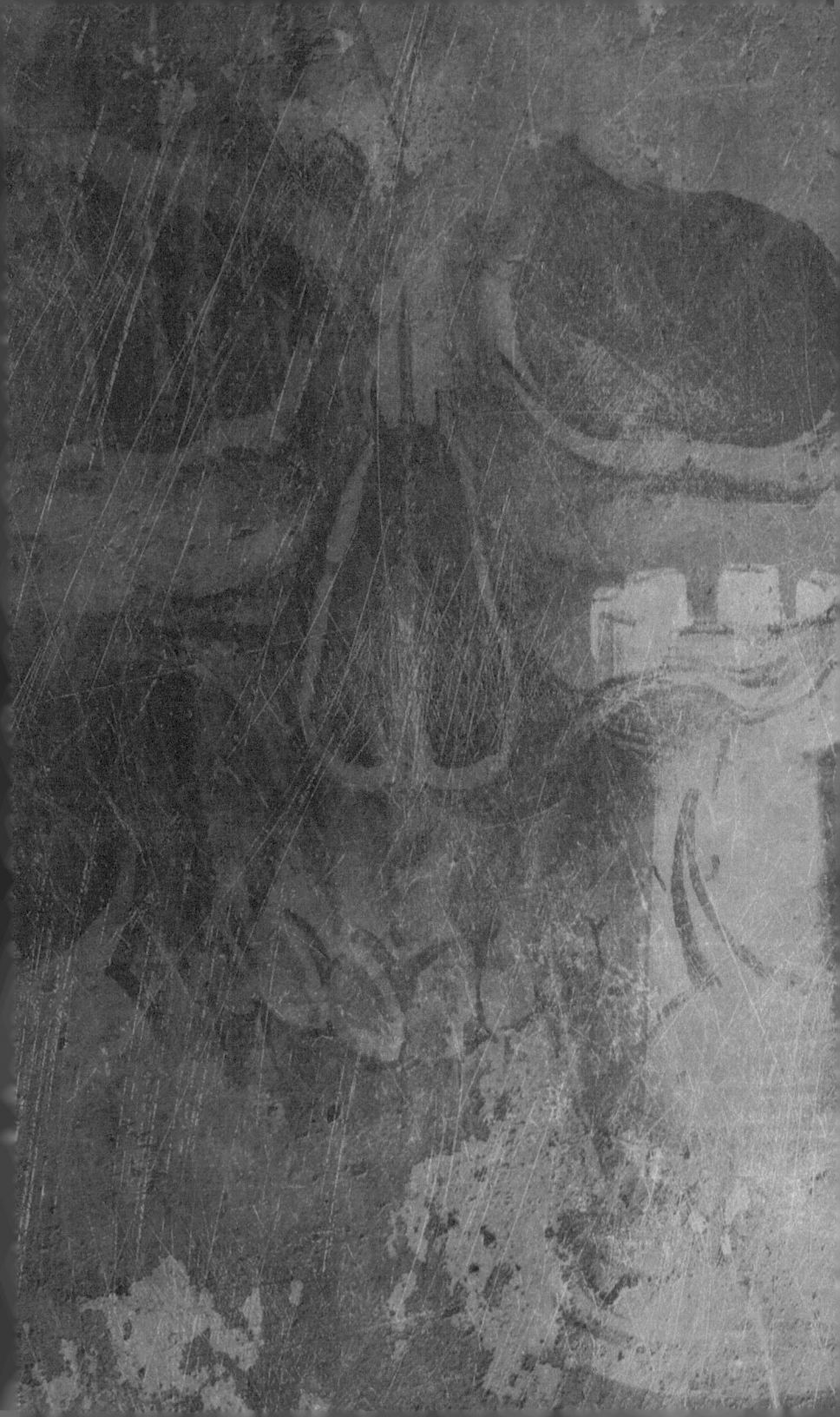

CHAPTER I

JAX · ZEUS

"YOU SEE NOW, *don't you? The Gray Man already has his replacement heir.*"

Just the simple act of swallowing is proving a feat right now, my throat working double time against the snarling mess of anxiety that's taken up residence there. It's a persistent, slow-creeping sort of dread—unleashed by the hand-delivered bombshell lying in wait for me at my office this morning.

A seed of pure chaos, eager to take root from within an unmarked envelope the moment I arrived at my desk and flicked through the mail.

At first glance, the unassuming package had seemed like a boon. Hundreds of pages, and each one filled with clandestine accounts, assets, purchases, contacts, meeting details. All brand-new-to-us information, and all of it designed to help paint an increasingly clearer picture of Sebastian's twisted intentions for our organization.

Untraceable, of course, but two months into my Crew's temporary exile—and desperate for any kind of lateral movement against my father—I was hungry and ready to count my blessings.

That was until I found myself being completely and utterly fucking blindsided by a single and concise set of DNA results from Lexington Diagnostics.

My very fate condensed into the equivalent of a two-page lab report, and casually slipped into my in-tray before the start of business.

A second biological Grayson child.

Technically, and perhaps *rationally*, I know this makes the kid family. My *half-brother*.

But that's not what I convinced myself of as I spent a solid three hours poring over every inch of Tristan Sinclair's file. The very one my Crew had put together during their Academy reconnaissance.

I only saw a son, now of age. A spare. Direct evidence of a Gray Man legacy contingency plan.

And my doom.

We'd figured for some time now that the power and protection afforded by my position would only stretch so far and for so long. Now, I can only assume that my team is being earmarked as Gray Men collateral as we speak.

Laying eyes on Sabine has certainly helped my blood pressure, and although my throat still feels as though I've been gargling broken glass, at least the steady war drum of my pulse is finally easing off. The payment for so many hours stuck in survival mode, however, is now every muscle across my back and jaw throbs with post-adrenaline fatigue.

But seeing the disturbed look on Sabine's face tells me

that getting any semblance of rest would be close to impossible, anyway.

I wince.

Fuck.

Logically, this is when I should look away. Break eye contact, stand up, regroup, and begin reviewing *our* contingency plans. After all, I can physically *see* that she's here. That she's *safe.*

But logic has not just left the building, but the entire fucking city, and those arresting gold-flecked, gray irises are doing a stellar fucking job of holding my entire body hostage. Always beautiful, but always locked down like Fort Knox, they're now quietly simmering with something akin to banked horror.

It's not an overt display of emotion by any means— but I can honestly say I've never quite witnessed this level of vulnerability from Sabine Winters before. Certainly not in the years following the Belgian's insidious 're-programming'.

It's almost...*disconcerting.*

In my periphery, I clock the minute tremor that runs through her fingers, the edges of the lab papers unceremoniously crumpling wherever she grips them. She hasn't even had a chance to read the rest of the documents yet.

"Sabine?" I croak again, the stress clear in my tired voice.

When she still doesn't answer me, my next breath feels like it takes an hour. But with her continuing silence comes an unexpected cascade effect on my own emotions. The longer I wait, the more that gnarled tangle of unease wrapped around my neck and rib cage warps, morphing slowly into something *else*.

Something that reads a whole lot more like...*satisfaction*. Preening like a proud alpha, and all because our ice queen's frigid walls appear to be melting thanks to a threat to *our* mortality.

Whatever it is, it's a harsh and greedy beast—one that, if I dare unmuzzle it, would howl my dark truth for all to hear. The truth being that for the last year, I haven't *only* wanted to protect Sabine Winters, our prized asset in an impending civil war.

No.

I've wanted to *possess* her.

And by the time I'd noticed the shift from familial affection to something...*more*, it was already too late. She'd lodged herself inside my chest like a piece of stubborn shrapnel; made a home among those quiet types of thoughts where obsession grows.

She's now the reason I spend every waking moment shoring up the walls of my self-control.

My need to compulsively second-guess each and every move on the board before I make it.

My one and *only* exploitable weakness.

My Achilles heel.

Which, of course, is why my father's strategy had involved plucking her directly out of my sphere of protection, and why giving into these darker desires of mine would only paint an even bigger target on both our heads.

Why right now, loving Sabine Winters—in *all* the ways I crave—would be nothing short of mutually assured destruction.

But that self-restraint I love to extol is dancing on a fucking knife's edge, and my thoughts are quickly turning intrusive once more. I groan inwardly as my cock kicks enthusiastically against the pleated front of my tailored pants.

Depraved images of all the ways I *could* have her, if I dared.

Consume her.

Admittedly, it'd be nothing but a half-life for either of us—but at least I'd have access to *some* part of her.

Despite the hunger that's now burning a path down my abdomen, at this very moment, I find myself needing to know how she's feeling. *What* she's feeling.

Because Sabine Winters is a fucking iceberg, and I don't think there's a single person in existence who knows exactly what lays beneath that severe, outer mask.

So, in place of mauling her, I grit my teeth and silently will my dick to back the fuck down, initiating an assessing sweep across her sharp features instead. I'm not sure what it is I'm hoping to find; reading micro-expressions and postural tells isn't exactly an option when it comes to Sabine.

But I'll work with what I've got.

What I *can* see is those mesmerizing eyes of hers are still a little glossy, a little dazed. Her skin's definitely more pale than usual, which I suppose is to be expected, given her recent shock. I do notice that the apples of her cheeks are flushed a light pink, though.

Curious. I didn't know Sabine even could blush.

My focus pulls down to that naturally pouty mouth before reluctantly continuing a clinical path down the front of a wrinkled shirt—one that's been haphazardly tucked into an equally creased skirt—all the way down to a pair of bare, sandy feet. My gaze returns along the lithe length of her, up past those subtly reddened cheeks, before ending on tousled, platinum blonde hair.

I stiffen then, clenched teeth grinding.

Jesus Christ.

She *looks* freshly fucked.

I inhale, my nostrils flaring.

Not a blush.

Freshly fucked.

The beast lowers its head, claws digging painfully into my chest wall.

Almost as if she can hear my thoughts, Sabine's lips part on a soft intake of breath. She leans back, the slightly scattered look in her eyes sharpening as she absorbs the latent hostility in my own expression. A host of stilted emotions plays out across her face: desire, then confusion...no, wait—*fear*?

But no sooner do those feelings breach the usually calm surface of Sabine's mask than they slip back under, her expression immediately cooling in their wake. All that remains then is that all too familiar apathy, and I can't help the heavy pall of disappointment that settles over my shoulders in response.

That blink-and-you'll-miss-it spark I'd glimpsed in her eyes? *I need more.*

I also need the identity of *whoever the fuck* she was just out with.

Chewing on *that* particular mystery has my pulse ratcheting right back up and my slacks tightening even further. So I stand abruptly, twisting my hips so Sabine doesn't take direct evidence of my runaway thoughts to the face.

Yet, the beast hisses, lowly. *Yet.*

Pushing an aggrieved hand through my hair, I tug on the strands in frustration. With my back still to her, I manage to pull in a single, settling breath before biting out, "Go take a shower, Sabe. We'll discuss our next movements after you've freshened up."

By some goddamned miracle, the reigning Queen of Back Talk doesn't utter a single word. She simply rises, rounds the couch, and heads in the direction of her bedroom—all in complete silence. The only sounds then are her feet as they pad softly away behind me and my own harsh breaths.

A moment later, I hear the shower kick on from behind the nearest wall. Without further thought, I find myself gravitating toward the sound, leather shoes eating up the remaining distance. My forehead thuds against the exposed brick, and my aching shoulders drop with a lengthy sigh.

However, before I can begin indulging in thoughts of Sabine less than a few feet away from me—*alone...*

naked...soaping up—I hear the gentle scratch of a key slipping into the apartment's front door lock.

I spin, Raptor in hand and aimed squarely between the amused eyes of a familiar intruder.

"Rhett," I grunt, mind still racing, and arm lowering only somewhat reluctantly as I take in his casual appearance. I suck down a growl.

Is this *who she's been with tonight?*

I've seen the looks they shoot at each other. The way they both always seem to conveniently disappear at the end of a Team night out.

"*Ohhh-ho,* Daddy Zeus is home!" my Second singsongs, completely ignoring the gun in his face and swinging the door shut with a large, booted foot.

I narrow my eyes. "...*Daddy Zeus?*"

Instead of answering, he tosses me a suggestive wink before bending down to scoop up Sabine's fallen set of keys. He drops them onto the small lamp table by the entryway like he lives here, and then he's stalking over to the kitchen, opening a cabinet, and pulling out a glass—again, like someone who's played out this routine a hundred times before.

The ease with which he moves around her space shouldn't incense me the way it does, but I can't help it. I've been forcibly iced out of Sabine's life by Sebastian's edict for months now.

Meanwhile, she's been here in Roxborough, free to do whatever she pleases.

Whomever she pleases.

They both have.

My jaw clicks.

"She's in the shower," I say gruffly, as if he can't hear the water running from a few feet away.

Rhett turns from the sink to lean lazily against the counter, drink now in hand. Striking eyes flick toward the bedroom before coming back to settle on me. He only hums in response, sipping at the water with exaggerated care. Then I'm being subjected to a slow, critical inspection; my hair and suit no doubt both looking as stretched thin and disheveled as I'm feeling.

A single blond eyebrow quirks at what he finds.

He's clearly enjoying my discomfort.

Bastard.

"Someone keeping you up at night, boss?" my world-class shit-stirring Enforcer drawls in that infuriatingly charming way of his.

What the fuck?

"Watch yourself, Orbison," I snarl back. Not even he's getting a free pass when it comes to keeping this Sabine-sized preoccupation under wraps. *No one* can know just how deep the cracks in my armor run.

It's the only way to keep her safe.

He doesn't so much as flinch at my bristling, holding up his free hand in mock surrender. He grins. "Your secret's safe with me, Capitano."

Jesus Christ. I'm way too fucking tired and on edge to be juggling *two* brats today. They're both as fucking bad as each other, and at this point, I'm not even sure whose attitude is rubbing off on whom.

What I do know is I sure as fuck need to stop thinking about them *'rubbing off on each other'* before my jaw slips and I crack a molar.

To give my shaking hands something to do other than wrap themselves around Orbison's thick, corded throat, I concentrate instead on sliding my jacket off and draping it neatly across the back of the closest dining chair. Rhett continues to smile across the rim of his glass as I carefully roll and cuff my shirt sleeves. The actions are calm and deliberate, unlike the current state of my insides.

Those are fucking *rioting*.

When his tongue darts out, gliding along his bottom lip while he observes me, the motion sends another angry jolt through me as I'm forced to picture Sabine's mouth all over again.

And what it might've been doing right before she got back to her dorm.

My gaze travels down the indolent length of him, discreetly searching for some material evidence of their sordid tryst.

A lipstick stain. Sand.

Why? Because she smelt like the beach, weed...and another man's cum.

And I need to know *whose*.

"Were you two just together?" I ask, coolly.

Evenly.

The perfect picture of restraint.

"I was just the getaway vehicle," Rhett shrugs, hooded eyes dropping to the drink in his hand. "I was just moving the Lambo off campus after I dropped her off."

With as closely as I'm watching him, however, I don't miss the spike of tension in his shoulders. Or the way he's studiously avoiding looking at me, as if that simple glass of water's suddenly become the most fascinating thing in the world.

He's throwing a massive front up, and it's not with that typical Orbison insouciance.

Just what in the hell is going on with the two of them tonight?

"Who, then?" I prompt when he doesn't elaborate.

"Miller," he answers after a beat.

"*Miller*," I spit back, though honestly, I can't say I'm surprised.

Of course, it'd be one of the fucking *Rox Boys*.

I take a heavy step forward, my teeth rattling and fists clenching against my thighs. "And what about Sinclair?"

My heart's pounding in my chest with thoughts of my half-brother's hands on her body. It should be *my* hands tracing the hollow arch of her back, *my* fingers digging into those two mouth-watering Venus dimples that frame the top of her peach-shaped ass...

"Sinclair?" he echoes, all nonchalance, and it does absolutely nothing positive for my blood pressure. Neither does that fucking eyebrow as it lifts once again in obvious delight.

Christ, I shouldn't want to commit such acts of violence against my best friend and team co-leader. I trust this man with my life, but the way he sees straight through me has me seeing crimson.

"Yes, fucking *Sinclair*. Has she been with him as well?"

Rhett straightens, abandoning all pretense along with the glass in the sink behind him before he crosses his gigantic arms tightly against his chest. The look on his face is knowing, but his voice is oddly solemn as he confirms my fear.

"Yeah, they hooked up at the Guardhouse, last weekend."

The very last of my remaining nerves fry to a crisp.

"And why do you look so fucking pleased about that?" I hiss.

"I'm...not," he hedges as if taking special care to consider his next words. But this is *Rhett*, so his pursed lips immediately tug up at the edges, shattering the sober illusion. "The only thing I'm pleased about is that Jackson Grayson is anything *but*."

Then that knowing smirk slides into a full-wattage smile, and my stomach unwittingly flips at the sight.

Like he knows he's got a direct line to my inner control, Rhett drops his arms and pushes away from his relaxed post against the counter. Evidently, at some point in our confrontation, I'd moved toward the threshold of the tiny modern kitchenette, and so my second-in-command is right up in my face with only two swaggering steps.

A single, inked fist wraps around my already

loosened tie and tugs, gently. It's not the first time Rhett's flirted with me, but this time? This time, I feel that tug somewhere *much* further south.

"It used to be enough, y'know? Burying ourselves in a few too many drinks, and a warm body or two for the night."

Somber olive-green eyes dart between mine, dissecting me in that studious way only he can. My loyal shadow for so many years, he must recognize each conflicted feeling reflected there as easily as he can his own.

I both love it and hate it in equal parts.

"Nothing lasting. Nothing serious. Nothing ever more important than just getting off," he rasps.

But it's no longer enough, I want to say, instead finding myself struck dumb by the sheer potency of being in such close proximity to the man I consider my best friend and right hand. After so many weeks apart, it's almost the same level of smothering relief as being reunited with Sabine.

His forehead meets mine. *It's not enough anymore,* he silently agrees.

It occurs to me that I haven't had the chance to properly catch him up on the events of this morning—opting instead to spend the day reading up about Tristan and his friends while plowing through a bottle of Jameson. And now, for some reason, instead of diving into the usual debriefing, tonight seems to be the night the first domino of our collective self-control has decided to tip itself.

All of the tension that'd been culminating for months before our exile, balanced so precariously, still uncertain on which way it wants to fall.

I swallow, and that rusted, barbed wire in my throat?

It's a jagged fucking thing, and it only tightens its grip further.

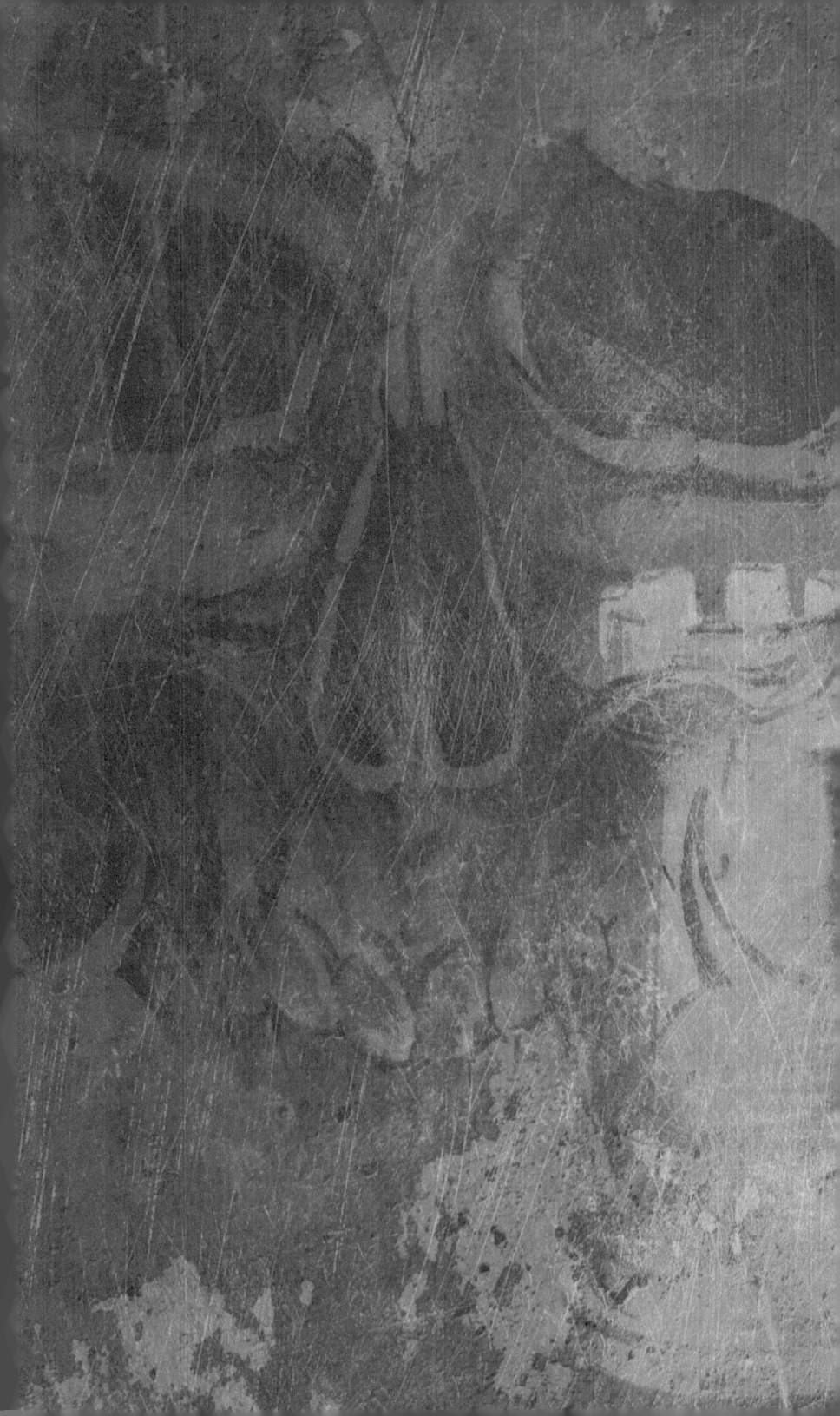

CHAPTER II
JAX · ZEUS

"PARTY OF TWO, or party of three?"

Rhett and I break apart as Sabine's throaty laugh floats across the small apartment, slicing through the growing fog of tension with all of the subtlety of a hand grenade. I groan inwardly when the fingers that were just wrapped around my tie drop, brushing against my abdomen.

But then I turn and catch sight of *her*.

She's wearing nothing but a soft, oversized men's t-shirt, leaving her long legs and feet bare. I can also see a hint of her elaborate back tattoo peeking over one shoulder, right where the stretched collar has slipped down her arm. Her freshly washed hair is pushed back and away from her face, showing off the jagged scar along her temple in a style that's as equally effortless and full of attitude as she is.

She saunters toward where we're standing in the tiny kitchenette, still close but no longer toe-to-toe. Her attention swings back and forth between us as she closes the distance, and it's almost heady, having her focus laced as it is with muted excitement.

I straighten, nervous anticipation pooling in my gut. There's no trace of that earlier hesitance anywhere on her face, almost as if our shocking conversation never took place at all.

This is the Librarian I'm more familiar with—all sass, all pure confidence.

"Don't mind me, I'll just..." she murmurs as she shimmies past before slinging herself up and onto the counter directly beside us. There's a quick tease of black boyshorts when the shirt she's wearing rides up. "You won't even know I'm here," she finishes with another serving of trademark Winters sauce.

Entirely unruffled by her interruption, Rhett slinks toward Sabine so that he can slot his hips directly between her knees. A large hand lands on each side of her tattooed thighs, caging her in. "I don't think anyone's forgetting *you're* here, babygirl," he purrs.

Her legs squeeze shut at the sound of his husky voice, and my jaw ticks reflexively.

He's not wrong though.

But just as they're drawing closer, gray eyes flick up over his shoulder as if instinctively seeking out my reaction—and if I didn't know any better, I would've said that slight falter I saw in her expression looked almost...sheepish.

Regardless, there's no ignoring the way the atmosphere in the small room has thickened with Rhett's sultry words.

It's *expectant*—and whatever it is that's been slowly awakening between the three of us expands even further —breathing in and out like it's a living thing.

Without warning, Rhett lifts a single hand, gripping the collar of his Henley and pulling it off in a single, smooth motion. He drops the shirt to the floor without a word, and my already erratic heartbeat skips once again as I'm greeted by the broad, inked muscles of his back, stretching and contracting with each movement.

Only this time, it's not skipping beneath the press of anger.

No, not...*anger*.

This time, it's beneath the choking surge of molten lust. Entwined with a healthy dose of dominance.

A need to claw back some semblance of control from this utter fucking shitshow of a day.

To punish Orbison for his over-familiarity with the object of my obsession.

To punish *her* for the hold she has over me.

And so help me—*to punish us all for my lack of restraint.*

Each thought comes with a renewed rush of blood to the groin; my intent no doubt crystal clear from the scorching look I now run down her torso, snagging on where their pelvises press lightly together.

Rather than stopping to overthink it, I'm stepping right up behind my best friend. Bracing myself against the counter with one hand, I then place the other directly between his naked shoulder blades. My palm glides over each of the twitching muscles there before finally settling against the back of his neck.

Rhett's skin is searing hot against mine, and I can smell the slight musk of his afternoon workout. Sabine's sandalwood scent, fresh from the shower, is stronger still, and it hangs around us all like a haze. I feel the moment a single breath shudders out of the man beneath my grip, his head gently dropping forward.

No resistance, just a deep knowing of exactly what it is I need right now. Easily handing me the reins.

One down. One to go.

Silently, I press downwards.

With a soft groan, Rhett lowers to his knees, hands automatically moving from the counter's edge to Sabine's bare legs as he goes. His palms run up and over the scarred skin there, before slipping beneath the shirt's hem to seek out the waistband of her underwear.

Meanwhile, my hand stays firmly in place at the back of my Second's neck. I don't dare reach out and touch her; the handle on my control is tenuous at best.

But my focus? *All on her.* Mesmerized by the rise and fall of her breasts. The flexing of her thighs. On that mocking glimpse of black material.

Rhett's fingers pause. Obediently awaiting my next instruction.

"Lift," I all but bark.

There's a split-second hesitation before I see the resolve gathering behind her eyes. That tells me she knows she's venturing into unfamiliar territory, and now she's feeling defensive. Desperate to test the limits of this new dynamic. To push back against the role I'm assigning her for this very unprecedented encounter of ours.

"What—" she starts, but I'm having exactly none of it tonight. She might be familiar with all of Orbison's play styles, but she's in *my* dominion now.

I lean down, dropping my chin so we're directly at eye level with one another. So there's no way she can miss my words. Or my intentions for her.

"For just *once* in your fucking life, Sabine, I want you to shut that bratty mouth of yours long enough to follow a goddamn directive," I grit out, my voice harsh, but still heavily laced with months of undisguised need. "Now, wrap those thighs around Orbison's ears, and the *only* two words I want passing your lips are: *'yes'* and *'sir'*."

Sabine's eyes flare wide with my words, and I'm practically scorched by the blatant heat I see reflected back at me. I watch greedily as her lids lower, her lips roll inward, and her legs stretch out on either side of Rhett's head.

So, despite having *the* most stubborn, independent streak of anyone I've ever known, it seems Ms. Sabine Winters *does* have it in her to submit, after all.

"Lift," I order again, and this time her hips tilt up without so much as a blink. Rhett snags her panties and drags them down her long legs, raising her ankles above his head as he goes. She helps him kick them off before they join his discarded shirt.

Freed of her underwear, Sabine moves to drop her calves back to rest on each of Rhett's broad shoulders. The motion causes the huge tee she's wearing to pool at her hips.

"Shirt, too," I hiss, and a heartbeat later it joins the rest of the pile on the kitchen floor.

My teeth sink sharply into my bottom lip, my brain struggling to reconcile its first glimpse of Sabine's fully naked form. Her pale chest rises and falls, focus flitting between the tousled head hovering between her thighs— and the fiery gaze now burning a slow trail between those perky, pierced tits and that gorgeous, glistening pussy of hers.

The source of all my most tortured fantasies.

I can tell she's simply dying to open her mouth and say something. *Anything.* No doubt she's used to calling the shots in bed. Or at least, she's used to always being given the *choice.*

It's a brave new world, princess.

"Lips sealed, and eyes on mine."

Her dusky eyes glimmer and her throat bobs as my command settles over her skin. Again, she only gives me a whisper of emotion, but I read it for the subtle flash of relief that it is. Slowly realizing that when she's with me, the burden of decision-making can be lifted, if only for these few stolen moments.

"Well done. Your reward for listening will be Orbison's mouth on your pretty little pussy."

Another breath heaves out of Sabine's lungs, and Rhett releases his own heady groan in anticipation. The combination of the two has both my chest *and* groin tightening to the point of pain.

I barely need to signal my assent, as no sooner do my

fingers press into the sides of my Enforcer's neck, than he's burying his nose against her clit and swiping deep with his tongue.

One of Sabine's hands shoots out to grasp a handful of dirty blond locks, and I find myself paralyzed again, riveted by the scene before me. I can hear the wet glide and contact of their skin. Smell the tangy fragrance of her arousal.

"I bet she tastes fucking decadent," I coax.

As Rhett's lips continue to weave their sensual dance, I let my palm drift north with the natural movements of his head. My fingers drag gently over his scalp before sliding firmly over Sabine's—connecting where they're still buried in his hair. Her breath hitches as she watches our grips interlocking before realizing her mistake and her eyes fly back to my face.

I *could* punish her, but there'll be a better time to explore that particular transgression another day.

When we're in a proper bed and I have access to my *collection.*

So I tighten my hold on Rhett's locks instead, purring down at him, "That's it, perfect, darling. Enjoy that sweet cunt, and then I'll have you taste us both together."

I'm rewarded with a desperate noise from deep within his throat—a reaction to my praise, the spur-of-the-moment pet name, or perhaps a combination of both—before his languid oral ministrations visibly speed up.

Sabine's head drops back in response, and I can see her composure wavering, her eyes struggling to maintain their focus on me. She's definitely close.

But her lips stay pressed together.

Let's see if she remembers her instructions.

"Such an obedient girl for us, but I think it's time. Are you ready?"

Without skipping a beat, she locks me down with those gray eyes and breathes the magic words. "Yes, *sir.*"

Holy. *Fuck.*

The next swallow I take feels like sandpaper all over again, and I squeeze her fingers, still laced with mine. "You can let go," I urge, my voice as strained as the front of these fucking infernal pants. "*Now.*"

Fortunately, it's only mere seconds before I witness her peak, tattooed thighs audibly snapping close around Orbison's head the moment she tips over. Her moan is long and low and raspy and, quite honestly, the most beautiful sound I've ever heard.

I only wish that she'd been making that noise while she was riding my cock instead of my best friend's tongue.

From the corner of my eye, Rhett rises gracefully to his feet, one hand gripping the bulge in his sweatpants. As he turns to lean against the counter beside Sabine, the change in position leaves me with an unrestricted, full frontal view of her pussy—swollen and pink and slick.

Then I'm sucking in a single breath before letting out a snarled, "*Fuck it,*" and it's the last deliberate action I make.

The beast takes full fucking advantage of my vulnerability and snaps its leash completely.

Foolish.

I was so busy monitoring *her* fall that I'd failed to clock how dangerously close *I* was to a full-core meltdown. I should have been tripping all sorts of emergency shutdown protocols before letting myself get to this point.

Instead, the edges of my vision darken and my hands seize Sabine by the waist, jerking her roughly toward me. I don't remember unbuckling my belt, nor unzipping my trousers, but between one heartbeat and the next, I'm plunging inside her.

Vaguely, I feel shapely nails clawing at the back of my shirt.

Narrow hips cinching around mine.

I hear the harsh, rhythmic breaths echoing between us and I smell her shampoo where my nose is buried against her hair.

I think I might hear Rhett's low, hoarse words of encouragement, but they're lost as soon as they reach my ears. Because despite all the intimacies of this moment, the most primal parts of my hindbrain have firmly taken over, and my entire consciousness has zeroed in on that one, perfect, singular connection between us.

I'm inside her.

Hot, tight.

And *mine.*

There's no gentle warning for what comes next. Our joint orgasms are as sudden and violent and all-consuming as my obsession. My vision blacks out completely, my only concern at that moment being the very real need to pump her cunt full of my seed.

And so the madness grows.

When I finally come back to myself, it's to the sound of jagged panting. And then to the image of Sabine's elfin face—eyes wide, pupils blown, high cheekbones tinged rosy pink.

She's a picture of pure satiation, and it stirs a pleased rumble in my chest.

Now I'm staring at her mouth, like it's begging me to suck on that plump upper lip. I'm desperate to tease my tongue along the piercing I know I'll find hiding behind it. I definitely should've kissed her long before we made it to this point, but they do say there's no time like the present.

I lean in.

A gravelly *"fuck,"* cuts in from our immediate left.

Annoyed by the sudden interruption, I turn my head to find Rhett, breathing like he's the one who just had a blackout fuck. My eyes drop to find his sweats shoved down, a cum-covered fist still wrapped around his dick, and slick fingers toying with the bars of his ladder. His hot gaze is locked to where I'm still buried inside Sabine.

Kiss forgotten, all three of us watch, fixated, as I make a slow, dramatic show of withdrawing my cock. Sabine's pussy—just as stubborn as the girl herself—never stops fighting to relinquish its stranglehold. It's not until the head forcibly slips free that our combined fluids can flow out.

I think I stop breathing altogether when Rhett leans over, scoops up the mess with two thick fingers, and then pushes the lot back inside. "Waste not, want not, baby," he teases her before turning his attention to me.

Our eyes lock, and my hand shoots out to grab his bicep, my grip rough. My head, at this point, is still pure chaos, and speech feels cumbersome.

"*Taste us*," are the only two words my tongue is able to form, but I still manage somehow to lace them with enough dominance that Rhett and Sabine both moan in unison.

Just as smoothly as he did before, Rhett kneels down between us. His fists—one still covered in cum—rest on his massive thighs, his hair an absolute mess from our grasping fingers. I expect his focus to pull back to our girl like a magnet, but as I step closer, his eyes remain trained on my still *very* hard dick. He watches as my thumb and index finger form a tight ring around the base of my shaft before sliding along its length, deliberately gathering mine and Sabine's combined releases as I go. As soon as I finish coating the head, I step forward and press it against Rhett's waiting lips.

And with another deep groan that Sabine and I both echo—Rhett proceeds to make an absolute meal of my basted cock.

His talented tongue laves and swirls and caresses, replacing our mixed fluids with nothing but his own saliva, and when he deems the job done, he slides off my length with an audible pop and a salacious grin.

Fuck.

My mouth hangs open.

I should really tell him how fucking amazing that was, how well he did for me.

How nothing between us can or will ever be the same.

But I'm still stuck in my post-coital fog, still at a complete and utter loss for words.

It's Sabine, of course, who recovers first and breaks our heated stare-off.

"Holy *fucking* bucket list, Batman."

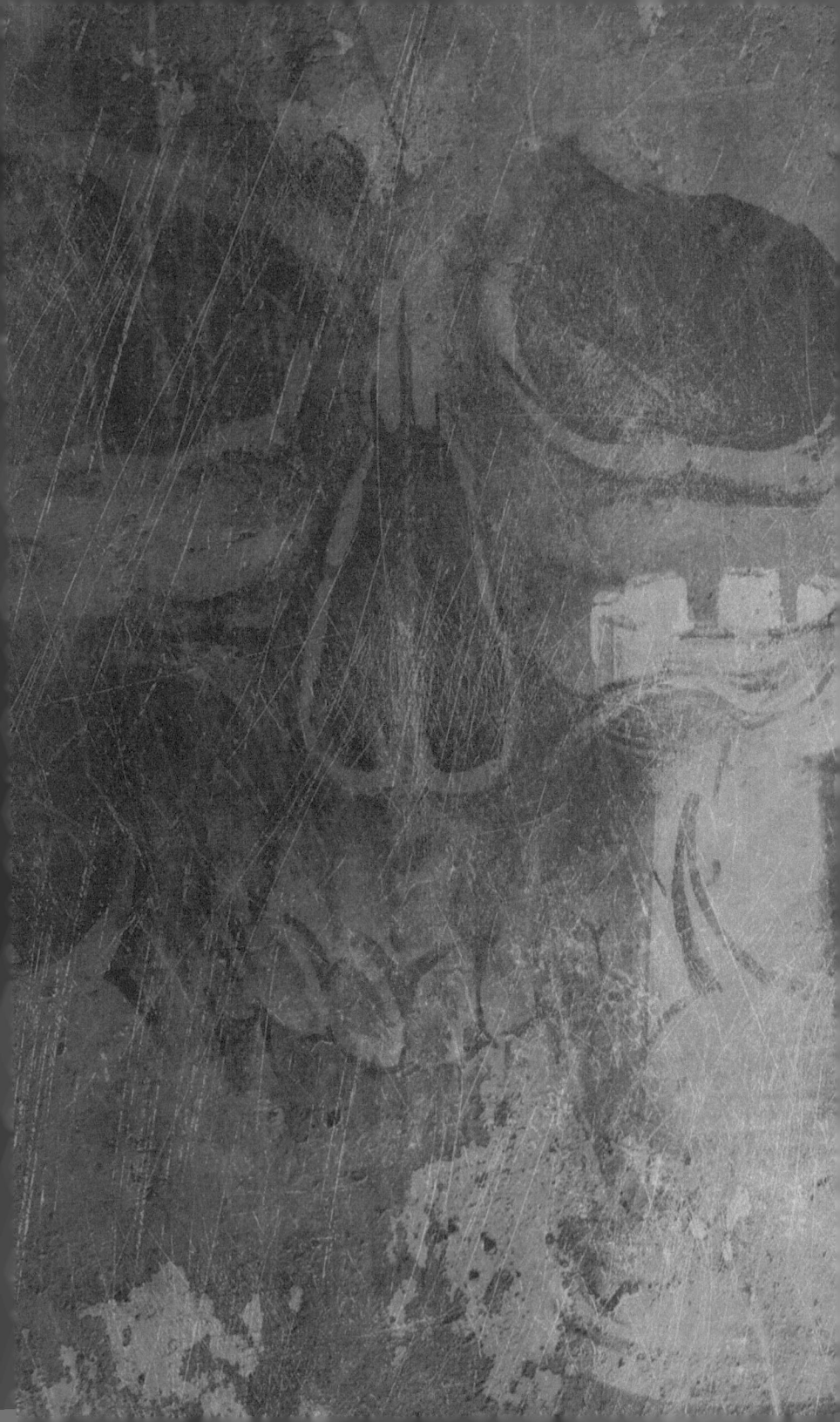

CHAPTER III

SABINE

"DON'T YOU MEAN *FUCK-IT* LIST?" Dionysus snickers as he stands, shooting me yet another of those wide, carnal smirks of his. It's a classic Rhett Orbison move that even on its own could threaten spontaneous impregnation—but then he goes and follows it up by lazily dragging his tongue over the hand he just finished jerking off with.

My teeth sink straight into my lip at the sight, and I quickly cross my legs. I'm a complete sucker for a man who doesn't balk at his own taste, so watching him lap up the aftermath like that? *Always hot.*

Not as hot as watching him do the same thing to Zeus's massive cock, though.

Good. Fucking. Lord.

I'm going to be walking in cursive for days.

The man in question only shakes his head at Dio's antics, tucking himself away while muttering darkly beneath his breath. Agitated fingers spear through equally dark hair.

Oh, hell no, mister.

Not even that signature eye roll of yours will be spoiling this absolute fucking unicorn of a moment for me.

Because not only is there now a gentle lull in the noise that infects my brain on the daily—it's all thanks to tandem orgasms, delivered by *these* two men in particular.

So I *double dog dare* Jackson Sebastian Grayson to try stoic-ing his way out of this easy chemistry—the evidence of which is currently pooling on the counter below me, despite Dio's best efforts to dam the flow with his fingers.

Which definitely shouldn't have been as much of a turn-on as it was.

"Whatever you call being party to some of my deepest fantasies come to life," I shrug, purposefully ignoring the furrowed brows aimed at the side of my head. I settle my weight back onto my palm instead.

"Two men, together? *Check*," I drawl, emphasizing with a languid air tick against my imaginary list. "But *you* two, together? That's *extra* credit."

Dio sweeps the two of us an appropriately sarcastic half-bow before sidestepping to the sink to finish cleaning up. "You're welcome," he shoots back over one shoulder as the tap flicks on.

Such a cocky motherfucker. But it's a sickening good look on him.

And now I'm wondering why he's never mentioned the two of them having a thing before today.

"Sooo...Exactly how long have you guys been

hooking up?" I ask, all super casual-like. I'll never admit it, but I *may* be slightly more jealous that they didn't share this with me than I am annoyed that I apparently missed all the signs.

"Oh, about thirty minutes, give or take," is D's deadpan answer as he flicks droplets of water in my direction. All while still completely nonplussed, as per the Orbison playbook.

My jaw unhinges.

Zeus, on the other hand, spins and paces directly away from us, only stopping when he reaches the threshold of the living area. The only view I have right now is the back of his head, but it's safe to assume, with the way his shoulders roll back, that he's busy tugging his armor back into place.

My first thought is he must be having a harder time processing their brand new dynamic than I initially thought, given how natural it seemed. They've been best friends and Crew partners for years, so I'm curious if it's something he was even aware was brewing—or if it came completely out of left field for him as it did for me.

But then he turns and it's *me* he pins with a challenging look, not our Enforcer. My spine immediately straightens when I see his pinched expression.

"That's all it was, then? Some sort of erotic wish fulfillment?" Zeus grates out, skating right on past D's little reveal.

I blink, and a small line forms between my brows.

I know that somewhere beneath the thorny, sarcastic

exterior exists a small part of my heart—as withered and emotionally stunted as it is—that's always carried a sort of pseudo-torch for the man standing directly in front of me.

A very much *unrequited* pseudo-torch, but a tiny, naked flame nonetheless.

So, to have him be the one to initiate all this? Even if all that eventuates from this little hook-up was just casual sex going forward? My younger teen self would be absolutely *crowing* right now.

Is it too soon to be updating our status to It's Complicated?

Zeus's gaze is becoming more and more a searing touch the longer it holds mine. Although he's normally so careful to guard his thoughts around us, it seems, for this moment at least, he might *actually* be opening up and allowing some of them to play out across his face.

What they are *not* saying is: *That was just casual sex.*

What they *are* saying is: *This was more.*

And with my deeply buried crush, I should be feeling fucking *ecstatic* right now.

But the problem is *more* requires…communication.

It requires empathy. Partnership. Giving, and not just *taking*.

It requires—no, *demands*—vulnerability.

All things *I* can't give him.

After all, the only committed relationship I've ever been in is with my ill-gotten Xanax prescription.

No. Zeus's been fighting so hard and sheltering us for

so long, and when this is all over, he deserves to find someone who *can* give him all those things.

They *both* do.

Which is why I can't let this get any more intimate than it already has. Not even with a kiss.

"A girl's got to have dreams—" I start, aiming for deflection, only to have Zeus cut me off with another angry huff.

"Stop, Sabe. Just *stop*," he snaps out, his frustration a palpable thing that settles in the pit of my stomach like a foreign object. My jaw grinds, and for once, I don't know what I should say to try and tease him back from the ledge. This is also not the first flicker of unease I've felt since coming home to find him waiting in the dark.

The image of Hermes's crestfallen face surfaces, unbidden.

Perhaps not even the first time today.

I almost jerk back when I feel Dio's warmth press in alongside me as he settles back against the counter. I look down at where his hot, damp skin meets mine. The simple show of affection isn't a characteristic one for either of us, and I find it oddly comforting.

I glance back up in time to catch Zeus's frown deepening. He's focused on the place our forearms touch. "Just me then," he observes, tonelessly.

"What?"

When his gaze returns to my face, all the heat that was simmering there just a moment ago is completely gone. His expression's no less fierce—it's just more of a cold burn instead. "I was the only one being used to check off your little sex list, then."

Alright, who in the actual hell body-snatched my *eternally indomitable, weather-all-storms, control freak* of a Crew Lead Grayson—because I have no fucking idea who this man is, with his hair all wild and crystal blue eyes flashing with possession.

Or why I seem to be sucking up all of the emotion leaking from that cracked composure of his like some kind of secondhand smoke.

I mean, that's got to be the only explanation for all the twisting snakes in my stomach right now...right?

Hey Google: can feelings be contagious?

"C'mon, Daddy Z, seriously? She's been mooning over you since she was sixteen," Dionysus cuts in with uncharacteristic annoyance, effectively shattering the kitchen's awkward silence.

My head instantly rears back.

"Dio, you better make your last will and testament known because you're officially about to become *very fucking dead to me*," I hiss.

The fucking traitor doesn't even bother feigning innocence. "Nah, babygirl," he drawls as he shrugs a massive tattooed shoulder at us both, "I guess your pussy's not the magical cure for blindness after all—because he *still* can't see what's right in front of his fucking face."

I don't know whose eyes go wider in response to that —mine or Zeus's. But apparently, D's not finished with his assault.

"I'm done watching the two of you silently pining for each other," he forges on, pointing an accusing finger in his best friend's stunned face for emphasis. "*You* know she has a hard time processing any kind of intimacy. You can't just ask her shit like that and not expect her to go on the defensive."

Then he turns to me, and I suck in a breath, bracing myself. The gloves are off, it seems.

"It was never going to be just a quick fuck for him, not when Zeus's feelings for you border on DSM-5 levels of obsession."

At that, my left temple begins to throb and I'm forced to keep my lips pressed tightly together in order to stave off the sudden mirth bubbling up my throat.

Because surely this is all a dream. One I'm about to wake up from—back to the harsh reality where *Jax fucking Grayson* only cares about me in the capacity of *ward* and *asset*.

Any second now.

And then I get my next surprise. Instead of an expression full of anger or guilt, our Team Lead only looks…exasperated.

"Okay, seriously, why the *fuck* do you keep calling me Zeus? Or…" His eyes darken as he presses the tip of his tongue against the corner of his lips, "…*Daddy*?"

This time I can't help barking out a laugh. It's the considering look on his face as he rolls the word around his mouth. I totally called it—he's *way* too dominant and enjoys reigning in my brat *way* too much.

Dio's brat, too, apparently.

Fingers crossed *that* leads to yet another entry being marked off the List.

"Uh, short story: I wanted to further protect our off-book surveillance of the Rox Boys by assigning them new aliases. I gave each of them a Greek god."

Dio leans further into my side, and I'm relieved to find a cheeky smile back on his handsome face. A small amount of tension eases across my shoulders.

Then he opens his big, fat mouth. Again.

"I wanted in on her budding harem, so I made her give me one too."

One of my hands connects with his chest and Dio's cheeks puff out with an exaggerated wince. Zeus doesn't miss a single part of the exchange, of course. The muscle along his jaw jumps, his eyes narrowing in our Enforcer's direction.

"I thought it was just Miller and Sinclair?"

Now my lips actually do part. "I swear to *god,* Orbison. Do you not understand the concept of *this stays between us?!*"

I wonder if I can reach that block of knives sitting on the counter directly behind him. And if these counters might be too porous for the impending bloodshed.

"You know I have to report everything back to the Bossman, baby, even pillow talk," he says, fighting and failing to hide his amusement at my indignant look.

I'm still deciding how best to carve that smug fucking look off his face when Zeus raises both a hand and an eyebrow. "Let me guess: Dio's short for *Dionysus*," he interjects mildly.

The giant, muscle-bound idiot's grin widens. "At your service."

Our Lead's gaze drops to his lips. "Fitting." The corner of his own mouth tilts, maybe even threatens to lift, but he still sounds much too terse. "And the others?"

"Tristan is pre-med, musical, revered by the student body. The golden boy. *Apollo*," I list them off, not blind to the way Zeus's face tightens at Tristan's name. "Callum's their weapons guy. He's big, angry. If they were to have an Enforcer, he'd be it. So, goes without saying—*Ares*. Lake is cyber and information, takes care of communication with their contacts. *Hermes*. Finally, Atlas is in charge of their money. Unlike the others, he's private. I also suspect he does most of their surveillance. *Hades*."

"Well, if your intentions were to form some sort of ancillary Crew, then it would only make sense for me to be Zeus, I suppose," he muses, with all the innate confidence and arrogance of a Grayson. The frown's gone, but now his look's entirely too self-satisfied for my liking.

"Don't know why you're automatically assuming leadership in *my* Pantheon," I grumble half-heartedly, but not exactly hating the way his eyes track down my body when I relax back onto my hands again.

"Because you like it when I tell you what to do," he mutters without skipping a beat, taking his first step back into the kitchen. With the way his eyes glaze, I'm not entirely sure he's even aware he took it at all.

Dio's head drops back and I feel his groan vibrate through my shoulder. "I can't believe *I'm* the one saying this, but we didn't expect to see you before the opening ceremony tomorrow night. Yet here you are—looking like the Herald herself just dropped a Kill Order with your name on it." He huffs out an exaggerated breath. "So maybe we turn *this*," he continues, circling a finger between the three of us, "down to more of a sweet simmer. Just long enough for us all to regroup, yeah?"

It's such a casually delivered jest, but the ensuing silence is so total, you could hear a fucking mouse fart.

Dio's eyes swing back and forth between us, assessing. His teasing expression slowly drops. "Wait—*seriously?!*" he exclaims, tanned cheeks now distinctly paler. "Who the fuck would even have the balls?!"

"Sebastian," Zeus replies flatly, wetting his dry lips and glancing away. Just like that, all the sexual tension of a minute ago is replaced by *actual* tension.

"Bullshit!" Dio spits out incredulously, volume rising as one large hand swipes through the air. "There's no way—*no fucking way*—The Gray Man's killing off his own fucking heir. He'd sooner rather get rid of his Codex!"

And before today, I would've one hundred percent agreed with him.

Until now, Zeus and I had both lived with and worked for the Suits fully confident that our importance to Sebastian's empire came with certain immunities.

Immunities like not being, you know, *forcibly retired.*

"There hasn't been an officially sanctioned hit," I cut in, and Dio's eyes slide reluctantly away from where he's studying Zeus's distant expression. He raises a skeptical eyebrow. "He's...found evidence Sebastian has a second biological son. One who's just come of age."

Dionysus's huge body rocks forward in shock. "You're fucking kidding. Do we know who it is?"

The look that passes between Zeus and I feels distinctly loaded, but I can't quite tell how said exchange actually makes me feel.

...Nervous?

...Guilty?

Fuck.

This is all too unfamiliar and raw, and I'm way too emotionally illiterate for this. Trying to understand what's currently happening inside my chest's like trying to decipher a set of hieroglyphics without the Rosetta Stone.

"Yeah, we do, actually," I finally manage after a harsh swallow. This goddamn acid in my stomach. Maybe I should be finding myself some TUMS instead because forcing down all these confusing sensations only seems to burn like bile.

"It's...Apollo," I force out, dipping my chin and glancing at him from beneath my lashes.

I have to bite down on my tongue as confusion, anger and amusement each take turns battling it out across his features—before eventually making way for *trouble-seeking*. Seeing his eyes glimmer with that familiar devilment is almost a relief.

There's just something so off-putting about a serious Dionysus.

I say *almost*, because of course the next words out of his cursed mouth have me wanting to reach for the knife block all over again.

"So inquiring minds *need* to know: Which of the Gray Man's spawn has the bigger dick?"

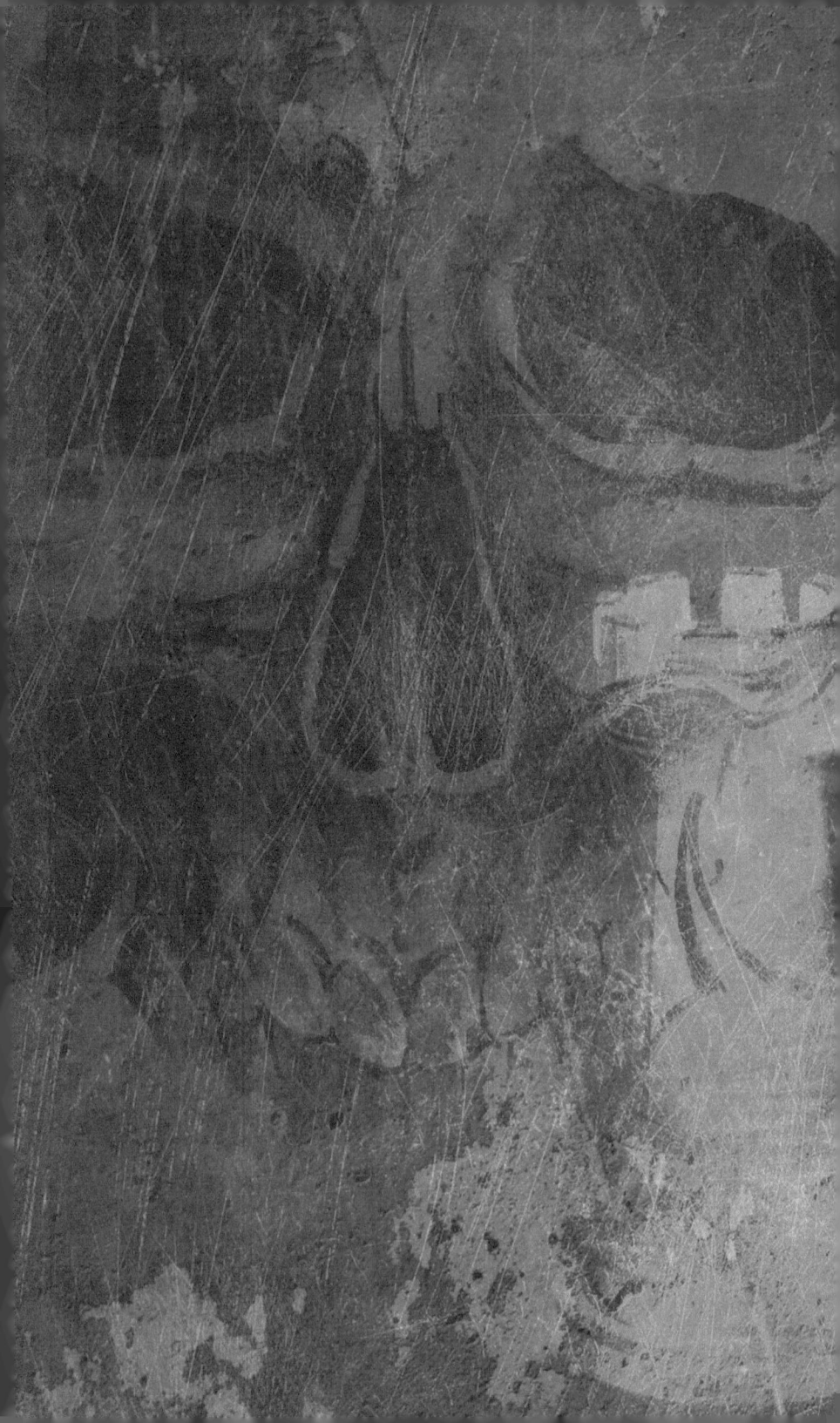

CHAPTER IV

A CURSE *on the maker of this goddamn dress, and a curse on their entire fucking bloodline.*

"Stop fussing, Sabine," Zeus snipes from the seat directly across from mine. His expression remains shuttered as he studies his phone, even though I've been huffing and puffing and drilling impatient holes into his forehead for the past thirty minutes. When his eyes *still* don't leave the screen, I decide to take advantage of his distraction and really drink him in.

Decked out in a bespoke tux of the deepest midnight blue, he looks like absolute sin incarnate and my teeth press greedily into my lower lip. There's just something about a well-fitted suit on an attractive man.

And coupled with that perfectly styled coif and neatly trimmed beard? He's back to serving *Well Put Together Team Lead*, and I'm fucking here for it.

It's not that I didn't enjoy last night's quick peek behind the curtain. I mean, the matching set of fingerprint-shaped bruises across the span of both my hips should tell you just how much I did. But so far today, I can't get a read on him—at *all*—and now I'm left blithely wondering whether the whole encounter was just a matter of me finally getting a taste of my own medicine.

No X's, just O's.

"*You* try sitting down in this thing," I eventually hiss back, trying and failing for the fiftieth time to adjust my gown's neckline so that I might be able to take at least one full fucking breath before I perish.

While the dress Dominic delivered to my dorm last weekend is objectively beautiful, I'm convinced its elaborate boning was handcrafted by Lucifer himself. Despite my tits being the reason push-up bras were invented, the bodice is still as immovable and unforgiving as a goddamn steel cage.

"Your father did this on purpose," I whine when he still doesn't look at me.

Dionysus chuckles, eyes crinkling with amusement as he watches my continued struggle. He slides his ass down the expensive leather seating, manspreading like the consummate dickhead that he is. One of his deliciously large thighs knocks obnoxiously against mine.

Mmm. Admittedly, another team member of mine who's looking like he's been practically gift-wrapped for the masses.

Dio's tux is a broader-fitting twin to his best friend's slim-cut fit, and for once, all that perpetually sex-tussled, dirty blond hair of his is slicked back neatly. His jaw's also remarkably clean of stubble.

I swear, the two of them together are enough to make

even the most stoic of angels weep, and for just a heartbeat, a small part of me wonders what might've happened if they'd both stayed the night instead of heading back to our Crew's shared Rox City apartment.

Nah, I tell myself with full confidence, *I bet Orbison snores.*

Studiously ignoring the small twinge of *what if,* I roll my eyes at our Enforcer instead.

He grins.

Finally, Zeus straightens, carefully tucking his phone away as he does. "Likely," he hums, finally deigning to acknowledge the devilry responsible for my ongoing torment. "He needs you uncomfortable, that way, you'll stay alert and observant for the full duration of the evening."

I huff, wishing I could slump back and cross my arms like Dio, but mindful of the layer of heavy-duty makeup concealing my expansive back and shoulder tattoos from prying Roxborough eyes.

I know *exactly* how his father's twisted mind works.

I am his favorite pet project, after all.

Knox, seeing me start to squirm at the mention of Sebastian, leans over and gently pats my hand. *Bless him.* I offer the big teddy bear a small but genuine smile.

Before I can muster a clap back, however, Zeus shifts again. This time it's to cross his legs. Long fingers interlock across one knee, his deep blue gaze sweeping carefully across our group.

I instantly swallow my retort.

Here we go.

It's been a tense afternoon—to say the least—with my Crew effectively being held hostage on the tarmac while we wait for the Gatekeeper to send through coordinates for this year's secret Symposium location. He's the only person with the authority to grant travel and trade rights within neutral Underworld territories, and no one can enter a host city until he gives the green light.

This also happens to be the first time the Junior Council has managed to occupy the same space since being forced to relocate to Roxborough. It's simply unfortunate the 'space' has to be the cabin of a private passenger jet sent by the Gray Man to escort us all to the event like the naughty children we are.

After sweeping the plane's interior for bugs, Zeus had then made ample use of the temporary incarceration to fill us in on the contents of the mysterious file he'd been sent. Unbeknownst to Dio and I, it hadn't *just* been the singularly explosive set of paternity results. He'd also been sent several other documents; some detailing Sebastian's latest moves on the Governorship, some his endgame bid for the Senate, and some with evidence supporting a recent toe dip into the skin trade.

That last was something that—*to our prior knowledge*—the Suits had yet to dabble in.

Information, weapons, drugs, prostitution: yes. But never before had we resorted to full-out human trafficking. It just hadn't been the Gray Men's 'style', or so our Crew'd been led to believe all these years.

Now, of course, we've been left with a whole slew of

new questions. The most important being: *So, just whose style* was *it?*

But also: *Who thought we needed to know about it?*

Despite all these new unknowns, Zeus seems to think this leak puts us in a slightly better position going into this evening's foray inside the lion's den. According to him, *any* edge over the Gray Man is better than nothing. No matter how small.

I, on the other hand, don't feel any more confident than I did last week. But if I'm honest, the only thing I *am* feeling right now is the aftermath of having had my entire rib cage fashionably and torturously rearranged since midday.

And I have several more hours of this misery left to go.

I'll show you 'fussing', mister.

After what feels like an eternity of holding my breath, Zeus finally breaks the expectant silence.

"It's being held in Themis this year," he announces, nodding grimly as the entire team sucks in a shocked breath. "Still waiting on the actual final location."

"*Fuck,*" Knox spits, prompting everyone to turn to him, eyebrows raised in varying states of surprise. Mine are personally hovering right at the jet's ceiling.

Our giant marshmallow of an Enforcer?

He *never* swears.

The tips of Knox's ears immediately turn pink in response, but I can't blame the slip.

'*Fuck*' is *exactly* what we're all thinking.

While technically a No Man's Land, the vast majority

of *Imperium in Imperio* factions still consider the city of Themis neutral ground when operating within its limits. That's because the small, unincorporated territory happens to be home to the ruling seat of *Concordia*: the lawmakers and peacekeepers for the entire Underworld, and led by the Arbiter herself.

The Symposium being hosted by none other than the *Imperium*'s very own Red Court means there's a very high chance that something truly significant is about to go down.

And in our world, significant is *never* a good thing.

"It's certainly contentious. Could be because of a high-profile trial we weren't already made aware of. But more than likely, the choice to host there is linked in some way to the unclaimed Southern crown."

Personally, I think the chances of it *not* being related to the empty throne are practically slim to none. It's been almost four months since the Green Knight's mysterious death, and we're no closer to crowning a new Sovereign than the day he died. A criminal leadership vacuum of this sort of magnitude is a truly special sort of anarchy, and the Arbiter's intervention would've become a necessary evil, sooner rather than later.

Besides, the Underworld is by no means short of gossip merchants. Even in exile, we've been able to keep our finger on the pulse. We would've definitely heard news of any upcoming Judgements well before tonight.

"Well, I guess the bright side is not even the boss would be crazy enough to pull some shit on the Arbiter's home turf," Dio muses, his dark humor a reminder of the probable death sentence now hanging over our Crew like some fucked up Sword of Damocles.

Zeus hums. "As far as we know, the Sinclair kid isn't aware of his connection to my father. So no, I doubt that's the sort of bombshell even he'd drop in the middle of a masked event known for its discretion," he agrees, though I see something like conflict flickering across his expression. "Still, it's probably best if we keep an eye on him tonight. Maybe run interference if needed. If we're lucky, Sabine can get to him first after you're all back in Roxborough."

His words are loosely disguised as a suggestion, but I still see what the order costs him in the sharp flex of his jaw. Nobody wants to take on the responsibility of protecting a person who may end up being responsible for your own demise. But at the end of the day, Apollo *is* still Jax's blood.

He's also just as much a pawn of Sebastian's as we are, and if anything, that simple fact will end up being more of a driving factor behind his decisions than a simple DNA report.

Without another word, Zeus rises, buttoning his jacket back over his silk waistcoat before leaving to inform the pilot of our destination. I shift restlessly in my seat as I watch him go, trying in vain to keep my own outfit's sharp waistline from stabbing into my churning gut.

The seat squeaks loudly beneath me, and I brace myself before glancing sideways at Dionysus, ready for more of his signature teasing. I needn't have bothered though. The asshole must've decided now is as good a time as any to take a nap because his eyes are closed, breaths already evening out.

How he can always manage to completely switch off without so much as a sleep aid, I'll never know.

Knox, however, is as far from sleep as you can get. He abruptly launches to his feet before sitting straight back down again, large hands clenching atop his thighs in distress. The dark, shaggy mop that normally crowns his head has been carefully tamed into a short tail at his nape, and—like the other two men—both he and Foster are wearing tuxedos designed to compliment the deep, inky blues of my dress.

All part of Sebastian's game of control, I'm sure.

My gaze flicks from our unsettled Second Enforcer and over to our introverted Security Officer. Foster's auburn locks are neatly parted to one side, and his sharp cheekbones look remarkably pale. Even after hours together, I'm still a little taken aback to see the pair of black frames perched on his narrow face. Typically, he hates needing glasses, opting only to wear them when he has to spend hours staring at his monitors.

"You alright?" I mouth as soon as his red-rimmed gaze flicks to mine. He doesn't answer, but he does grant me a small nod. For just a split second, I swear his eyes slide over my chest before darting back up to the small window at his left.

That's fucking weird, even for Foster.

But further introspection of my Crew mate's oddball behavior is interrupted by the stern figure of Zeus striding his way back down the narrow aisle.

His shoulders are straight, ticking jawline now set in place.

"Wheels up in five."

Oh shit.

He's in battle mode.

Looks like it's finally time to get this shitshow on the road.

THE MOMENT the town car pulls up to the mysterious final location—sent via a second encrypted message after entering Themis—is the moment the rest of my Crew collectively begins to lose their shit. My poker face, on the other hand, has hundreds of practice hours logged, and it slips into place as soon as my heeled toe hits the roped-lined entranceway.

Of course, I don't manage so much as a step forward before both Enforcers are up and out of the vehicle and crowding my back. I don't know why they bother; no paparazzi will be greeting our arrival on this red carpet.

Zeus places a firm hand on my hip, and as they begin escorting me up the guided walkway, I swear I can almost *hear* the internal crises he and Knox are sharing as they unfold in real time.

Foster's glasses fog as he takes in the building before us and his breathing speeds up.

Dionysus, undeterred by this latest curveball, is instead in his fucking element. "Lady and gents, get ready because *shit. Is. About. To. Go. Dooown,*" he trumpets, head tipped back and palms cupped around his mouth like some kind of deranged sportscaster.

Luckily for me, the single saving grace of this accursed gown is that the bodice's design doesn't impede the movement of my arms at all. *"Babe,"* D manages to wheeze out when I land a nice jab to the idiot's ribs. He should know better than to stand so close behind me when my elbows are almost sharp enough to qualify for concealed carry permits.

"Keep it down, *jackass,*" I mutter back, though my focus remains locked on the imposing colonial brick monolith now rising before us.

Unfortunately, he's not wrong. Shit *is* about to go down.

Because as it turns out, tonight's event is not only being hosted *by* the Red Court—it's being hosted *at* the Red Court.

"Masks on," Zeus instructs in a perilous tone, and the stark reminder that we're all about to step into a building teeming with hundreds of Underworld VIPs is more than enough to sober up the entire group, including our resident lord of misrule.

I comply, ready to head toward the main doors, when long fingers reach out to snag my wrist. Crystal blue eyes flash darkly from behind the feathered disguise now covering the upper portion of Zeus's handsome face. He leans in, warm lips brushing the shell of my ear before delivering a heated, *"Be good."*

The murmured warning sends a lick of arousal down

my spine, each hair on the nape of my neck flaring in response.

God. Damn.

I have to tilt my chin away from him, battling against the pleased smirk that's threatening to take over my mouth.

Was I completely off in my assessment earlier? Was last night *not* a one-and-done for him, after all?

Wait, no. *Fuck.*

This is precisely why I don't do the whole dating thing. I never have to worry about this sort of confusing song and dance when I'm the one who's calling all the shots.

Sadly, the bratty scowl I shoot back at him is wasted, hidden by my own matching half-mask. Regardless, the rebellious intent must still be perfectly evident because he nudges me firmly up the front steps.

The entire perimeter of the massive, copper-colored building swarms with unmasked *Concordia* guards and officials, all dressed in black attire with logos in their signature red. Directly outside the front entrance, there's a petite man in a smart, aubergine suit who's busy greeting each guest before permitting them to step inside.

"Invitation," *Marcus Nielman, 43*, prompts with an impatient flick of his wrist.

Zeus holds out the ornately embossed black card he received on behalf of the junior representatives of the Gray Men syndicate. Sebastian and his Senior Council will enter together, with the more traditional members of the *Imperium in Imperio* being very big on keeping the younger generations separated and 'in their place'.

Another terse gesture from Marcus and then we're joined by a set of guards who usher us onto the second checkpoint. This time, we're subjected to a biometric eye scan and mandatory equipment check-in since no single person is permitted to enter a Symposium event while armed.

Names are never formally exchanged during this entry process, though an identifiable record of each attendee is kept for the weekend on the off chance a guest finds themselves in violation of the Law of Hospitality. So, with no official electronic guest list to pull from later, my presence at these sorts of events becomes more important than ever.

The third and final checkpoint is a secondary weapons pat down.

I'm not sure if it's just because we're all a little on edge or if the guys maybe sprinkled extra testosterone on their Wheaties this morning, but *both* Dionysus and Zeus let out matching growls when the *Concordia* attendant gets a little handsy while checking my skirts for hidden blades.

"Down boys," I scold, throwing them a mock glare over my shoulder, though somewhat mystified at their behavior. Albeit not as mystified as poor *Niles Whiting*, 26, I'm sure. I shoot the man with his sweaty hands on my exposed thigh what I hope is my best chagrined smile. "My apologies, I haven't finished house-training them yet. They're still get a little nervous around crowds."

Wisely, Niles doesn't utter a single word in response. His neck does remain a mottled scarlet though, as he hurries through the rest of my full body pat down at double speed.

Finally, when the five of us are each officially cleared for entry, our group is signaled to continue on through to the main atrium.

Soaring domes of stained glass, russet-colored stone blocks, and gothic chandeliers give the red-lit chamber a harsh, almost foreboding atmosphere. There's absolutely no warmth to the massive, decadent space, despite the fact this year's event is very much underway and it's already filled with writhing bodies.

In fact, it's how I would imagine stumbling onto one of the outer rims of Hell must feel.

Quite fitting, really.

Nobody acknowledges our entrance. Most guests are either entrenched in conversation, covertly watching one of the public displays of debauchery, or are themselves indulging in one of the sundry vices on offer.

Zeus keeps a possessive hand pressed to the small of my back, using it to steer me past a cluster of Victorian fainting-style couches and toward what appears to be an empty space next to one of the eastern wall's alcoves. Smoke and low chatter ring the elaborately masked heads of the Underworld members occupying them.

No matter my Crew's heavy feelings on the subject, it doesn't change the fact that we're here—*formally*—on behalf of the Suits, and as their Librarian, it's still my job to *observe, observe, observe*. That means my focus needs to remain as sharp as it would during any field mission, and not a single lackey in attendance can escape my notice.

So my face remains carefully neutral as I instinctively trace over each of the men's faces, absorbing identifying features and ignoring the half-naked Courtesans scattered at their feet and draped across their laps for efficiency's sake.

They all appear to be middlemen for Southern factions. Mostly Irish, but a few of them I know are tied to the stateside chapter of the British Islington crime firm.

To ensure I don't miss anybody important, however, I do need to stop and start carefully sectioning off the room in its entirety, which is best done using mental quadrants. Probably why Zeus picked the gap on the eastern wall in the first place; it'll work well as a starting point, giving me a straight shot of the entrance, the bar, the small curtained stage that's been raised for the event, as well as the stairs that lead to the upper chambers of the Court.

When I finally reach our designated spot, Dio and Knox take up their posts, immediately bracketing me like a pair of overly muscled bookends. Their matching black half-masks do absolutely nothing to hide their matching intimidating scowls. Zeus, conversely, plants himself directly in front of our group. One hand casually slips into his pocket, his shoulders angling in a subtle offer of privacy. I'm not exactly sure where Foster ended up during my trek.

Having the rest of my Crew close by does help settle some of the acid that's started eating away at the center of my chest, but my lungs still feel tight at the thought of having to face the Gray Man himself at some point tonight. Knowing I can't afford to be off my game for even a moment, I pull in a single, fortifying breath—an open invitation for my old friend, the killing calm, to slide on in and join me as my plus one for the evening.

Unfortunately, just standing around like finely dressed wallpaper always feels awkward at these types of hands-on parties. As if having heard my thoughts, Foster chooses that exact moment to re-materialize, silently thrusting a flute of champagne in my direction. I accept it with a bewildered *thanks* before he's gone again, melting back into the crowd like a trained spook.

Okay, then.

Obviously, I can't imbibe, but I'm still oddly grateful he's given these idle hands of mine something to do, despite his weird behavior.

Zeus eyes my decoy drink, then glances toward a passing server whose tray holds nothing but tall, elegant, crystal-cut glasses. "I'm going to go grab a whiskey so we can keep this looking as casual as possible," he mutters before he too disappears, this time in the direction of the open bar.

And now that I'm no longer being blocked by his tall, protective figure, I finally get my first real, unimpeded view of this year's Symposium, in full swing and in all its hedonistic glory.

A tingle of adrenaline skips its merry way across my

scalp in anticipation, and I roll my shoulders, ready to begin working. Usually, having to catalog such a large group of people would result in a hefty mental recall cascade effect, just from the sheer volume of faces alone.

In this instance, however, having to first sift through a sea of obscuring masks and elaborate formal wear usually helps slow down the barrage of data. There's no way I won't go to bed later without a splitting migraine, but I should hopefully at least make it through to dinner before my brain starts leaking out of my ears.

Well, here goes nothing.

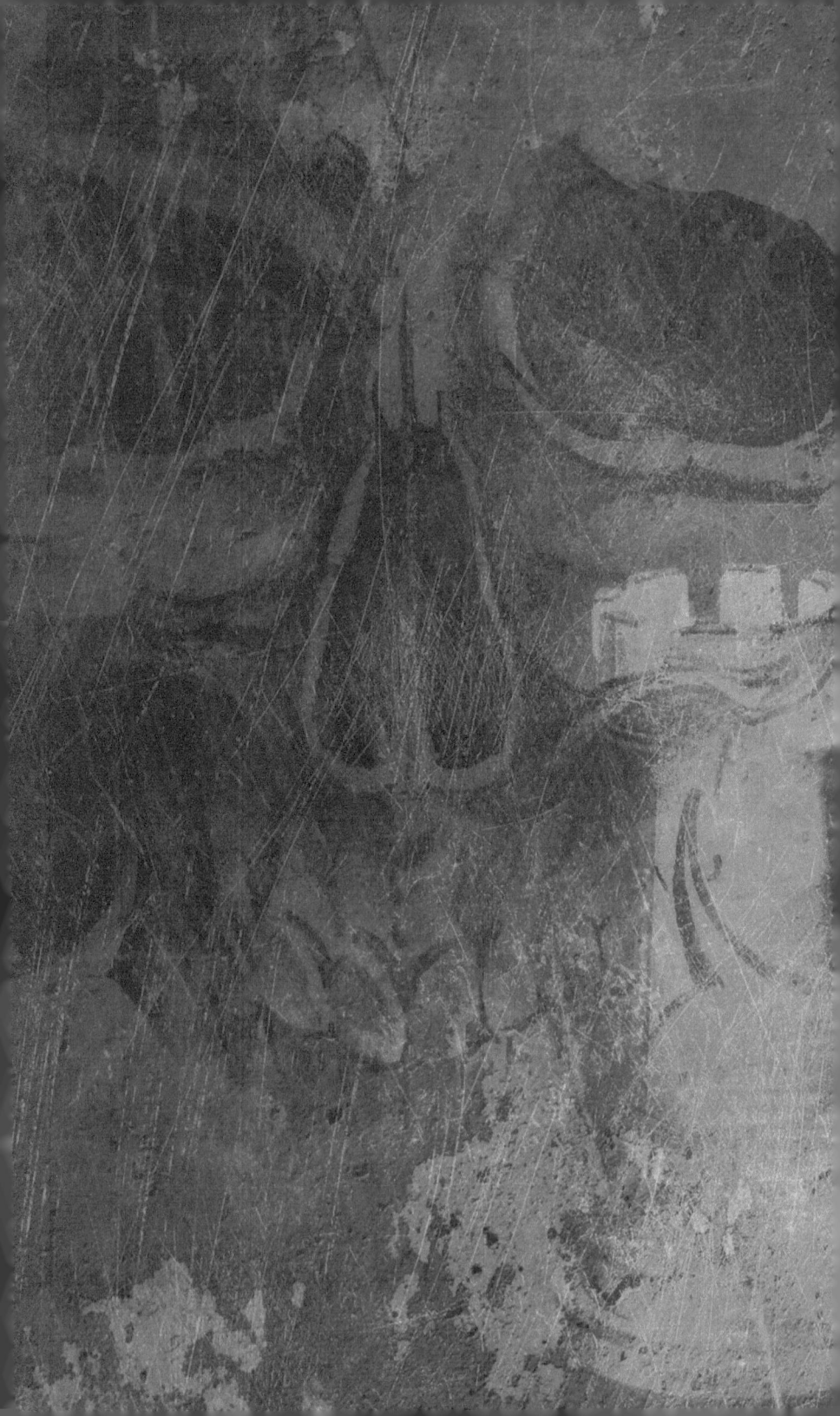

CHAPTER V

AFTER SECTIONING off the atrium and adjoining alcoves into four distinct areas—intending to use the grid search method to approach each quadrant—I decide the guests in my immediate vicinity are as good a place to start as any.

Luckily for me, only the most powerful or notorious receive an annual invite to come and safely rub shoulders with their enemies. Even accounting for larger factions, it means there are always way more key players present than not, with most of them requiring a lot less mental power to pick out of a crowd than the average Underworld denizen.

Case in point.

A mere dozen feet from us stands a young woman sporting a blonde pixie cut, the lower half of her face covered by a golden veil. *Cassandra Jane Priam, 27. Currently unaffiliated. Multidisciplinary doctoral degree in Mathematics.* More commonly known as The Oracle, thanks to her unmatched ability for pattern recognition and statistics.

Cassandra holds herself stiffly, too polite to interrupt the three middle-aged men currently arguing over her head. *Anthony, Christopher and Lawrence Moros, 46. Neutrally aligned. Premier bookmakers and owners of the Underworld's largest gambling outfit.* Known collectively as the Fates, the identical trio of brothers are no doubt trying to puzzle out the Red Court's long game—and all the ways they can monetize it. I'd even wager good money they're harassing the Oracle for probability data as they wait for the big reveal.

I'm just lifting my champagne flute to my lips when there's a sudden flurry of movement from nearby. Both of my Enforcers immediately go on red alert, each pressing in protectively before a goddess in a sleek, copper wrap —complete with matching serpentine headdress— appears like a vision through the parting crowd.

Aurora May Ellis, 24. Bounty hunter. Specializes in poisons and paralytics. True affiliation unknown, speculated Maenad. If you're an Underworlder who's serious about needing someone found—and/or retrieved—then *this* curvaceous, fiery-maned femme fatale is the person to call.

Medusa.

I may or may not have a teensy, tiny boss bitch crush.

Without so much as a word, she hooks a toned arm around the Oracle's waist, spins her, and then proceeds to whisk her away, not bothering to glance in the Fates' direction as she does.

To the casual observer, it might look like the simple intervention of a woman already fed up with every single man in the building. But to me, all it does is further feed my suspicion that it's not just Medusa but *both* women who are Maenads: members of a secret group comprised entirely of female thieves, hackers, and assassins.

As yet unconfirmed, but I do still gleefully file away the entire interaction and then reluctantly move on.

Just as I'm completing one of the north-south legs that dissect my southeastern grid, what could only be described as a *tremor* begins to make its way through the crowd. There's a palpable drop in chatter that follows the ripple like a cold snap, practically confirming that someone both prominent and recognizable has just arrived.

My attention naturally shifts toward the entrance, hoping to catch a glimpse...and my tongue almost sticks to the roof of my mouth.

Because striding into the atrium—with all the confidence that comes from wearing one's notoriety like a cloak—is a group of individuals so infamous in our world that I'm sure *every* mouth in the general vicinity is now bone dry.

Knox and Dio must feel the exact moment I tense, each pressing a large shoulder to my own.

"What's up, babygirl?" D rumbles against my ear.

"The Whitechapel Four," I murmur back, concentrating on keeping all the exposed parts of my face arranged in as blank an expression as humanely possible. I'm almost positive they can preternaturally sniff out weakness and *fuck*—as the Gray Man's mythical Librarian, I'm one of the biggest liabilities in attendance.

As a rule, *Imperium* members are expected to swear allegiance to a single criminal outfit or syndicate, as recognized by either the Northern or Southern Sovereignty. Anyone failing to do so must then register as a Neutral player and agree to offer services indiscriminately.

Strictly speaking, the average *serial murderer* won't fall under either governance.

Unless they're a group of certified psychopaths who find themselves mysteriously pivoting from serial killings to highly sought-after Underworld contract killings, of course.

The Scalpel. The Ghost. The Ferryman. The Muse.

The crowd parts around them like iron filings repelled by a giant magnet, granting the Four a violently wide berth as they make their way across the now silent room. They're led by a woman with black, pin-straight hair, a smirk on her cherry-red lips, and as they move closer, I finally understand what's ratcheting the usual tension up to an all-new level.

The Muse's ivory cheeks are streaked with crimson, the effect almost a perverse mimicry of a weeping holy statue. But it's not her *eyes* that are the source of the bloody 'tears'—it's the horrific fucking 'mask' she wears.

One clearly handcrafted from a slab of human flesh, and recently—if the bloody rivulets snaking down her swan-like neck are anything to go by. Almost involuntarily, my eyes track their downward progress, down to where they meet the modest neckline of a gown in ruby red. It's a simple dress, paired with what appears to be a startlingly intricate, bone-white corset.

On closer inspection, I realize that's because the fucking bodice is literally *a preserved human rib cage*.

"Gnarly," Dionysus breathes in my ear.

"No fucking kidding," I mutter, still surreptitiously trying to turn myself into that finely dressed wallpaper I normally hate so much. I'm not exactly squeamish when it comes to human viscera, but the idea of being close enough to somehow draw their attention is a tad bit daunting.

The other three flanking her are no less terrifying. The Scalpel and the Ghost both sport matching meat masks and blood-stained tuxedos, the latter stopping periodically to snap his teeth at anyone stupid enough to be openly gawking at them. The Ferryman, on the other hand, is in full head-to-toe combat gear, including a complicated-looking gas mask. But there's no missing the festive streaks of red adorning the mask's air filter or neck gaiter.

It's almost like the four of them arrived at the Red Court, remembered tonight's party was a masquerade, and decided to drop the nearest body in order to whip themselves up some homemade masks. All before stepping inside and falling subject to *Hospitium* for the Symposium's duration.

When they finally leave our line of sight, an agitated movement of bodies begins filling the space left in their wake. I adjust my angle slightly as the guests shift positions, and find myself immediately drawn in by the impossibly tall figure of *Papa Kado, 49, parin* of Louisiana voodoo gang, the Ghost Boys. Already a solid foot above a crowd on a good day, Kado's height is only further emphasized tonight by the towering leather stovepipe hat that sits jauntily above a loa skull mask.

Any other year, and I'd be surprised to see Ghosts here in the flesh, what with how loud they are in their disdain for Underworld politics. Kado and his gang of Neutral mischief-makers tend to do their best work from the shadows, and outside of contracted jobs, they *very* rarely wade into the greater gangland cesspool.

It just further supports our theory that this evening's opening address from the Arbiter will be a memorable one.

Milling about next to the merry band of floating skull visages is a group of disgruntled-looking 19th Street Disciple members, including their leader *Fernando Luis Santos, 41.*

Hmm. Another brow-raising addition to this year's guest list.

Unless the order of things has *drastically* shifted on the west coast, the 19Ds don't hold nearly enough sway to warrant receiving a black card on their own. In fact, the only way a small-time group like this particular Latin gang attends a Symposium is via sponsorship. From someone with *actual* power and influence over our half of the Underworld pie.

And nobody in the *Imperium* sponsors out of the goodness of their cold mafia hearts. No, sponsorship means *quid pro quo.*

Through that renewed lens, I start scanning the atrium again. My neck prickles uncomfortably as I begin clocking more and more representatives from mid-range Southern organizations.

The Nomads; a group of gun-runners led by *Hodan (29) & Mahmud Omar Dihoud (28)*, the brothers recent Somali transplants to the south-west.

Sal Rual Felipe, 38, and his Cuban Marielito gang out of Miami.

Even the Romano Mafia family is here, and they barely have control over their own city.

"Lots of charity cases this year," I remark aloud, earning an affirmative grunt from Knox.

"Bottom feeders jumping at the chance to ride a brand new sovereign's coattails up and out of the streets," he snarks, careful to keep the scathing observation beneath his breath.

I huff, shaking my head. Whoever's been promising all these weaker groups a seat at the Big Boy Table is playing a dangerous game indeed.

Side-stepping, I continue along the latest gridline. I feel rather than see Rhett and Knox moving with me, flanking me like obedient, hulking shadows.

As the crowd parts, I spot another head of prominent red hair, only this time it doesn't belong to Medusa.

Michael Angus 'Smiley' O'Sullivan, 46. Sloane's father and patriarch of the O'Sullivan crime family. The Mob boss appears to be engaged in an intense conversation with *Cashel Marcus Reilly, 34* and *Connor Ian Reilly, 25,* and everything about the sight has my brow pinching.

Before his death, the Green Knight'd not only ruled the Southern half of the Underworld, but he'd also been Head of all Irish-American Mob families operating within his Sovereignty. When it came time to annex the fallen monarch's empire—with no apparent heir—the O'Sullivans and the Reillys had both sought claims on the Maker's Bay estate and its assets.

Bloody claims, and with casualties on both sides.

And yet, here they were, not only on speaking terms but with each of the Irishmen wearing matching metal eye masks, differentiated only by the colors of their individual family crests.

It's subtle, but a declaration nonetheless.

The previously warring Irish families are teaming up, and suffice to say, two such prominent mobsters joining forces would bode very well for a potential Crown bid.

My eyes dart over the group once more, looking for Sloane's fiery mane, but there's zero sign of the O'Sullivan princess herself. It's unlikely she'd be allowed out of her father's company at a gathering such as this, which tells me she's more than likely not even here at all.

Which is very unexpected. I'd assumed now that his only daughter was eighteen—and with his designs on the Green Knight's legacy—that Smiley would be busy trotting her out in an attempt to woo potential allies. Are the O'Sullivans closing ranks instead?

Unless…

My gaze slides back to the Reilly brothers.

Unless she's already *promised.*

As much as I'd love to, I can't spend too long

watching a single group of targets when I only have a finite amount of time to catalog everyone here. So, after watching the Irish bosses bicker over the rim of my champagne glass for a few minutes more, I finally force myself to shift my attention elsewhere.

Almost immediately, it's snagged by a group of dark-haired gentlemen, each one standing with their backs to the wall.

At first glance, their postures seem relaxed, open, their heavily tattooed hands grasped casually in front as they each observe the party. But as I continue to watch them, I notice their black eyes never stop roaming over the attendees.

Almost as if they're looking for something.

Or someone.

My scalp prickles. I don't recognize *any* of these men *or* their elaborate ink, and that sets off every alarm in my already loud as fuck head.

Because if I've never laid eyes on their likeness before? Then they're one hundred percent a new and unknown entity in our world.

And there are few things I find more unsettling— especially when the name of the game is literally being able to identify every single player of said game.

Zeus chooses this exact moment to return to my side, and I let out a tense breath, adjusting my dress with my free hand. "West wall, near the Rothko painting," I murmur, not bothering to greet him.

His eyes make a careful circuit of the room as he takes

a slow sip of his newly acquired whiskey. "No clue, but second from the left's definitely in charge."

I slide my gaze across the group again—and of course, he's right.

The way they've arranged themselves against the wall makes you want to dismiss them; write them off as nothing more than low-rank muscle patiently waiting on their boss to return. But there's a certain arrogance in the set of the second man's chin as he studies those guests standing closest to him.

He's not a man used to waiting on *anyone.*

"Knox?" Our deputy Enforcer holds a special interest in international syndicates. The ones that lay outside the scope of my locally focused database.

He hums, considering. "Could be a South American outfit, possibly Colombian. Could also be Mexican, though. I've seen cartels working out of both regions that are starting to combine their markings."

It's not exactly conclusive, but one thing's for sure— they're definitely not *Imperium*—so who the fuck vouched for their admittance tonight?

I follow the unknown leader's line of sight for a moment, noticing he's now tracking an Underworld favorite with an eagle eye as they move through the atrium.

Angelo Marcus Chiron, 39. Neutral. Former military field medic. Emergency medicine specialist. Also fondly known as 'Doc'. He's probably patched up most of this room at one point or the other, and if the new guy has plans for him, he's going to quickly find himself with more enemies than friends. Especially since the beloved trauma surgeon already went missing once this year.

"Trick's finally here," Zeus cuts in, yanking my focus back to him. "Near the bar."

Sure enough, *Patrick Arnett 'Trick' Mahoney, 49,* leader of the Strange Aces MC, is standing not even thirty feet from us. A few Spades are scattered around him. While they might all be wearing tuxedos and harlequin masks, their neck tattoos are a dead giveaway.

Trick himself is tall, broad, inked, and still in very decent shape for his age. He's stroking a thick, auburn beard as he laughs at whatever his companion's saying. A small line creases my forehead when I realize the person he's currently entertaining is *Alexander Morrow, 36.*

Not much is known about the elusive businessman or his three closest friends, only that the four of them are considered the closest thing to corporate mercenaries.

"Who's he talking to, Sabe?" Zeus asks, his hot breath a welcome warmth against my neck. If I'm honest, I keep expecting a Sebastian jumpscare every time the sea of people shifts.

"One of the Four Horseman."

"Well, that's not good," Dio chimes in.

"Nope," I agree, voice dripping with sarcasm to mask my own annoyance at seeing the mysterious Horseman speaking with our greatest rival. It stings that despite being prominent Underworlders, I know next to nothing about the men *or* the nature of their relationship with the Club.

Before I can dwell on it further, my towering stilettos are carrying me forward.

Knox immediately squeaks, Rhett whistles, and Zeus curses beneath his breath, each desperately trying to stay in step without treading on my gown as I prowl directly toward the head of the Aces.

"Sabine. Careful, darling," Zeus warns as he reaches out to grip my elbow. I ignore him, concentrating instead on the soothing *swishswishswish* of my dress's train as I cross the marbled floors. The sound syncs with the quiet pulsing of blood in my ears and the click of my heels.

By the time I manage to navigate my way through the throng surrounding the bar, Morrow has disappeared. Mahoney's now blessedly alone—save for the few trusted Aces with Hearts on their throats that are hovering nearby, no doubt playing the parts of Enforcers for the weekend.

I'm not worried about a handful of faceless henchmen, though.

"Ah, was wondering when one of his Suited cronies would come up and say hello," Trick greets us, reaching for his drink with an unnervingly smug twist of his lips. One large, tattooed hand dwarfs the handblown Glencairn, the other adjusts a sparkling black, white, and red *pierrot*-style mask. The design resembles a jester's hood, only modified to leave the wearer's mouth uncovered. *The Joker.*

I plaster on what I hope is my most polite smile and forcibly lower my shoulders. The black feathers crowning my own mask might mark me as a Gray Man, sure. He might even know *who* I am, considering there aren't many women high enough in the Underworld ranks to warrant an escort such as mine. My blonde hair's another tip-off, if he cares enough to notice.

But there's no way this man knows exactly *what* I am.

It's in *really* poor form to call out another guest's identity, but when honey-brown eyes slide lasciviously down my figure, I find that in this moment, I really don't care to stand on formalities after all.

"Mahoney. Making new friends, are we?" I drawl.

"Ah ah, birdy," he tuts, ignoring my not-so-subtle faux pas and taking a noisy sip of what I wager is a glass of his favored Bulleit. "That'll be *Your Grace* to you, soon enough."

And there it is.

After so long playing the role of constant thorn in Sebastian's side, it seems the Strange Ace himself is finally putting his money where his mouth is. Which means Trick Mahoney must have succeeded in gathering *a hell of a lot* more support for a leadership bid than our previous intelligence showed.

In fact, some might even argue that gaining the favor of the famously selective members of *Ordo ab Chao* is more of an ominous sign than the Irish deciding to band together.

It would certainly warrant this newly inflated sense of entitlement.

Are we digging our own fucking graves by underestimating the man standing in front of me? Or, is he just playing head games with what he thinks is a passing group of Gray Men—hoping we'll run straight back to our boss, twisted narrative in hand?

It's the kind of thing the Gray Man would do if he weren't so busy icing us out.

Fuck. I need more, but I can't exactly declare, *"I saw you over here chumming it up with Alexander Morrow,"* without potentially breaching my cover. So I try again, hoping he'll at least acknowledge his former drinking companion. "What, because you think you've got the Neutrals on your side?"

He chuckles, running a large hand over the exposed part of his beard. It's a deep, raspy thing, letting me know he sees straight through my ruse. "Be foolish to ignore such an untapped source, birdy girl. But I dare say cooperation on all fronts might just be the way of the future."

Damnit all to hell.

He's tap dancing around what I want to know as only an experienced Underworlder can. The thought of addressing a glorified biker as *Your Grace* should have me in stitches, but not having the whole picture has a frustrated growl wanting to claw its way up my throat instead.

Before I can formulate a new line of questioning, however, Zeus's hand lands on my hip, hooking me away. Trick's booming laughter follows us as my Team Lead directs me toward the other end of the full-service counter.

"Not another word," he hisses in my ear, and my

teeth snap shut as I seethe. "Keep working," he urges, nudging me to find another target to profile.

Hovering at the end of the bar is *Ivan Dmitriyevich Antonov, 40*. The stout figure of the *Pakhan* is surrounded by both a thick cloud of cigar smoke and his *Sovietnik*—a group of his closest and most trusted advisors. The Russians swear shaky allegiance to the North, but aren't shy about striking deals with Southern entities if the price is right. His countenance seems reserved tonight, eyes slowly roving the room from behind his simple bronze half-mask.

Like a well-oiled machine, my Crew keeps me focused and moving, and I continue on with our rotation. It's not long before I stumble upon another oddly paired couple.

Chatting over matching tumblers of dark red whiskey are *Alessandro 'Sandro' Michele Alessi, 38*, head of the Alessi Mafia *famiglia*, and *Asano Kento, 65, kumicho* to the Northern-based Asano Yakuza.

While the Asano organization enjoys quite a nice spread of influence across the North, the New Jersey Italians' only strength comes from having cemented themselves as one of Midas's top sycophants.

There's nothing worse than a power leech, and Sandro Alessi is the king of leeches.

"Poster boy for bottom feeders everywhere," I mutter, spinning to place my now flat champagne flute on a passing waiter's tray. Before I get the chance to offload it, I feel all three of my Crewmates tense, sending every single hair on my body standing on end.

"Hello, little rook."

The greeting drags its fingers down my spine like a languid caress, with honeyed tones that hold just the slightest hint of a taunt but always leave trails of ice in their wake.

Fuck. My. Life.

My nostrils flare as only now—when it's much too late—do I realize the crucial mistake I've made. I've made myself vulnerable by moving from the relatively safe edges of the room and wading directly into the snake pit to confront Trick.

Opening myself up to encounters such as these.

There's no point trying to ignore his presence completely; avoiding this man's poisonous orbit is a peer-approved, double-blind study in pure futility. And since he's *Imperium* royalty, that makes him somewhat of a regular workplace hazard.

So I turn, slowly, buying myself a moment before having to face the gilded monster himself.

Fortunately for me, I know how to dance with the Devil.

Sebastian Grayson's been teaching me for years.

"Midas."

CHAPTER VI

ATLAS · HADES

BY THE TIME we clear the final entry checkpoint, I've been touched by no fewer than fourteen people.

Sweat dots my upper lip, my heart beating out a frantic tattoo against my sternum. The boning in the brocade vest I spent months so carefully tailoring now feels like a prison in its intricate corsetry.

Aside from a single encrypted message insisting on our presence—and that our masks tonight be gold—it's been total radio silence from this supposed benefactor of ours.

Ever since the incident at the Guardhouse check-in.

He *did* come through with a chartered flight for the four of us, but all this cloak and dagger is doing is only further convincing me that we're little more than pawns in some tyrant's endgame.

Tristan, on the other hand, loves extolling the humble pawn. The unrelenting strategist banks on the fact most players continuously underestimate its net worth—forgetting all about the only piece on the board able to be promoted above its original station.

Forgetting that in the right hands, a pawn could easily be the difference between a win and a loss.

Personally, I don't know if I quite agree with putting that much faith in a lowly foot soldier. What I *do* know is that it doesn't make being here tonight any less dangerous. No one can argue that we're not completely out of our element.

And what's worse—*she's* here.

Somewhere.

I'm not exactly sure if this nauseous grip on my stomach is dread...or anticipation.

Callum's hand curls protectively over my shoulder, reading me like a book. Normally, that familiar touch of his would come as a welcome one, grounding me before the anxiety takes over and the edges of my vision white out. Right now, however, it's all I can do not to flinch.

"How many candles you think are in that big ass chandelier right there?" comes his deep baritone from my right. I feel his fingers flex against the fabric of my overcoat. My brow knits, but the question has my focus drifting to the vaulted ceiling against my will.

The massive, empire-style lighting all look to span at least twelve feet each. Each one contains hundreds of crystal bulbs arranged in rising patterns of bronze sconces. I'm about to begin mapping out the bottom tier's generous circumference when I'm gently tugged away. It's Callum again. He's hovering there with a pinched expression as his gaze roams over my face.

"What?" I ask blankly, but he must find whatever it is

he's looking for, because some of the tension around his honey-brown eyes lessens the longer he studies me.

"Good," he eventually grunts, turning away to scan the room we've just entered. I squint at the side of his head, wondering why my skin's no longer crawling. Finally, it registers I was so distracted by Callum's challenge that my panic attack never found its foothold.

Ever the caretaker, I already know he's not expecting a thank you, and without another word, he uses his huge form to begin herding me toward Tristan and Lake instead.

I do my best to ignore the chattering crowd as we weave through the throng, choosing instead to focus on the figures of my brothers. The two of them have claimed a spot in the opposite corner of the atrium, not far from a large obsidian dais that was likely brought in especially for the event.

Tristan's running his cool gaze over each of the guests nearest them.

Lake, on the other hand, looks ready to bolt, shoulders high and long fingers flicking his Zippo open and close in agitation. After he'd disappeared from the stadium yesterday, he hadn't resurfaced again until well after midnight. He'd been cagey with the details and has stayed skirting the edge of mania ever since.

It's honestly a miracle Tristan got him here at all—or in one piece. He's even managed to smuggle him into a slim-fitted tuxedo jacket despite his vocal protests.

As soon as we reach the two of them, Callum

immediately circles in, eyeing Lake like a dogcatcher with a net.

"It's a masquerade, and we don't even know what color she's wearing," Tristan's explaining very calmly, like he's talking down a skittish child. True to form, he seems completely unfazed by the fact he's currently surrounded by some of the most dangerous people in the country. "I want answers just as badly as you do, but we need to be careful."

My jaw tightens.

Answers are the only reason I even agreed to come tonight. I'm just afraid we'll end up leaving empty-handed.

Or worse, walking away with even more questions than we came with.

"You two hold this position, Atlas and I will do a lap."

Lake's blond curls bounce dramatically as he pitches forward. "Seriously?" he scowls, face screwing up in annoyance. One of Callum's massive hands shoots out, gripping him by the nape. The corded muscles along his neck and chest strain as he struggles to contain that crazed energy.

Our brother's so close to the edge that it's a wonder we can't physically see the void rising up, ready to swallow him.

"I'm serious. *Don't. Leave. Cal's. Side*," Tristan instructs firmly, authority evident in every clipped word. He tilts his head at me, signaling his intent to leave. He turns before adding a final, "And *fuck*, just—*behave*."

"I just—"

But Tristan's already moving off, ignoring his continued protests. I mean, it's not an unreasonable command. We're surrounded by pockets of debauchery and there are plenty of lascivious looks being shot in Lake's direction thanks to the outfit I helped create.

No guess who he's peacocking for.

Tristan and I don't speak as we ease our way through the mass of bodies, our path naturally following the edges of the large chamber. I'm always appreciative of the fact that my brothers know me well enough that we don't really need to. Both hands slip casually into the pockets of my dress pants, my head on a swivel. It's not long before I'm casually dropping my pace, keeping a step or so between us.

This is me at my most comfortable—slipping through a crowd unseen; the silent observer. Already the press of people is becoming less suffocating.

The guests we pass are a swirling mix of formal and elaborate designs, each group of masks forming a statement for their owners. I'm not so well-versed in the factions to identify them on sight, though I'm positive each of the colors chosen are significant. Unlike our simple gold pieces, it seems to be a sea of feathered and bejeweled Venetian masks—some tasteful in their brocade patterns, others favoring the towering harlequin-style headdresses.

Commedia dell'arte has also been a popular choice I note, passing a huddle of raucous Pantalone wearers, marked by their grotesque cheeks and exaggerated noses.

They're followed by a group of more modest *pagliaccio* half-masks in silver.

I even spy a group of twisted *shikami* Noh masks.

Just as we're moving past a pair of men wearing matching metallic gold Voltos, I catch a snippet of their conversation and my whole body lights up with a renewed shock of adrenaline.

I may have only met the man in person the one time, but I would recognize him by voice alone.

"Not a chance. Her guard dogs are sticking to her like flies on shit," he grates in that unmistakable, gravelly Italian-American accent.

I'm cautiously angling my head in their direction when I see his companion roll his eyes. It's the only part of his face that's still visible behind the full coverage of their masks. But then I clock his companion's thick, dark, wavy hair with its signature white streak.

Correction—I recognize both of them.

The Donato brothers.

Twin black gazes stay intently focused elsewhere as they speak, and almost involuntarily, I turn to follow their line of sight.

A dire mistake.

It feels like every organ in my body has plummeted south, sending me reeling. I stumble forward, chasing after Tristan and snagging his elbow.

Fuck, keep it together. You knew this was coming.

He turns, eyebrows raised, giving me an expectant look.

I tip my chin, before flicking my eyes back toward the two men. "It's Raphael and Gabriel," I hiss. "I think they're planning something with Sabine."

But even as the words leave my mouth, they already sound bizarre to my own ears. Why would two Lieutenants of the Alessi crime family be interested in an orphaned high school girl?

Tristan's nostrils immediately flare when he also sees what has the two men so fixated. My spine and knees feel like Jello, and I'm forced to settle for the armor of a dark scowl as he drags us both into place behind a nearby statue.

I thought this part would eventually get easier, but it's just as much a punch to the gut seeing her in this unfamiliar place as it is having to see her haunting the halls of the Academy every day.

More so, actually.

I've always enjoyed puzzles. By their very nature, I know they'll have one single, predetermined solution.

Predictable.

Logical.

Safe.

Sabine Winters is *not* a puzzle.

Sabine Winters is a labyrinth—an endless maze I blindly wandered into at twelve years old, and one I'm yet to escape. How could I, when each of her walls are constantly shifting, and the path never stays the same?

The day she disappeared and all the ones that followed are seared into the very bones of me.

The tart smell of strawberry chapstick.

A woolen-gloved palm, sliding into mine.

Her teasing laughter.

White-blonde hair whipping in the cool December air, as she spins and walks away for the final time.

And then her absence.

I side-eye my brother's rigid profile, the Donatos temporarily forgotten. I find myself avidly wishing at this moment that I could read his thoughts as he unabashedly drinks her in. Wondering if they're half as conflicted as mine seem to be growing the longer I trace her figure.

And despite my trepidations, I'm finding myself extremely...*jealous* that I'm not the one who made this dress for her.

I absolutely should not give a fuck if she was dressed by the finest fashion houses in the country.

I should also not give a fuck that she's here with someone else.

But for some reason I do.

I really fucking do.

It's a hideous, constricting thing that slinks around inside my chest, poisoning my resolve until all I can think is *but, she's mine.* Planting thoughts that each have my dick stirring, and I loathe that years later she can still make me feel this way.

That she makes me feel anything at all.

The woman in question stands tall and regal, her platinum hair in soft waves and wearing a floor-length ballgown in a blue so deep it looks black beneath the red light of the chandeliers. The dress itself boasts a narrow bodice, a defined, sweetheart neck, and a basque waistline. One shoulder and the upper layers of the skirt are decorated with long plumes that match her mask exactly.

The rest of the dress is shot through with clusters of diamonds, and when they catch the light, they wink like galaxies in deep space.

The effect is otherworldly.

She looks like Nyx. Goddess of the Night.

Sabine certainly looks as if she's holding court—closely surrounded by three huge men whose combined body language reads like they're facing down a threat. And from the way they've positioned themselves around her, that threat must be the fourth man, whose back is to us. I can't see any distinguishing features, aside from a mane of golden blond hair that's just past his collar.

Only the lower half of Sabine's face is visible to the room, but her mouth is pressed into a hard line. As are her shoulders.

"Who the fuck is that she's with?" Tristan practically grinds out from where he's pressed up beside me. His frustration feels hot on my neck.

"Those might be the two men Cal and Lake saw her with at the diner," I reply, quietly. The descriptions certainly match. *A blond and a brunet, both tall, muscled, tattooed.*

"What about the third guy? And those masks—are those meant to be ravens?"

I shrug, unsure about both. Sabine and her

companions wear matching disguises, each richly
decorated with long, black feathers. They do look like
they would come from some kind of corvid, but I can't be
entirely sure which.

I also have no idea who the extra man beside her
might be. Cal only mentioned seeing her with two
heavily inked, Enforcer-looking types. Whoever this
other guy is—she must be comfortable with him. He's
practically welded himself to her side, one shoulder
angled forward like a shield and the other arm snaked
around her waist.

Exactly like a possessive boyfriend might stand.

In fact, all three of them are crowding up in her
personal space like they each have a right to.

Is this *who she's made her new life with? Who she left us
behind for?*

Those thoughts send battery acid eating its way
through my lungs. I blink rapidly when there's a burning
sensation at the back of my eyes. I have a job to do and I
need to remain impartial.

Otherwise, we'll never get our answers.

The blond-haired man must've greeted her because
her crimson-framed mouth parts.

A single word.

Midas.

Midas?

Oh.

Oh fuck.

When she was verbally sparring with Monelli and
Reynolds in the alleyway, she'd mentioned both the

North and the Arbiter. It was painfully obvious that not only did she already know about this world, she was well acquainted with it. And with that level of confidence, perhaps even more than we were—considering we'd only been initiated a few months before.

But this here? This was more than simply knowing about *Hospitium* and treaties.

This was something else entirely.

"Did she just call him what I think she did?" Tristan breathes. He's not as practiced at reading lips as I am, but the way she drew his name out, not even a novice would've missed it.

"Midas," I confirm, my voice sounding oddly thin to my ears. Like some of the oxygen in the room has just been sucked out.

It certainly feels like it.

"How—did she just—a fucking *king of the fucking Underworld*—?" he manages to sputter out after a few ragged breaths. His chest heaves while my own fingers dig harshly for purchase on the cold stone before me. He never could handle not knowing which of a deck's cards were already in play. And here she stands before him, holding onto her full hand.

Possibly even with a trick card or two still hidden up her sleeve.

I wait quietly as he struggles through a spectrum of emotions: *shock, anger, frustration*, before landing on *determination* and forcibly gathering up the broken shards of his composure.

He turns then, catching my wide gaze, the *real* unspoken question hanging in the air between us.

The one that's been dogging us all since her unexpected return to Rox City.

Who the fuck is this *Sabine Winters?*

CHAPTER VII
TRISTAN · APOLLO

MIDAS. *Sabine. Alessi.*

I squeeze my lids tight, needing a moment while my equilibrium finishes righting itself.

Fuck.

Connection. What's the connection here? There has to be one. Why else would both Alessi's bulldogs *and* one of the highest-ranking men of the Underworld be circling her like well-dressed birds of prey?

Atlas has fallen silent beside me. He'd already been skirting the edges of his control, having endured the dozen or so pat-downs needed just to get inside. I can see the minute cracks in his composure now: fingertips trembling against the stone, brows pulling down as he absorbs each detail of the confusing scene playing out before us.

Soft ripples creeping across the surface of an otherwise quiet lake.

While those waters are often dark and murky, I've always found comfort in knowing how deep that particular lake bed goes. In fact, I could really use some of that quiet intensity of his now, could use it to smooth over this open, jagged sensation tearing up my chest. As it is, it takes me several shaky breaths just to clear the obnoxious fucking ringing of my world tipping on its axis.

When I swallow, my throat feels like sandpaper.

Christ.

"I can't hear anything, we have to get closer," I rasp, but I'm already up and leaving the statue's meager cover. I trust Atlas will be right behind me, despite how lost in his head he looks right now. But it's not until we're across the gap in the crowd, and almost close enough to reach out and touch one of the world's most powerful men, that I'm finally able to hear their conversation above the rest of the party.

We still can't see his face properly from this angle, but I can tell from his profile that—unlike the rest of the partygoers—he's not wearing any type of disguise. At all.

"I don't believe he's here yet," Sabine's saying, both her tone and body language oddly rigid.

"It's not like Sebastian to let you out of his sight for so long," the man we now know to be Midas hums back across the rim of his glass.

Sebastian?

Everything about Midas—from the way he holds himself, to his voice—is like a big jungle cat in repose. Relaxed, yet brimming with power. Ready to spring forth at a moment's notice. Our girl must sense the same from him.

I know she's only been back in our lives for a

heartbeat, but I've yet to see her present herself with anything less than complete self-assurance. Even with Sloane coming at her from day one, she's taken everything on the chin, nerves taut like steel.

She didn't so much as flinch when Reynolds literally held a gun to her head.

But something about this man's presence seems to melt straight through that steel like a hot knife through butter.

"It's been, what, two months now? That's certainly plenty of time to get yourself into *all sorts* of trouble, isn't it, little rook?"

The danger implied by that sultry cadence alone sends all the hairs on my neck rising. There's a way in which he delivers each subtly probing question that makes it clear they're more than simply small talk between guests.

They're a threat.

Sabine narrows her eyes ever so slightly before visibly stiffening, catching herself. It's a *blink-or-you'll-miss-it* moment, almost entirely hidden by her mask, but even just that small flash of her usual spine has my dick kicking in response.

There she is.

There's the girl ballsy enough to address the Crown Sovereign by nothing but his chosen name.

She remains cool and dismissive when she replies, "School's got me busy toeing the line."

"Ah yes. Odd choice, starting your senior year at a

brand new school," he muses, before taking a deep, deliberate sip of something amber and expensive.

My spine jolts, the observation—again so casually delivered—sending a whole new chill creeping across my skin.

Because why would *he* be keeping tabs on *her*?

Is he having our Academy watched?

"Just needed a change of scenery. As you can imagine, it's a little much always having these guys breathing down my neck," she returns with a forced shrug and a little wave in the direction of the men still very much crowding her in.

Midas is silent for a moment. I imagine his brows lifting as he waits for her to elaborate. "And? Made any new *friends*?" he prompts when she fails to do so, taking a smooth step toward her.

The group at her back immediately bristles at his attempt to close the distance between them. Something that has my forehead creasing. There's no arguing the man himself exudes very clear and obvious danger, and understandably, most people would feel cornered if they had the direct attention of the leader of half the fucking country's criminal population.

But does this level of caution toward Sabine's person seem...dare I say....*excessive*?

"I'm still finding my way around."

Again, she lobs back a perfectly polite but total non-answer. She obviously has experience playing political dodgeball. More importantly, it's becoming increasingly clear she's not afraid to spike a few back herself.

Midas takes another slow mouthful of his drink.

The anticipation has my insides feeling like they're performing an entire gymnastics routine. Sabine looks like she's bracing herself while he considers her. Even Atlas shifts uncomfortably, his elbow knocking against mine.

"Well, you'll honor me with a dance, won't you?" Midas drawls right as I'm beginning to think the man's about ready to move on. His posture remains relaxed, which does seem to ease a small amount of the tension holding those around him hostage.

My lips thin with irritation, however. I don't care how powerful this guy is, I don't want his hands on or anywhere near her.

"Two left feet," Sabine shoots with a pained smile that's more a baring of teeth than anything remotely apologetic.

"Hmm," the Sovereign chuckles, undeterred. He lifts his glass for another unhurried sip. "I don't mind leading."

The chatter surrounding them drops ever so subtly at his rumbled laughter. It now seems everyone in their general proximity—including Sabine's companions—is holding their collective breath, waiting for her rejection.

Even Gabriel and Rafael are watching soundlessly, and those assholes love hearing their own voices. They might not be privy to her exact identity as we are, but no doubt they're each dying to know exactly why the Northern Sovereign has taken such a keen interest in her.

Midas extends a single hand in invitation while at the

same time smoothly depositing his unfinished drink on a passing tray. It's a move that says he's confident she's not even contemplating the idea of refusal. The poor waiter squeaks in surprise before barreling through the press of bodies.

Sabine stares down the hand like it's a serpent reared up, fangs bared and ready to sink its venom directly into her flesh. Like she's very *much* thinking about telling him exactly what he can do with it.

Two thudding heartbeats later, she stonily passes off her own champagne glass. As soon as her hand slips into his, he yanks her in against his body, and the aggressive power move has all five of us stepping forward before we can stop ourselves.

The guy previously glued to her side throws out a low armbar in warning, bringing the two bulky Enforcers to a halt. The three of them exchange frustrated words beneath their breaths, though their eyes never leave the back of Sabine's head.

"*Relax*, it's a simple waltz," Midas teases lightly as he pulls her along, but there's a coiling undertone to his humor that's almost serpentine. "You're as stiff as all this marble around us. Almost makes me want to take you home and display you on a plinth."

I bite my tongue so hard I taste copper.

"I tried telling you that I'm not a great dancer," Sabine grits out, the lie written all over the downturned purse of her lips.

Midas, still ignoring her weak excuses, spins her

deftly away from her keepers, and Atlas and I finally get our first front-on view of the monarch's face.

Golden skin, golden hair and the type of flashing, intelligent eyes whose color is impossible to pin down under this type of lighting. To most, that set of features would seem safely handsome and charming. And I'm sure he's more than charismatic enough to pull it off in normal circumstances.

All I see is the perfect predator.

An empty gaze, focus honed sharply on the prey currently within his clutches, all while seasoned instincts keep him keenly aware of his surroundings.

As if to prove that point exactly, those fathomless eyes lift and find mine through the crowd unerringly.

I suck in a breath at the veiled menace I see there; my feet rooted to the spot, my stomach heavy with ice-packed dread. Ambient sounds fall away, and I watch as each of the muscles along Sabine's exposed neck and back seem to tense. There's an echoing tightness that spirals along my own limbs and spine.

His face splits with a newly mocking smile, one framed by a set of sharp, white incisors.

One hand drifts down, stopping just above the swell of her ass.

And then he fucking *winks*.

The moment that follows seems to hang forever, the suspense only breaking when a jittery man in a crimson host's mask appears suddenly at Midas's side.

"Your Grace, her Honor wishes to speak with you," the messenger rushes out, wringing his hands and bobbing nervously. Midas doesn't acknowledge the interruption, the poor man visibly aging by the second.

The king of the North's unerring focus is instead back on Sabine. It's another painstaking minute before he deigns to break the silence. "Do remember, little rook— *these violent delights have violent ends,*" he purrs cryptically.

Then, with what might have been another sly wink, he turns on his heel and strides past the sweeping staircase that's been roped off from the rest of the party and toward a set of curtains. The mass of guests between us and the stairs immediately melts back, leaving a generous path before him.

My brow furrows as I'm left staring daggers at the back of Sabine's white blonde hair and feathered mask, turning the random Shakespearean line over and over.

"*And in their triumph die like fire and powder, which as they kiss consume,*" Atlas murmurs from beside me.

I grunt in acknowledgment.

Only why *Romeo and Juliet*? Did this man—who reportedly controls almost half the known criminal syndicates in the country—consider himself and Sabine...*star-crossed lovers*?

Nothing about their interaction spoke of romantic interest.

At least not consensual.

My teeth gnash against the inside of my cheeks.

His hand on her ass. And that fucking wink.

But then something else wrestles its way to the

forefront of my simmering thoughts. What had Midas called her?

Little rook.

Rook? So *not* a raven, then.

My mind latches onto that seemingly innocuous nickname, trying in vain to remember where I might've heard the word *rook* before in reference to the *Imperium*.

Nothing.

I'd need Atlas and Lake to check through their notes as soon as we get back to campus.

Or.

Or I can get the information straight from the hauntingly beautiful source herself.

Before I can take more than a single step, however, I'm intercepted by a large, foreign hand clamping down on the back of my neck. My eyes immediately cut to the side, only to confirm there's an identical tattooed grip against my brother's nape. Atlas's shoulders are up around his ears.

Fuck. I know I wasn't on my best guard just then, lost in thought, but Atlas normally is. This guy must move like a fucking ninja or else he got lucky and was able to use the swelling noise of the party after Midas's exit to cover his approach.

"Evening, lads," our captor sings from behind our heads with a flirty lilt. He follows up his cheerful greeting with a single warning squeeze of both hands. "You must be two of Sabine's little lost Rox Boys."

My heart rate slows just a fraction as I process those words. There's a very good chance he's one of the men we saw accompanying her just now—and *not* someone from Alessi's crew.

Still, he managed to catch *both* of us with our figurative pants down, and I don't like it one fucking bit.

"And who the fuck are you?" I growl back, skin prickling with shame beneath his firm touch.

My eyes dart back over to where I thought they were last standing. Sure enough, only the two dark-haired bodyguards remain. They're tracking Sabine's stiff approach as she returns to their side. I'm also attempting to track her steps without moving my head.

The stranger only chuckles. Obnoxiously. "Wouldn't you like to know, pretty boy? It's Sinclair—right?" He punctuates the second question with a firm shake of his hand, and *Christ*, it feels like my whole skull rattles.

But I'll be damned if I let this asshole keep calling the shots here. I shrug him off roughly, and as soon as the twin death grips fall away, Atlas and I spin defensively.

My gut was right.

It's the large blond, who's clearly enjoying himself, the black feathers of his face mask unable to hide the mirth glittering behind his eyes. Couple that with the dark smirk he wears like a slash of war paint, and his whole demeanor has me feeling like we've blindly stumbled into the trap of some unhinged trickster god.

Which probably explains why I suddenly find myself right up in the shorter man's personal space.

"She's *ours*. *Always has been*," I spit, my words dripping with all of the hot, possessive venom now searing out the hollows of my rib cage.

I'm fully expecting the asshole to laugh again. Instead, all I get is more of that incessant fucking smirk.

Fuck, do I want to wipe it right off his smug fucking face.

"I need to talk to her," I grind out, wondering, not for the first time, if he's going to prove to be an actual barrier between us and our girl.

"Apollo, my man. A word to the wise: This alpha bullshit? It doesn't work on her." He pauses, looking thoughtful for just a second before adding with another sultry grin, "Unless you're Zeus. Then she's folding like a house of cards."

I have exactly zero idea who this Zeus fucker might be, but my brain's now fixated on the fact this motherfucker just addressed me by the same callsign Sabine gave us as she fled with us from the Guardhouse.

Apollo.

Is she the one who gave *Zeus* his name? And what about this guy? What's his alias?

For some reason, it's that thought—the thought of her also bestowing matching pet names upon these perfect fucking strangers—that sends the hottest jet of jealousy coursing through my chest yet.

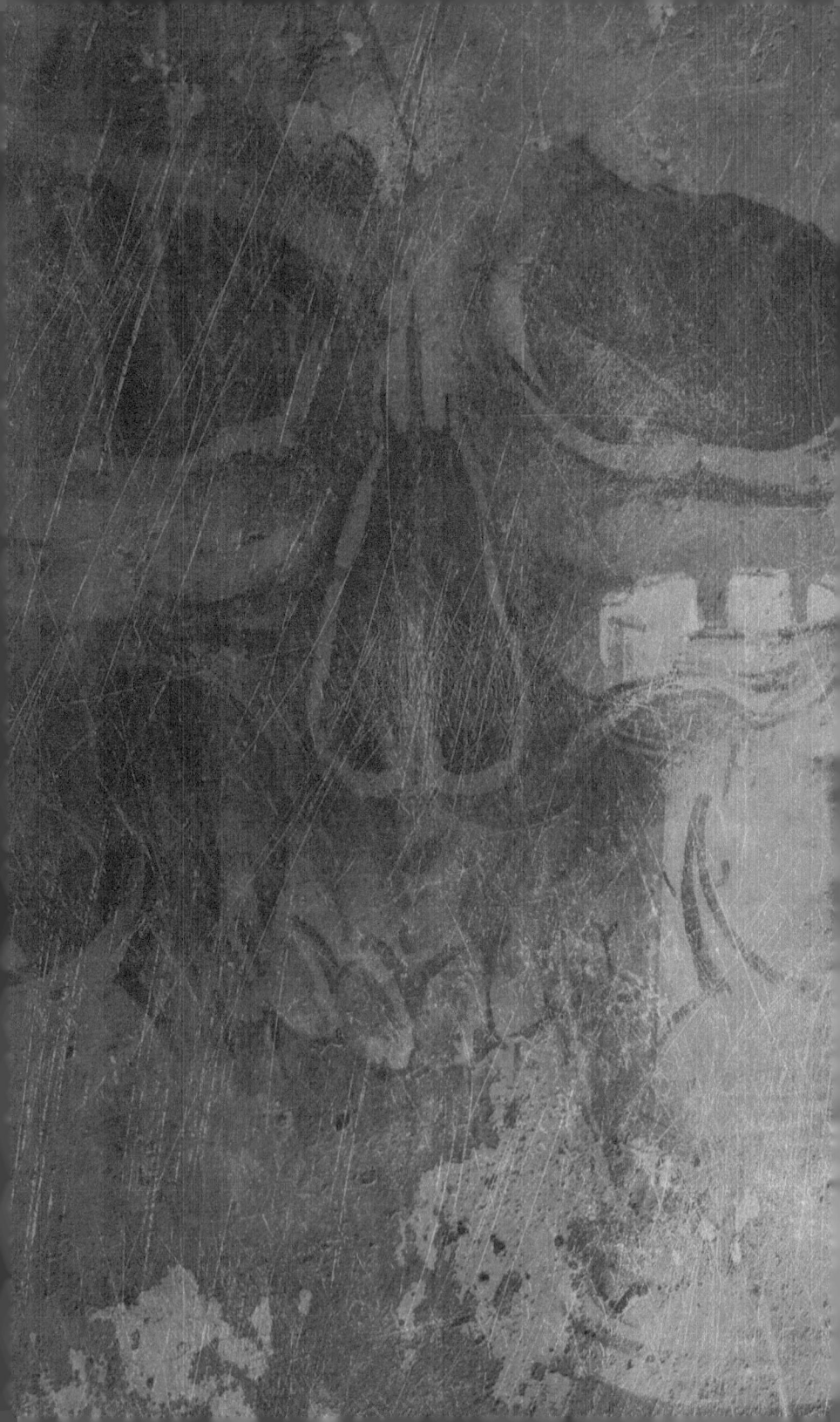

CHAPTER VIII

SABINE

NAIVELY, I'd thought the biggest mental hurdle of the evening would be keeping my composure around Sebastian. But that was only because I forgot to factor in being accosted by everyone's favorite golden-haired despot.

I'm seriously considering begging Zeus to let me break my 'no drinking' rule, but the stern look I get as I'm eyeing the decoy glass in his hand says he knows exactly what I'm thinking and to put that errant wish to bed.

"What the fuck was that?" he mutters darkly as he reluctantly hands over the flute.

"I think he's got someone watching me at the Academy," I wince.

"*Fuck*," he spits before draining the rest of his drink.

"Yeah," I agree, every inch of my exposed skin still crawling from the encounter. "Where's Orbison?"

Zeus's jaw ticks. "On your six, keeping Sinclair and Rhodes occupied."

"What? Why?" I ask, my voice weirdly high. There's

an odd thrill of excitement skating down my neck at the thought of these two sides of my life finally colliding.

"It looks like the two of them were about to storm over here," Knox remarks, watching with amusement while I rotate in my unwieldy gown as casually as possible. As Midas left to meet with the Arbiter, it occurred to me that I've yet to clock a single identifiable Suit so far tonight—but that doesn't mean I'm not being closely watched.

As I finally finish painstakingly rearranging my skirts, I glance up to where Dionysus is busy manhandling a stony-faced Apollo and Hades, and my entire expression slams shut with an Oscar-worthy display of nonchalance.

I was *so* right. Apollo *does* look pornographic in a tux.

The newly revealed Grayson wears a traditional black tuxedo suit, cut well to his athletically broad shoulders, and paired with an ornately embossed black tie. His dark hair is neatly styled to the side. Even with his identity partially obscured by a simple, metallic gold half-mask, the resemblance to his older brother is unmistakable. Not for the first time do I wonder how the fuck I didn't notice the connection sooner.

D still has him pulled up by the nape, alongside Hades. Hades, who's out here exiling souls from bodies left and right with how criminally good he looks in that brocaded corset vest of his. In head-to-toe black, with his long hair slicked back in a neat bun, he's wearing a gold mask that perfectly matches his best friend's and is no doubt hiding a grade A scowl.

The two Rox Boys might be slightly taller than D, but

with how flushed Apollo's neck looks and how rigid Hade's shoulders are, there's no doubt about who has the upper hand there.

Unfortunately, seeing the three of them together is proving hazardous to the scrap of silk masquerading as my lingerie, and as much as I'd love to sit back and enjoy the show—discretion remains key.

We don't need any opportunistic Gray Men reporting back to Lexington that the Rox Boys have my inner thighs doing their best impersonation of a Slip 'N Slide.

Or—*fuck*—back to Midas, for that matter. He seemed *entirely* too interested in my 'academic life'.

No, I can't have *anyone* thinking my fledgling Pantheon remains anything but a mandatory recruitment project for the Suits, so I instead fix my attention back onto the three *Concordia* agents I'd noticed during my earlier room sweep.

Baron Teague, 29, Maddox Williams, 28, and *River Lee, 28.*

There's nothing particularly scandalous to be found inside any of their modest Gray Men dossiers. What initially had the trio snagging my interest was the way in which they've each been obsessively tracking Medusa from the moment they came on shift.

I chuckle lightly into the champagne glass. Either the infamous bounty hunter's facing disciplinary action, or these Peacekeeper boys are nursing three massive, stalker-level crushes.

Can't say I really blame them, though.

The things that woman can do with the right paralytic.

"What's so funny, troublemaker?" Zeus murmurs as he leans in, his voice a low, husky kiss behind my ear. His large hand caresses down the length of my spine, gently soothing over the ghostly afterimages of Midas's touch.

My lashes flutter as it settles back onto my hip.

Any minute now, and I'll wake up to find this newly blossoming dynamic of ours has all been nothing but a blissful dream.

Before I can formulate a mostly mature, *mostly* non-horny response, however, the massive, red-lit chandeliers overhead begin to dim, and an expectant hush falls over the entire gathering.

A frown pulls at my brow. I'd hoped to have finished getting a lay of the land before the opening ceremony, but I realize I still haven't laid eyes on Hermes *or* Ares.

Or our Gray Man Council, for that matter.

Zeus's grip on my hip tightens expectantly and I wince as I feel the first dull throb behind my eyes. A sign I'm starting to approach the limits of my forced sobriety.

In my periphery, Dio's massive form rejoins Knox just as the sound of curtains being drawn back dramatically has everyone's focus moving to the black-marbled dais. The crowd shifts in anticipation, and I lose sight of Apollo and Hades.

When the velvet drapes part completely, it's to unveil the towering form of an ornately carved hourglass on a low marbled rostrum. The supporting framework of the massive structure is crafted from dark cherry oakwood, with each of its pear-shaped bulbs spanning dozens of feet in both directions and only separated by an extremely narrow and delicately blown stem.

The top half still contains each one of its crimson 'grains'—but everyone knows the grains of 'sand' aren't sand at all. They're a mixture of metal oxides, slate, and most notably, the pulverized bones of fallen Underworld leaders. Each 'grain' has then been carefully stained the same deep red as *Concordia*'s signature color: the unmistakable color of blood.

It's no secret that the entire tableau has been designed as a macabre reminder of the nature of our world. A symbol of the fleeting lifespan of man versus the everlasting legacy of the *Imperium in Imperio*. The belief that it will endure no matter the discord between North and South—an eternal empire within an empire.

Seeing the Green Knight's final resting place up close has those same soft fingers of dread brushing against the base of my skull as when I read the paternity results for the first time.

Because an hourglass only has one purpose.

But *what* exactly will it be counting down?

The crowd—already uneasy following the curtain's reveal—shifts again when a lone, hooded figure steps out from behind the hourglass, cloaked in the same crimson as its bloody sands.

Their face remains in shadow, but as they take their place at the front of the dais, there's no mistaking that air of power.

"Welcome to the 63rd Annual Symposium," the Arbiter intones, her voice a somber lilt as it echoes across the open atrium. The solemn greeting is met with a scattering of polite but nervous applause. "I only wish the occasion could be marked by a more joyous state of affairs. Alas, I fear that we will soon have nothing short of civil war on our hands."

This is it.

This is why we're in Themis this year.

She's never really been one to mince words, and true to her nature, the Last Word of the Underworld dives right to the heart of the matter. "It is no secret the former Southern Sovereign died without issue, nor that his estate has remained hotly contested."

My jaw clenches when she clasps her hands before her, as only someone who has come bearing grim news would.

"In the absence of an heir, in both blood or name, suitable Sovereign nominations must then not only find a majority, but do so within a timeframe as deemed reasonable by the standing cohort. The Southern Crown has now lain in dispute for a total of one hundred and fifteen days."

No. He wouldn't.

Like an unwitting magnet, my eyes seek out Midas's blond hair. He's situated right next to the dais itself, nursing a new whiskey and looking entirely too fucking pleased with himself as the *standing fucking cohort.*

The trepidation that follows creeps along my scalp until it feels like all the hair on my body is standing on end.

Despite his leonine demeanor, Midas and the Gordian

Knot are more akin to a pack of hyenas: always circling, testing the waters, stealing scraps—all before going in for the final kill.

In fact, he's so well known for his risk-averse, hands-off approach to business, that I would've put *actual* money on his organization continuing to sit back and monitor the chaos in the South. Right until its explosive conclusion. Content to wait while we finish tearing ourselves apart from the inside first—leaving them free to swoop in and clean house in the aftermath.

For him to make the first move like this, means he knows something we don't, and the realization lodges in my throat like a fishbone.

Whatever else the Arbiter says next turns to static in my ears as I scan the area around the platform and inadvertently lock eyes with the Gray Man. He's standing opposite the stage in dark contrast to the golden Northern Sovereign.

"He's here," I breathe, not needing to elaborate on who *he* is, and trying to move my lips as little as possible. Sebastian's penetrating gaze has not once left my face.

How long has he been watching us?

Unlike Midas, he does have a mask—a black-plumed replica of the ones my Crew is wearing.

"I see him," Zeus replies, and I hate how empty he now sounds. Gone is the firm but flirty Jax. He's shutting all the playfulness down and slipping the role of the indifferent son back on his shoulders like heavy battle armor. "Keep listening," he urges.

I force my focus back to the dais. "And to see through

this historic changing of the guard," the Arbiter is saying, "the younger Southern cohort must now carry forth the burden of their fathers' debts."

The cold shock of seeing my guardian in the flesh for the first time in months is met with a new wave of existential dread.

Fathers' debts?

"*Fuck*," Dio hisses at the possible implications of those cryptic words. Zeus's fingers dig reflexively into my hip bone beneath the edge of my bodice, right as my own go numb against the delicate stem of my champagne glass.

Jackson.

The perfect pawn for whatever price the Red Court has in mind for determining the next leader of the South.

Either he comes out on top for the Gray Men—or he dies trying.

Again, a win-win scenario for Sebastian.

The ominous pronouncement seems to have been all the signal needed for a second figure to approach the stage, this one in a hooded white cloak. The Herald quickly takes up position by the massive base of the hourglass before beginning her own rehearsed speech.

"It is by request of the Northern Sovereign that the Red Court formally intervene in the matter of succession for the Southern Crown. It is thus the decree of the Red Court and her esteemed Grace, the Arbiter—that the issue of Southern succession now be settled by participation in and completion of"—a dramatic pause—"*The Twelve Labors.*"

The room immediately comes alive with a mixture of

excited and intrepid conversation. The last time the Labors were initiated was in 1968—after both Sovereigns and their heirs were assassinated during the opening ceremony of that year's Symposium. The attack had sparked an all-out war between the Northern and Southern factions at the time and was the reason the Law of Hospitality was invoked in the first place.

Twelve weeks of increasingly difficult tasks in an officially sanctioned *Hunger Games* between vying factions.

Twelve weeks of every man for himself.

"To formally place a bid for the Crown, representing factions may nominate no more than *three* legitimized heirs for participation in the Labors."

Wait.

Heirs, plural?

A second Grayson heir.

"*Shit.*" I feel like my corset has crushed the last remaining air from my ribs.

"Don't look," Zeus warns, "he's still watching."

I swallow roughly. I couldn't, even if I was feeling ballsy enough to risk it. I don't know where Apollo ended up during the opening address, and aside from the little bubbles of space afforded to the most influential players standing closest to the platform, the rest of the throng is impossible to see through right now.

But this throws a *major* fucking spanner in the works.

There's no way we can risk waiting until we get back to Rox City to have our conversation with Tristan. Not if there's even the slightest chance an allowance for multiple nominations might have Sebastian pushing up his timeline—and dropping that bombshell *tonight*.

"No limits have been placed on the number of auxiliary team members, however, alliances with both Northern and Neutral entities *will* be strictly prohibited for the duration of the Labors," the Herald continues, her loud voice cutting cleanly through the rising chatter of the crowd.

"Although inter-faction interference during the execution of a trial *is* permitted, participants may not wilfully conspire to cause direct harm to another. Harm befalling participants during the natural execution of a Labor—while unfortunate—will *not* be considered a punishable offense," she further clarifies, and the excitement swells once again.

"Nominations are to be officially submitted within seven days. The Labors will begin following the release of the roster, and will continue until the last grain falls, or a single participant remains—whichever transpires first."

The room sobers a little, faced with the real possibility a significant portion of the next generation will be heading home from the Labors in a cushy pine box.

"The encrypted details of each Labor will be relayed electronically, one trial at a time," she continues. "Transmissions will be sent at 7pm, Pacific Standard Time, on the Sunday following the conclusion of each Labor."

So potentially, this whole ordeal could be over in as little as three months.

Unless, of course, not every heir makes it through to the end and they don't need to run all twelve trials.

Fuck.

Without staying to take questions from the increasingly agitated crowd, the Herald turns and disappears back past the curtain screen. The Arbiter, left standing vigil on the dais, raises a single hand and the murmurs of the crowd fall completely silent.

"Thank you, everyone. You may now move through to the next hall. The dinner service will begin shortly." And then she too turns, retreating from the stage in a flourish of crimson robes.

Released from her hold, the atrium once again explodes with a mixture of heated opinions and excited conversations. When the lights brighten again, I warily scan the nearby crowd, but the noise is quickly becoming deafening and does absolutely nothing to help my burgeoning headache.

No doubt the Fates are already doing the rounds, drafting up a list of projected nominees, and handing out their death pool odds. There's only one thing more universally loved throughout the Underworld than mutual bloodshed—and that's betting on it.

And right now there's at least one crime scion in the room who has no idea his hat's about to be thrown into the ring.

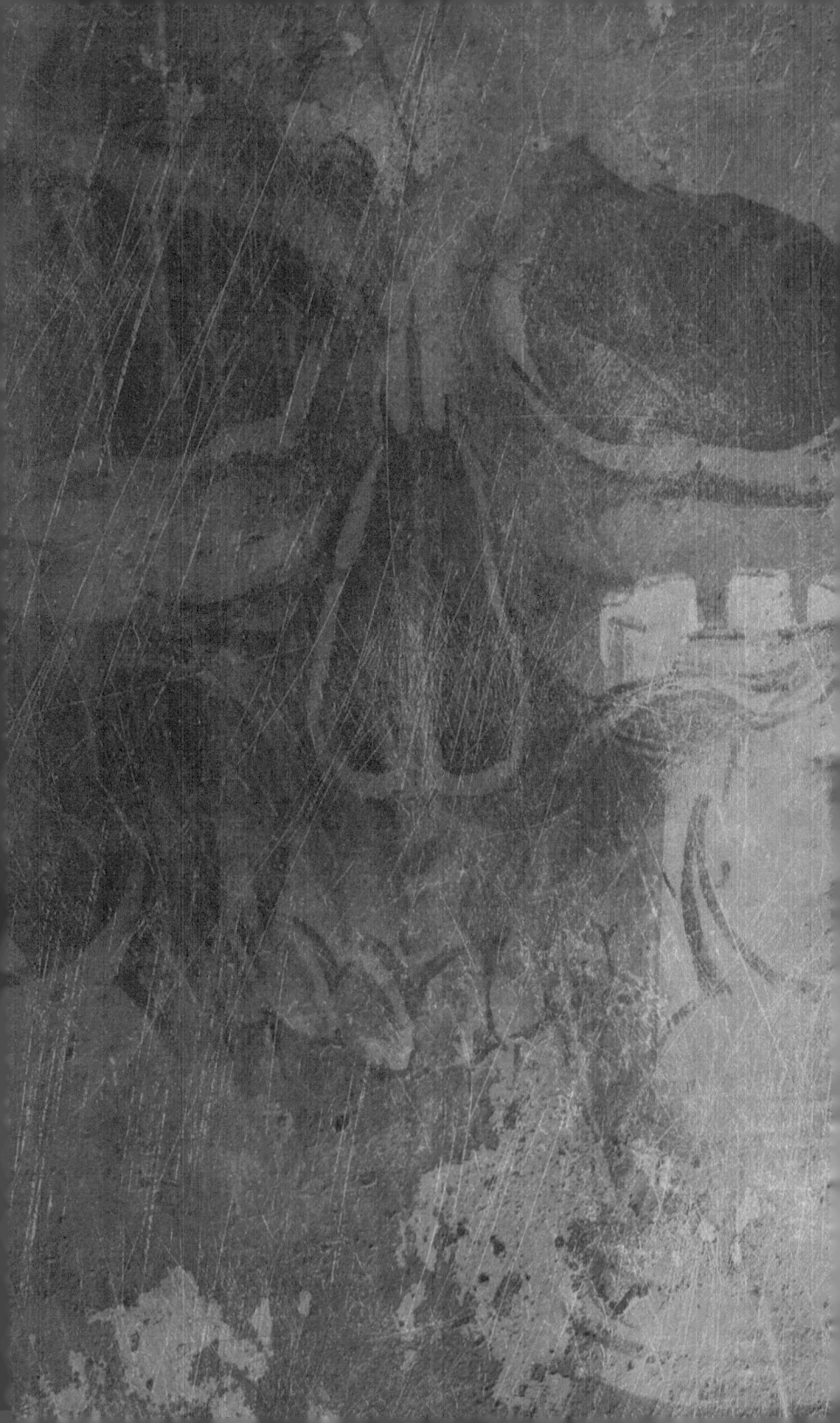

CHAPTER IX

STUDIOUSLY IGNORING the boogeymen still gathered near the stage, I'm carefully hunting for signs of the Rox Boys when Smiley O'Sullivan and the Reilly brothers once again steal my attention.

Considering the nature of tonight's announcement, I'm expecting to find a renewed discord between the rival Mobs. But unlike the vast majority of guests around them, their smiles and postures appear relaxed and confident.

Entirely too unfazed for a group of Irishmen whose driving tenets have always been *muintir ar dtús, muintir go deo. Family first, family forever.*

That small, uncertain buzzing at the edge of my thoughts starts to grow in intensity. It's not the usual information overload ache either; it's the gnawing, gut feeling you get when you know you've missed something important.

I startle when Zeus's hard bicep tucks me in against his side. With lips brushing my temple—hoping to be heard above the swell of the party—he directs my focus in the opposite direction. "Two o'clock, second alcove."

My eyebrows jump, my mask sliding up a little with the movement. *He spotted them before I did?*

Before I get a chance to verify, he starts hustling us toward one of the alcoves that are tucked off the atrium's eastern wall. Both Dionysus and Knox quickly fall into step around us.

"Jesus," I mutter, trying not to break an ankle as he hauls me along like a man on a mission. I chose these heels for their height advantage, not agility. "Slow down, will you?"

"You want the Suits snatching up the Boys?"

"Of course not," I huff as my bodice shifts, the boning pressing uncomfortably against my ribs. If he doesn't slow the fuck down, I'm going to find a way to make *him* spend twelve hours in this thing and see how *he* likes it. "But you did find them? *How?*"

I'm choosing not to focus on the fact he seems to think they're holed up in one of the private indulgence rooms.

What do I care if they've got two dozen Courtesans in there with them?

I'm not their keeper.

"Miller," is all he says. He sounds like he's grinding rocks between his teeth.

"Miller?" I ask, perplexed.

"You'll see," D sings.

"Okaaay," I drawl, just as we reach the veil of crimson gossamer used to screen off the entrance to the alcove. "Should we maybe—"

Without further preamble, Zeus shoves straight through the flimsy privacy drape, dragging me inside with a taut arm still wrapped around my torso like a bandoleer.

The noise from the main party drops away slightly, the ancient red bricks creating a natural sort of sound chamber for its occupants. The lighting in here is also significantly dimmer than the rest of the building; the deep, red hues lending a more debauched air to the small anteroom that normally only serves as a receiving area for the Court.

It takes a second for my eyes to adjust and then another for it to register that there are only the four Rox Boys in front of me, each posted up in a different corner of the room.

And not one of them is engaged in anything remotely illicit—unless, of course, you count Hermes's outfit.

Dio presses up against my other side, covering up a groan by coughing into his fist. *"See?"*

And *Sweet Lady Karma,* do I.

I see *so* well that I'm going to need to upgrade my earlier lingerie situation from *Chance of Flash Flooding* to *Search and Rescue Operation*—because I swear they just straight up floated out to sea.

Aside from a pair of decadently skin-tight, leather biker pants, the only thing Lake Miller is wearing is a *godsforsaken* waist trainer.

Black velvet paneling, strips of intricate brocade framing the fasteners, and a smartly cut underbust.

No undershirt. No overcoat.

Just tailor-made sin that leaves the entire upper torso bare and sets the stage for those caramel button nipples of his to steal the show.

Boys in corsets?

My kryptonite.

"Sabine?" comes Apollo's terse voice, reminding me why I'm here in the first place. *Rude.*

"Yeah," I confirm with a sigh, reluctantly tearing my focus away from his friend's nipples and reaching up to untie the black silk ribbon holding my feathered disguise in place. "We need to talk."

Stormy eyes run over my newly exposed features, assessing. They narrow from behind his golden mask when they move onto my companions, taking in both my Enforcers' protective stances and Zeus's possessive hold.

When Dionysus blows him a mocking kiss, he steps out from between two loveseats, fists clenched and chin lifted like he's expecting another confrontation.

I hold my hands up in surrender. "They won't touch you," I insist.

Apollo only scoffs, shooting daggers in D's direction. But I don't miss the way my words have Hades shifting in my periphery, aura like a cornered animal.

Fuck.

"They won't touch you—*again*," I clarify, attempting to shoulder both Zeus and Dio away as discreetly as possible.

"*Sabe*," Zeus warns, lowly.

"Maybe you should step outside and watch the door," I say to him pointedly. We only have so long before we'll be expected in the dining hall, and we're going to get exactly nowhere with all this loose testosterone and caveman posturing.

When their large frames only tense up further, my eyes roll to the heavens. "If either of you growls again, I swear I will have you *both* fucking neutered."

"We're not letting you out of our sight, babygirl," Dio argues right back. He's wearing a wicked smirk that I know is purely for the Boys' benefit.

"No one's getting in here, you idiot," I snap. "Now get out, we're on the clock."

"That's not what—" he tries to protest.

"I know it's not, but I'm safe with them. *Trust me.* Knox?"

Our Second Enforcer exhales dramatically, then obediently grabs hold of Zeus and Dio by their suit collars and begins tugging them both backward. He despises team conflict, but he's on my security detail for a reason.

The moment the drape settles back into place behind them, Apollo hisses, *"Who the fuck are they?"*

"Look," I start, inching toward one of the couches. I choose a spot close to the entrance that lets me keep all four of them in my line of sight and perch myself uncomfortably on the armrest. "It's a long fucking story —one that I don't think we have time for right now—but there *are* some time-sensitive matters that *can't* wait."

Apollo slips his hands into his pockets, bristling. He's clearly unhappy about the dismissal.

"What sensitive matters?" Ares grunts, and my eyes

cut to where he's glowering at me like a dark cloud. In this lighting, the neatly combed strands of his auburn hair appear almost blood-red, his amber glare now the color of grain whisky.

As soon as his gaze meets mine, he shifts into a defensive stance. Forearms fold tightly across the broad width of his chest, massive biceps trapping the yoke and sleeves of a bespoke tuxedo in a valiant fight for their lives.

My mouth waters, but I have to get this done before one of the Senior Enforcers shows up to drag me off to dinner by my ear.

I slide my focus back to Apollo, watching carefully for his reaction. "Your father, for one. The Labors for another."

When his face visibly pales, shoulders pulling taut, my spine immediately straightens.

Does he already know?

"What about my father?" The question is purposefully even. Normally, I'd say he had a reasonable poker face, but the stress now written all over his body language gives him right away.

"Your father will most likely be entering you into the trials for the Crown Succession as one of his designated heirs."

That pulls a startled laugh from his mouth, cracking through some of that cool confidence he was trying to cloak back around himself.

"My father's a monster, but he's not part of the Underworld," he assures me in a derisive tone, with his full chest. Despite only having been around him for a short time, it's what I like to think of as *Classic Sinclair.* "Well, not officially, at least. I wouldn't put it past him if he had dealings. But there's no proof. Not in his office, anyway."

In his office?

Shit.

That means he has no idea, then.

I slump back down, causing my waistline to pinch.

"What?" He frowns at my defeated look. "Why do you look disappointed about that?"

"Why do I look disappointed you don't believe your father has Underworld connections?" I repeat, not at all sardonically. My fingers lift to my temple, rubbing along the scar there.

"Yes, exactly." Apollo's now looking down his nose at me like I'm a petri dish devoid of all intelligent life.

Time to rip off the Band-Aid, I guess.

"Because I thought for a moment there you already knew what I'm about to tell you." I sigh. "Martin Sinclair isn't actually your father, my guy."

The small room is deadly still for only the span of a heartbeat before it explodes with angry Rox Boys. I wince, checking the veiled entrance for signs of my guard dogs, but it seems my own Crew decided to trust me, after all.

I almost feel like a bit of a voyeur then; getting lost for a moment as I watch each of them converge on Apollo. The fierce bonds of their shared brotherhood are palpable, the four of them orbiting each other with the kind of bone-deep familiarity that only found family can.

When I look back up, Ares is right in my space. I gaze up at him from my seat on the armrest.

And *up*.

Fuck, he's big.

I'd pay good money to see him and Dio go head-to-head sometime.

"What would you even get out of saying some shit like that, Winters?" he demands. A muscle right below his gold mask jumps. The tattoos kissing his jawline pull with the movement.

"Nothing, actually," I say, awkwardly pushing up to stand up so he can't loom over me like a giant wall of muscled formalwear. He still has a couple of inches on me, though, even in these shoes. "And it's true. I can bring you proof as soon as we're back in Rox City."

Unsurprisingly, all four of their expressions remain decidedly skeptical.

"I know you don't owe me your trust. In fact, you don't owe me *anything*," I quickly amend when Apollo looks like he's about to argue with me. "But to be perfectly honest, I don't owe you anything, either." My eyes move between them, trying to ignore the powerful effect their combined presence has on me. "I'm only at your Academy to do a job. And no, I wasn't given a choice in the matter."

I'm never even given the *illusion* of choice. Not since the Gray Man sat down across from me on that winter's day five years ago.

What would that kind of freedom even look like? What would I choose? *Who* would I choose?

If only one of the choices was not having to choose at all.

"What job?" Ares barks.

"We'll have to put a pin in that until we get back, but for right now, I need you to listen."

Apollo steps right up beside Ares, standing shoulder-to-shoulder with him and blocking my view of the final two Boys. His eyes are hard as they dart between mine. Probably trying to inspect my face for tells.

Good luck with that.

"Fine," he eventually agrees, tone laced with frustration. "Then who the fuck *is* my father?"

My stomach tightens, wishing I knew how much time I had left. I'll just have to stick with the *CliffsNotes* version for now.

"Sebastian Grayson."

"Are you talking about the Mayor of Lexington? *That* Sebastian Grayson?" Ares sneers, following it up with an uncharacteristic roll of his eyes.

"What else aren't you telling us?" Apollo prompts when all I do is nod.

"Originally, we didn't think he'd risk a public confrontation by approaching you this weekend, but the Herald's decree has just thrown a spanner in the works. Now, there's every chance he'll corner you before you leave tonight. Most likely at dinner."

"Is she fucking kidding with this shit?" Ares spits.

Apollo ignores him, raising his hand in a silent bid for me to continue.

"He probably won't go so far as to make the big reveal at the dinner table, but he may still invite you to eat with him under the guise of wining and dining you as prospective recruits."

"You don't think so? Why not?" Apollo asks, tensely. He looks about ready to crawl out of his skin.

"He doesn't know that we know, and I don't know if he's ready to reveal his hand just yet."

"And how long *have* you known?"

"That you *were* his son? I only found out yesterday. Someone sent your paternity report to Zeus anonymously."

"Zeus?" His tone sounds oddly strained when he repeats Jax's callsign.

He's probably annoyed I didn't give him the head moniker.

Just more proof of his bloodline.

"Your older brother," I clarify with a rueful twist of my lips. "The disgraced heir."

And for the first time, the Head Prefect allows some of the surprise to color his expression rather than defensiveness. "Okay, fuck. So I have a brother." He blows out a breath. "But none of that explains why a *city mayor* would be invited to the Symposium—or why he'd be recruiting."

"Or how *you* know him."

The quietly delivered question comes out of nowhere, and my chin jerks up in surprise.

It's the first time I've heard Hermes speak tonight—

only his voice is devoid of all the usual roguishness I've come to expect from him.

Now that I think about it, there were no playful quips upon our arrival either. No flirty banter. Of course, I'd been too caught up in the theatre of his outfit to notice whether he had a closed posture or a mournful set to his plush mouth. But when I dig into my visual memory banks for a snapshot, it's all there in high-definition.

A corona of wild curls. A stubborn jawline and the rigid press of bronzed shoulders against red bricks. The new, feverish shine in an already too-bright gaze.

Maybe it's a lucky thing I can't see him around Ares's protective bulk, after all.

I pull in a deep breath through my nose.

Best just to be direct.

"Sebastian Grayson is the Gray Man. And I'm his Librarian."

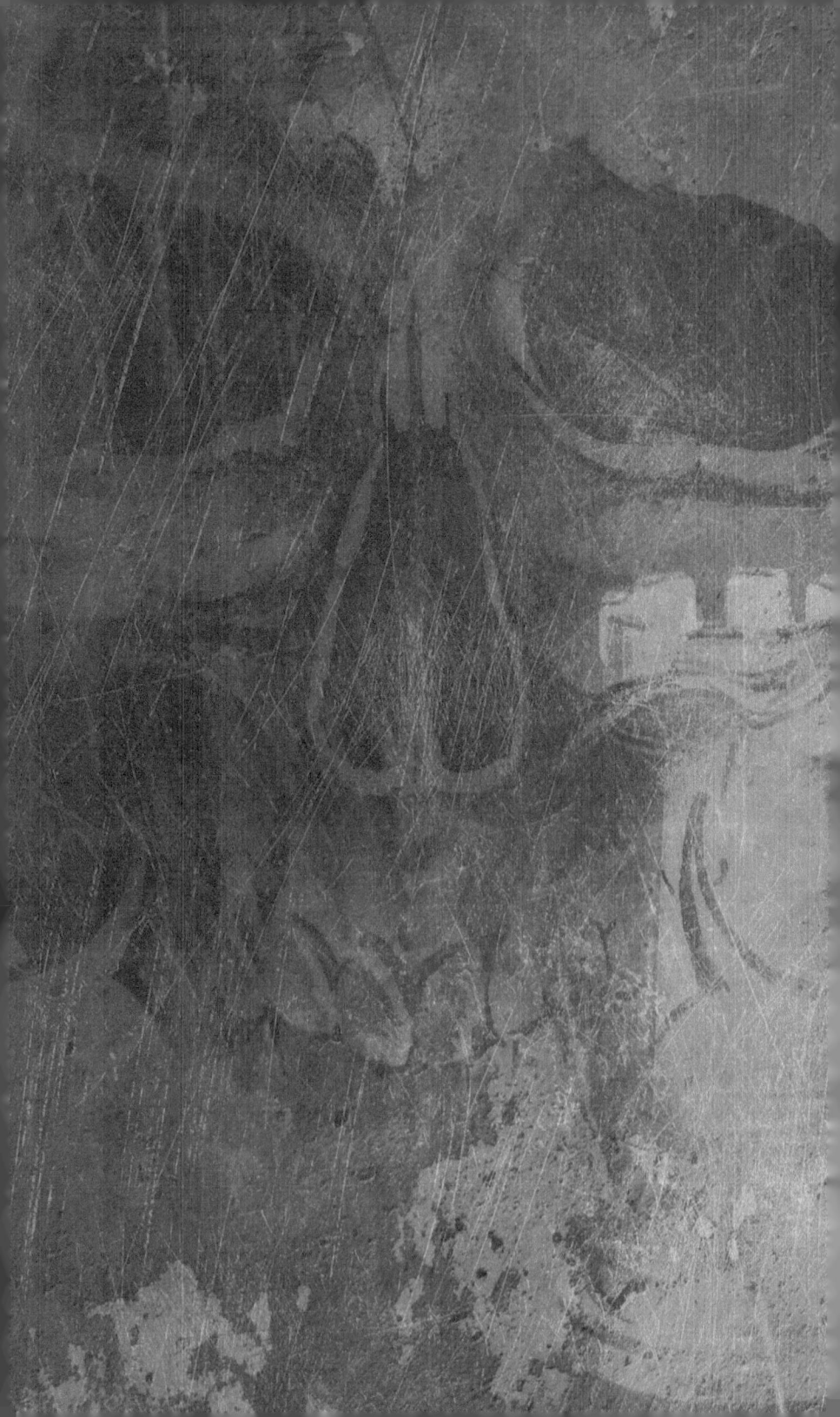

CHAPTER X

SABINE

ARES GROWLS, inked fingers dragging down chiseled features in frustration. The way his gigantic arms curl has me a little concerned for his jacket seams; the poor things look just about ready to surrender.

"*The Gray Man?* So Tristan is just swapping out country club-brand evil for mob boss-brand evil?" he grouses the moment he's calmed down long enough to speak.

"I guess? I don't know his father personally, though I *am* well acquainted with his sire," I hesitate, wondering if I should elaborate. I'm pushing my luck the longer I stay, but I can't just let them jump straight into the snake pit without at least a warning, right?

There's no anti-venom for this type of fuckery.

"So, I need you to believe me when I tell you that there are only three men in this world who can still *truly* evoke my fear response—and he's one of them."

"What the fuck does *that* mean?" Apollo snaps. His arms are now folded tightly across his chest. He's not as obscenely muscled as Dionysus or Ares, but the guarded pose still does a stellar job of showcasing just how broad his athletic frame is.

Without a mask to hide behind, I have to work overtime to keep my expression as serene as possible. "Not important."

"And who're the other two?" Hermes demands, stepping into view. His fingers are laced behind his head as he prowls back and forth. With his arms raised, the busk of his corset rises, blessing me with an even clearer view of the lines of his Adonis belt as they dip below his waistline.

Christ.

"Also not important," I repeat, clearing my throat when my words come out a little too huskily.

"*Midas.*"

My eyes jerk to Hades's as if magnetized, finding him now hovering at Apollo's side like an apparition in all black. The lines of his tailor-made outfit are immaculate —save for the way his dress pants pull too tightly around the fists now shoved inside their pockets.

"You looked uncomfortable when he asked you to dance," he says, voice raspy from disuse, "and relieved when he left."

Well, fuck. Trust the ever-silent, watchful one to pinpoint exactly which of my loose threads to tug at first. His focus now feels somehow even more intense, the weight of that knowing gaze a lead apron on my chest.

When I neither confirm nor deny his brother's observations, Apollo, of course, takes that as an opening to bulldoze his way back into control of the conversation.

"What did he want with you? And don't say just a dance. We heard his twenty questions. He was oddly interested in you."

I purse my lips, casually examining my nails. Perhaps my promise to explain *everything* had been a tad hasty, considering we've only known each other a couple of weeks—and not even well at that.

The problem is each time I contemplate walking away, there's a troubling tug behind my sternum.

"He knows who I am. Well, he at least knows that I'm valuable to Sebastian, and that makes me potentially valuable to *him*."

Apollo's brow pinches. "Because you're a librarian?"

Amusement fizzes, tipping up one side of my mouth as I glance back up at him. "Not *a* librarian. *The* Librarian."

"You make it sound like a title."

I hum, considering. "Not so much a title, it's not like a job I applied for. It's...what he made me." I hold up a hand before there's another interrogation, "But that's also for when we're back in Rox City. Just know that most of the Underworld knows the name, but not my identity. That's strictly need to know."

"Okay," Apollo says, yielding for now. "But that creep Midas still thinks you're *valuable*. Are you in danger?" he asks darkly, absently flexing his crossed arms.

Hermes resumes his pacing, and I'm so preoccupied with the agitated bounce of blond curls that I don't see the way Hades's shoulders stiffen or when Ares's glower deepens.

My next swallow feels a little rough as I muse on that. *Good question.*

"Honestly? The Suits guard me like an heir, so I've always assumed he thinks I'm Sebastian's daughter rather than a ward. I don't know why he hasn't made a move before, but I *do* know he prefers the long game." My eyes slide back to Apollo. "Regardless, your father is the more imminent threat."

"The Suits, that's who you've been with this whole time?"

Most kids in Roxborough or Lexington grow up hearing scary stories about the Gray Man and his smartly dressed army. He's the Twin Cities' Bogeyman and the Gray Men—or the Suits as we like to call them—are the weapons he uses to haunt us.

I lift my mask, showing them the black feathers. "Yes, and if you see one of these tonight, they work for your father. With the exception of the three standing outside, you can't trust any of them."

Ares's shoulders roll back at that. He looks about ready to start staging an armed insurrection against the Suits himself. "And he's entered Tristan into these trials? What do we need to do to get his name off that list?"

"I said he'll *most likely* be nominating him since he's allowed to nominate up to three heirs. And he won't have a choice if that happens; a succession nomination's binding. It's like putting your name in the Goblet of Fire, so to speak."

"*Fuck,*" he curses under his breath, turning his whole body toward his best friend. "We can protect you—"

"How?" I blurt, cutting him off. This is *the Gray Man*. Four seniors and a few loose criminal connections aren't going to cut it.

"What?"

"I know you guys seem to have a lot of sway at the Academy, and I'm impressed you've managed to dodge the Aces for so long. But being big fish in your little Rox pond won't help you when there are actual sharks out there," I say forcefully.

Ares only smirks. There's a challenging glint in his eye like he thinks he's finally got one over me. "We're *sponsored*, Winters."

"No *shit*," I drawl right back, "or you wouldn't fucking be here. By *who*?"

"The Alessi Family."

I groan. "You're actually kidding me right now."

Why are the pretty ones always so stupid?

He visibly bristles, but I only scowl, wanting to knock that stupid gold mask from his face.

"The Alessi Family? As in the *New York Alessis*? New. York. They're from the *North*! That means they won't be able to participate *or* interfere in the trials. Besides, the Alessi crime family are practically nobodies compared to the Suits."

I turn away from them, needing a second to piece my thoughts together. That niggling uncertainty is back, clawing for my attention.

None of this makes sense.

Sponsorship is expensive, requires influence, and is heavily vetted. Whoever sponsored Tristan Sinclair and his friends would only do so if they *really* wanted them here tonight.

And they knew they could pull it off.

The only thing of note the Alessi mafia family has ever contributed to the *Imperium* are the Donato twins. And they can't even claim them anymore.

Someone else knows about the second Grayson heir.

"You're better off going to Martin Sinclair for help," I mutter.

"No!" Apollo and Ares bark at the same time.

"Jesus, fuck," I huff, turning back and taking in their outraged expressions. *I was only joking.*

Scanning the room, my gaze then lands on the entrance, reminding me of the men outside.

"Alright, then. I guess if Sebastian *does* nominate both of his sons, we'll all technically be on the same team, if temporarily. You should probably accept *our* help at least."

Instead of answering, Ares and Apollo have a silent conversation with their eyes, while Hermes pauses with his hands on his hips. He hasn't said another word, and this might just be the longest I've seen him go without speaking since I've known him.

Hades continues looking through me with that uncanny X-ray vision of his.

When Apollo returns his focus to me, there's a little more color in his expression, and eyes that I now know are a shade of Grayson blue are filled with resolve.

"We obviously still have questions, and evidently, you've got the answers."

A flash of that first day in the courtyard: *Sabine Winters is* dead. *So who the fuck are you?*

"Obviously," I echo, with a curt nod to cover my unease.

"But, yes. It's probably in our best interest if we... work together," he concedes, watching as I slip my mask back into place. Just as I finish with the ribbon, I hear a flurry of movement on the other side of the privacy screen.

My arms drop back to my sides.

Time's up.

"*UGH*," I groan, leaning into Zeus's muscular hold as he ushers me toward the dining hall. My head had started pounding the moment I'd stepped out of the alcove's dim lighting and back into the main atrium. "I don't think I can do dinner. I'm about five balding mobsters away from an epic migraine."

"You know as well as I do it will be a thousand times more painful—*for both of us*—if you don't show your face. Just get through the main service and I'll have Orbison drop you off at the hotel."

"Can I at least start drinking now?

"No."

Was that a whimper? I'm pretty sure it was a whimper.

"*One* drink, *with* a plate of food, and then you are going straight to bed."

I sag, letting him take even more of my weight. Because as much as that commanding tone had me deflating in his arms like a slutty balloon, I can still feel my skull starting to split like an overripe piece of fruit.

Damnit.

I really could've used the drink *before* we had to head in and throw ourselves to the wolves.

Or *wolf*—singular.

The Big, Bad, *'Possibly the Next Southern Sovereign'* Wolf, to be precise.

I tilt my chin, studying Zeus's tense profile as he expertly steers us around another group of rowdy mobsters—this one comprised of three members of the American *Cosa Nostra* sharing lines off the small of a petite Courtesan's back. "And where will *you* be?"

His eyes cut to mine, stern gaze dropping to my lips for just a nanosecond. But I caught it, and the dominance in his expression has my mouth watering against its will. I swallow.

"Running interference," he answers evenly, his own throat bobbing once.

"*Jax*," I whisper.

"I rather liked *Zeus*," is all he says, punctuated by a rueful grin.

"You don't—" He cuts me off with a single, knowing squeeze to the waist.

I shiver when Dio then runs a knuckle down the length of my spine. "*Hospitium*," D reminds me, "and Knox will be stuck to him like glue. He'll be fine, babe."

Logically, I know Sebastian won't lay a hand on him

here—not without major consequences. But that paternity report has still sparked a small, foreign flame of anxiety deep inside my chest. It all but puts a bounty on Zeus's head, and the protection of neutral ground ends the moment we leave Themis.

"I'll be fine," Zeus echoes before purposefully putting some distance between us. We've reached the doorway of the antechamber hosting tonight's dinner service, and as soon as the four of us move through the set of Georgian double doors, a mousey *Concordia* hostess wearing a blood-red cravat practically teleports her way to our side.

Jessica Crabit, 29's chocolate brown doe eyes instantly zero in on Zeus. "Sovereignty, sir?"

"South," Zeus instructs her, glancing around the hall. Although there are quite a few revelers still enjoying the debauchery outside, it looks as though a good majority of the tables have already been seated.

"And party, sir?"

"Gray Men."

There's no missing the flash of pity on Jessica's sharp, elfin face.

"Leadership or ancillary?" she asks, more timidly.

"Second gen leadership," Zeus clarifies, and she pales as though he just asked her to escort him to the gallows herself.

To her credit, she doesn't miss a beat—bustling off almost as quickly as she appeared and leaving me cursing at the thought of having to chase her down in this unholy combination of dress and heels. Zeus follows calmly in her nervous wake with the long, unhurried strides of a mafia prince.

I have to practically jog to keep up.

The hostess comes to a halt in front of a grand cluster of tables, each one covered in a black cloth and bearing an elegant placard inscribed with:

Southern Sovereignty:
The Gray Men

"Here, sirs," she gestures politely to one of two intimately set tables, both positioned slightly apart from the rest of the seating reserved for our faction's party. Both, surprisingly, are still empty.

Zeus dismisses her with a nod, reaching for the chair directly in front of me. Before he can finish sliding it out, however, Dionysus shoulder checks him out of the way.

"Your ladyship," he croons in my ear with a dramatic hand flourish.

"*Dude*," I jeer, at the same time that Zeus scolds, "*Orbison.*"

"What?" He flutters his lashes at us with faux guilelessness.

Zeus rolls his eyes—no doubt seeking strength to deal with his Second's antics—but my focus has already been drawn by the weird number of place settings at each of the two tables.

Six.

There should be five for the Junior Council and four for the Senior.

Which reminds me—"Has anyone seen Foster?" He'd disappeared after shoving that drink into my hands, and I hadn't seen him again since. It's been hours.

"He's doing bug sweeps on all the Gray Man suites at the Delphi. Sebastian's orders," Knox supplies. He scratches his neck, a grimace pulling down his mouth.

"What the fuck?" *There goes all hope for a ceasefire.* "He has two dozen other tech guys on his payroll that could've done that with their eyes closed."

"Are you really that surprised, though? Low skill, low effort. How better to remind us just how little he values his Junior Council?" Zeus drawls. "Plus, it's kept our group split for the better part of the night."

I huff, angrily maneuvering myself into my seat and trying not to puncture a lung on the boning of my dress as I do.

He's definitely not wrong, but now I'm even more confused about the seating arrangements. If Sebastian had no intention of letting our entire Crew eat together, why were there not four seats? And even with the possibility of having the Rox Boys join him, why two tables of six?

Dionysus leans over my shoulder, ogling my cleavage as he helps to push the chair in. "You know you almost look like you own a pair of tits when you sit down in that thing," he stage whispers, knowing full well I can't stand back up and retaliate without the assistance of at least two grown adults. His eyes twinkle behind his mask.

"Oh, you *did not just*—" I start, jerking my arm back,

but the asshole twists to keep his torso out of the direct area of impact.

"Sit *down,* you brat," Zeus hisses, taking his place to my left, and—*I swear to orgasms*—the tips of Dio's ears turn pink. He drops down on my other side without another word.

Knox then makes a show of cramming his giant body into one of the empty spots directly opposite, eyes ping-ponging between the three of us. His chin begins to quiver with the effort of holding his tongue.

I smother a grin.

Always such a slut for the tea.

"Just *ask,* Morales," Zeus says with a long-suffering sigh, toying with one of the many cutlery sets arranged before him.

Knox sucks on his lower lip before immediately launching into his inquisition. "How long? Who made the first move? Each of you and Sabe? Or is it *both* of you? Like you and Rhett—or you *and* Rhett? Or like, all three of you *together* together?"

When he's forced to pause and take a breath, Zeus quirks his brow, his black mask shifting up with the movement. "You done?"

I'm fully expecting our gossip queen to keep peppering him with questions. Instead, his dark beard splits with an oddly satisfied smile, full of teeth.

"Why does your face look like they just announced a new season of *One Tree Hill*?" I ask, chuckling.

"Woman! Don't *even* joke about that," he pouts, aiming one huge index finger in my direction. "Seriously though, you know I love a good slow burn, but *this*"—he circles that accusatory finger between the three of us—"has been giving me *major* bangxiety."

Then the giant teddy bear of an Enforcer leans in, propping his chin up on two massive fists. With the crown of his head covered by feathers, he looks like he's about to perform a cabaret. "Tell. Me. *Everything*."

But hearing that even *Knox* noticed our push and pull has my gut tightening and my chuckle backsliding to an uneasy laugh. Was I the only one who thought my years of pining had been completely, totally, one hundred percent unrequited?

"Who?" I deflect with a mocking smile. "Orbison and I? That's old news, sweetie."

"*Saberella*," he groans, and his playful eye roll melts away a little of that weird feeling in the pit of my stomach.

"Okay, *jeez*." My hands go up in mock surrender. "Uh, the three of us did kind of hook up," I hedge, subtly flicking my eyes to my left. I'm trying to gauge exactly how much to divulge, but oddly enough, our leader's expression remains open and relaxed. "But last night was the first time, I swear."

Knox scowls at my half-assed admission. "When I said tell me *everything*—"

But I don't get the chance to defend myself because then Dionysus leans in with a signature smirk, reminding us all that he's just as much a provocateur as Knox is a busybody.

"You wanna hear how Daddy Grayson had her riding

my face, right there on the kitchen counter, do you?" he teases his fellow Enforcer, acting out the scene with hands and tongue in true showman fashion.

"How feral he was at the sight of her dripping down my chin? How he just fucking *snapped* and fucked our babygirl's brains out—clean through the back of her skull?" He's biting his lip as he mimes a head explosion.

"*Lord have mercy,*" Knox whispers, and everything below my waistline clenches like the steel cage of my bodice at the memory.

Lord have mercy, indeed.

"Or maybe you wanna hear how he put me back on my knees and had me clean the two of them off his very *long*...very *thick*...and very *veiny*...*cock*," Dio drawls, really just rolling that last word around on his tongue for added effect.

Our deputy Enforcer dramatically crosses himself. "I just *knew* he'd be a Dom. Too much Daddy energy," he says, shaking his head. He leans back in. "Tell me, is he cut?"

"Cut," D purrs with a lazy nod while stretching an equally languid forearm across the back of my chair.

"Jesus, fuck," Zeus grunts from my other side, and I almost snort aloud at the sound of his exasperation. "I also *wax*, Morales. Since we're apparently dissecting my every inch right now."

Dio chuckles. "Of which I can confirm he has a good eigh—" His playful words cut off as he spots the four men now bearing down on our table. His arm immediately drops away, all humor gone.

Knox doesn't bother turning to see where we're looking—the stiff postures along our side of the table tell him everything he needs to know. In an instant, he too switches gears from *Tea Drinker* back to *Underworld Enforcer*.

Tendrils of dread begin to writhe low in my gut as we silently track their approach.

Game faces, ladies.

CHAPTER XI

SABINE

THE POOR HOSTESS escorting the Gray Man and his Councillors to their seats looks like she's on the verge of passing out. Since our seating plan puts the Seniors furthest from the door, their path leads them directly past our table. Of course, Sebastian views that as the perfect opportunity to stop and spike the heart rates of his favorite Junior Officers-in-exile.

Even after this many weeks apart, his domineering presence still feels both as familiar and as suffocating as ever. The dark blue eyes that bore into each of us are like ice spears, reminding me of those parts of the ocean so deep no light from the surface can reach them.

Sub-zero and unforgiving.

Next to him, his Second-in-Command *Dominic Licata, 49,* and the rest of their Council are about as intimidating as the *Concordia* agents lined up along the edges of the dining hall.

Which is to say: *not at all.*

Nobody dares breathe as we wait for one of them to break the taut silence between us. It's Sebastian who finally does, but only after we spend an eon pinned beneath that cold, calculating gaze.

"Jackson. Sabine." His tone is perfectly neutral, and in true Gray Man fashion, he completely ignores the rest of his Juniors. The *Concordia* employee takes that as her cue to escape.

I know there's no way he'd compromise his prized asset by addressing me as *the Librarian* so publicly—but to my ears our given names still sound like war drums.

The beginning of the end.

A death knell.

Suddenly my throat's developed a very real craving for a glass of ice water.

"Father," Zeus acknowledges him, just as evenly, somehow also managing a respectful tip of the chin.

"Sir," I croak.

He passes a considering look across the men seated around our table before zeroing back in on me. "Join me for dinner, won't you."

It's not an invitation.

Invitations come with the right of refusal.

RSVP: Dearest Gray Man, I must respectfully decline on account of a sudden case of watery bowels.

It's also only tossed in *my* direction. *Fuck.*

My chair scrapes loudly in the ensuing silence, but then Zeus is there—his touch warm and steady as he helps me back to my feet. In the time it takes us to disengage my skirts from the plush seating, Sebastian's already seated himself at the Senior table, leaving five place settings distinctly empty.

Instead of joining his boss, however, a silent Dominic swoops in for the seat I've just vacated. When the remaining Councillors—Sebastian's main money man, Head Accountant *Barlow St. Ives, 51*, and systems analyst, Head Architect *Stephen Almani, 45*—step forward and take the empty spots on either side of Knox, the reason for the bizarre table split becomes clear.

The Gray Man *is* planning a dinner ambush—but I'm the only other Suit getting a front-row seat.

Sweat dots my brow. It's no more than a few wobbly steps to reach the empty seat that Sebastian indicates— but I may as well be walking a Green Mile on execution day.

At least I'll look fabulous for my funeral.

Eight weeks ago, I might've told you that I was finally starting to build up a small immunity to the Gray Man's sinister presence. That I was moving about more freely; thinking less and less about the consequences of chasing down scratches for the itch inside my head.

He still unnerved me, yes, but after years of exposure therapy, I could at the very least enter my guardian's direct line of sight without every single piece of my training flying straight out the window.

Now it seems even just a couple of Sebastian-free months has been more than enough to weaken all those Gray Man antibodies. The void I'd tried inviting out tonight has jilted me, leaving me in no better shape than the broken teen he'd dumped on his son's doorstep all those years ago.

Zeus eases me into the chair at his father's right, and I

manage to take a single, hiccuping breath before the bodice pinches me in new and exciting places. At this point, I think I'm resigned to just never filling my lungs properly, ever again.

Sebastian catalogs every microsecond of the interaction.

"*Enough*, Jackson," he snaps, not bothering to keep the contempt from coloring his tone.

My throat bobs when a finger trails gently down the back of my arm. But then it withdraws, along with the comforting presence at my back. I glance up through my lashes as he turns to leave. The tension in his jaw alone could haul an eighteen-wheeler the length of an interstate highway.

He knows he has no choice but to leave me to fend for myself out here in these metaphorical woods; the only thing missing is the red cloak.

My, what soulless eyes you have.

"Jackson's communications on the Roxborough project have been few and far between. Report your progress," Sebastian's glacial tones slice through my morbid musings. Gooseflesh prickles the back of my neck and the sweat quietly gathering there begins to chill. I'm suddenly grateful I wore my hair down.

The Roxborough project—said so dismissively. As though holding our lives hostage, and forcing me to harvest 300 souls for his organization like I'm some kind of Gangland Grim Reaper is just a little weekend hobby for him.

"Sir, I've submitted updated accounts of where I'm at

on student and staff numbers. Those haven't changed," I say, dry swallowing.

His Senior Council still sits in silent vigil at what should have been the Junior table, while behind us, I hear the soft murmuring of some of the more highly ranked Suits as they arrive and find places to sit. Only a portion of the very upper echelon of the Gray Men are permitted to attend tonight's Symposium. I concentrate on keeping my breathing even and my focus entirely on him.

"Yes, I'm well aware of your dismal numbers, Sabine," he chides, holding up a hand to halt the pale-faced waiters who were about to descend on our tables. "Talk to me about the Rox Boys."

I knew it was coming and yet I can still feel my own pulse through the soles of my feet.

"We got word they had a meeting with two unidentified syndicate members, inside Ace territory. Two Clubs stumbled on the meet, pulled guns on them, and they exchanged fire. Both the goons and the Aces were reported dead at the scene."

He doesn't ask who shot whom. The only detail worth his notice is the fact a pair of Strange Aces drew weapons against the boys. "So they're not working for Patrick, then."

"Seems unlikely, given how it went down."

"What do we know about their visitors?"

"This Front Man, Morelli had a New York accent. The Enforcer's name was Reynolds. Morelli could be from any one of a dozen Northern Mafia families. Neither name lined up together in the Codex."

I'm not expected to keep a record of every disposable Underworld grunt, otherwise the sheer volume of information I would be forced to parse would be completely untenable. Generally speaking, that means we only keep track of those players likely to survive in the long term, and so tend to restrict data to the middling ranks and up. Like the two Clubs, the Northerners were most likely too low down the *Imperium* totem pole to warrant an entry.

Sebastian raises a single, sculpted brow.

"They were directly outside a building owned by the Aces. There was surveillance in the alley," I explain, trying to keep it as close to the truth as possible. The base of my skull throbs with the effort of keeping my voice even and my facial expression locked up like a bank vault.

I watch while he silently presses an index finger to the soft gold metal of one of his signature cufflinks—a familiar tell. It lets me know that the level to which this conversation is annoying him is fast approaching one of actual concern.

My vision crackles along the edges, spidery fingers of adrenaline tap dancing along my spinal cord in warning.

Please don't ask to see the tape.

Please don't ask to see the tape.

Please don't ask to see the tape.

"And *what* exactly were they meeting about?" he asks instead.

As soon as we get out of here, I swear I'm having Dio

CHAPTER ELEVEN | SABINE

stop off at the nearest gas station so I can buy myself some scratch-offs.

"We could only pull bits and pieces of the conversation, which is how we got names, but there really wasn't a lot there for Brannon to work with. We do know that whoever their boss is, is pleased with them, and that he thought they'd run into more trouble with the Aces."

I don't add *or the Gray Men.*

The cogs are working overtime behind his rimy gaze, and after another breathless wait, he reclines—dark and languid as a panther. He lifts two of his fingers, finally clearing the wait staff to approach. In unison they all rush back in, setting out crystal-cut tumblers and enough top-shelf liquor to fill the giant hourglass outside.

"Champagne?" a ruddy-faced *Brian Stellars, 36,* offers me from over my shoulder.

"She'll have water." Sebastian's decree only sinks my heart further.

Should have fucking insisted on that one drink before *we headed in here.*

"So a possible connection with a Northern Mafia," he muses aloud, as he examines his drink. "Who have you seen them with tonight?"

I down half the glass of iced water Brian serves me in one aggressive gulp, temples pinching with pain. The attendant attempts a polite refill from his carafe, but Sebastian waves him off. And not for the first time, I wonder at the exact manner of my inevitable demise.

Would the autopsy report read *Death by Ball Gown* or *Death by Cottonmouth*?

The single-serving platter of delicately wrapped sashimi that appears in front of me certainly doesn't do my growing nausea any favors.

Looks I don't get to order my own food tonight, either.

"I haven't seen them speak with anybody of note. Just watching and learning the ropes by the looks of it," I hedge, roughly. It's up for debate these days as to whether or not he still considers *me* someone 'of note'.

"If they're as promising as they look on paper," he hums, "and so keen to wade right in, then we won't stop them from getting their feet wet."

I nod, dumbly. *Yes, that's totally who they are; just an eager set of future prospects.*

"I believe it's time for you to get closer to them, maybe ply them with a little insider knowledge if you have to."

I tense, waiting for it.

"I trust you will use discretion," he sniffs. "Turn on the charm—*if* you can."

Ouch, there it is. "Of course, sir."

A full minute goes by with his disapproving silence bearing down on me. I don't know if my lungs even inflate.

And then another.

The edges of my periphery start to go gray.

When he's finally satisfied with my acquiescence, Sebastian turns, eyes blessedly moving away. He takes a measured sip from his tumbler, but he won't touch any part of the food spread before him. The Gray Man never eats in public.

I pick half-heartedly at a tempura prawn entrée. My normally healthy appetite is being completely strangled by the close proximity of the man next to me. Perhaps keeping my hands occupied and trying to catalog those diners I can still get a good look at might help stave off the creeping noise in my head a little longer.

With each minute that slowly passes in silence, a little more of the strain in my chest eases. My neck and traps start to loosen. I don't think I'll be able to *fully* relax until I'm safely away from here and locked inside my hotel room—*several drinks deep*—but at least the incessant urge to scream is finally beginning to abate.

I'm sifting through an ancillary table of Strange Aces, each of them Spades by the look of the ink on their necks, when there's a masculine scream from the front section, followed by raucous laughter. I press my spine against the ornate backrest of my seat, trying not to smirk. Unlike the Sovereignty tables, which are split into their respective factions, the Neutral diners are each seated individually. And by the sounds of it, some unlucky fucker just got stuck sharing a table with the Whitechapel Four.

Of course, just as I feel like I might actually try eating something, Lady Luck decides that's the moment the Rox Boys are going to manifest directly within the Gray Man's sightline.

Ares, Hermes, and Hades all flank Apollo as a unit, and I can't help but admire, yet again, just how well they fit together. Or how effortlessly confident they would appear to anyone who's never met them, considering both their age and circumstances. I remember my own first Symposium: walking around on eggshells the entire time, convinced I was about to commit some accidental gaffe and have the Peacekeepers chasing me for it later.

But after so many weeks spent familiarizing myself with their body language, I can see there's a whole new level of tension there. It's in the stiff set of their shoulders and their matching tense strides.

No doubt they've spent the last thirty minutes or so in an emergency debriefing, deciding their next moves. They're on edge, which means that hopefully they've taken my words to heart and they've come in here nursing a healthy dose of caution.

Fuck knows they'll need to make a habit of it, especially if they want to continue living and working in this world.

Now that I know who their sponsor is—*or at least, which Sovereignty they belong to*—it's no surprise that Jessica, our harried hostess, is leading them over to a small table on the opposite side of the hall, nestled amongst the gold-laden seating reserved solely for Northern guests.

Two of the waitstaff approach them, ostensibly to confirm their meal plans.

Unfortunately, they're just too far away for me to comfortably read their lips, so I slide my eyes to my left, trying to get a current reading on the pH level of Sebastian's temperament instead. I'm honestly expecting to see nothing there but total indifference, so imagine my surprise when it's *naked disdain* that I find simmering from behind the eyes of his rook disguise.

"Now explain *that*," he grits out, so acidly, that it has my stomach plunging to the floor and my gaze cutting back to their table in a heartbeat; wondering what could have *possibly* gone wrong in the few nanoseconds since I last had eyes on them.

It doesn't take long for me to realize exactly what has set Sebastian off.

Or rather *whom*.

My teeth instantly click together in annoyance.

Even from this distance, with their faces hidden by full-coverage, Volto-style masks, there's no mistaking the duo now standing at the Rox Boy's table. The unique, white Mallen streak that interrupts the front of one of their dark coifs gives them both away. Because where one goes, the other is never far behind.

The Donato Twins—*Gabriel Michale Donato* and *Raphael Bruno Donato, 25*. Formerly sworn to the Alessi Family of New York, but as of late, loyal to the banner of another much, much more prominent Northerner.

The Underworld's infamous Golden Boys, otherwise known as Midas's personal hitmen.

Oh, boys. Just what the fuck have you gotten yourselves into?

My mind spins, trying to land on the most likely scenario in which Rafe Donato, of all fucking people, would be slapping a hand down on Ares's shoulder like they're the best of fucking friends.

None of them are good.

Is it possible we weren't the only ones sent evidence of Apollo's secret siring? Have they been sent in at Midas's bidding—to cut down that sapling before it has a chance to take root?

But I can't voice a single one of these thoughts because Sebastian's under the impression that's exactly what it's been—a *secret* siring.

When I still don't answer, the Gray Man's icy voice penetrates the din, sweeping across both Council tables like a tundra wind.

"Dominic, go and fetch the Boys."

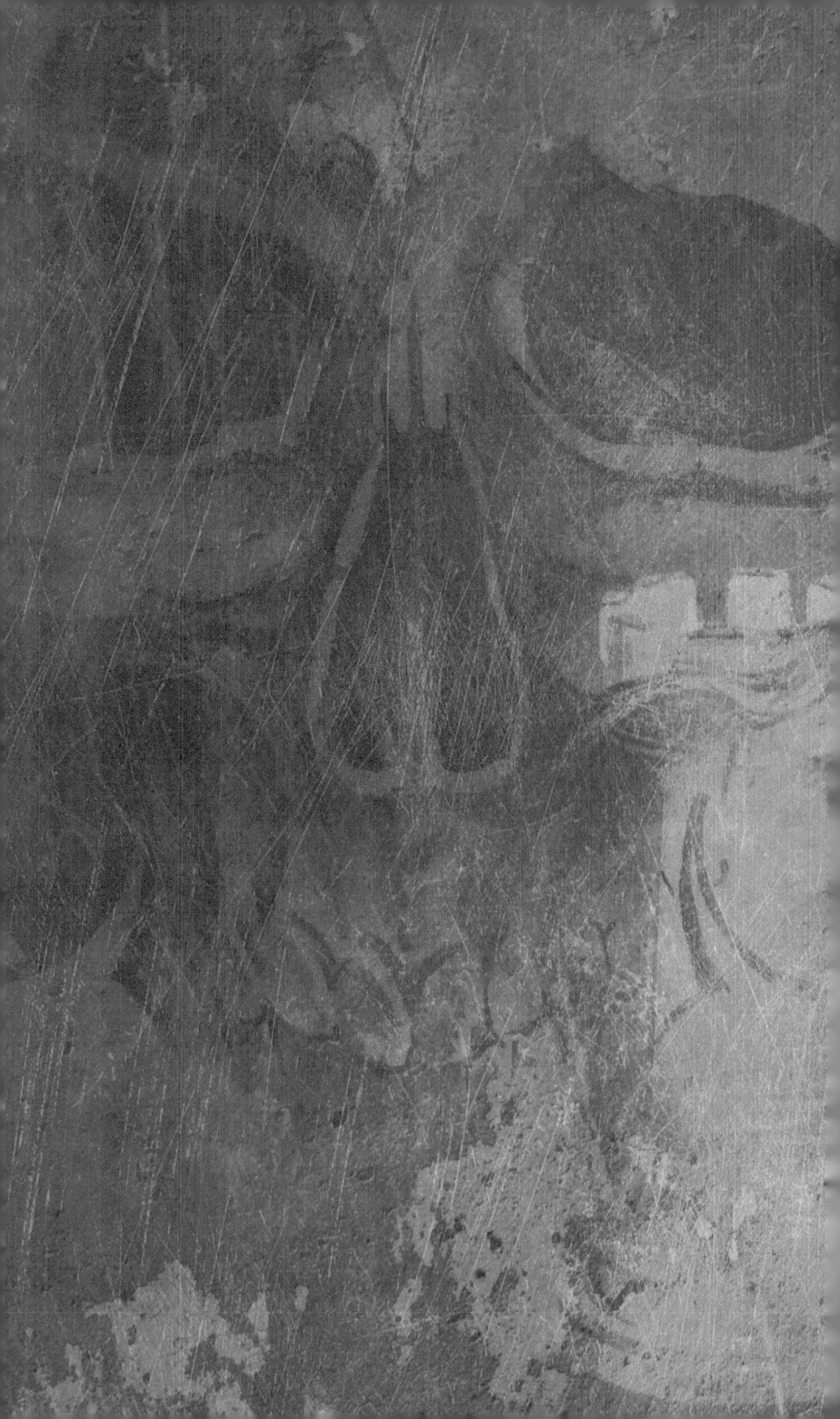

CHAPTER XII

CALLUM · ARES

IF THERE'S one positive coming out of tonight's announcement, it's the validation we did the right thing by digging in our feet against the Aces for all those months. Their nonstop recruiting efforts are now making a hell of a lot more fucking sense; no doubt Trick was looking to throw the four of us on the frontlines with the rest of his Club grunts, guns drawn and ready to bleed out for the cause.

Not our monkeys.

We might've dodged that particular bullet, but it doesn't mean we're out of the woods just yet. His MC still holds control of Roxborough, which means the City of Sin's dirty streets are about to run an even darker shade of red. Not to mention, our hands are still plenty full dealing with both our employer as well as the man we *thought* was Tristan's sperm donor.

And now we have this new problem to add to the list: *Sebastian Grayson.*

Tristan's *actual* sperm donor.

Allegedly.

Figures that just as we're managing to carve out a somewhat viable escape plan, we'd find ourselves standing on the sidelines of a motherfucking turf war. And not just any turf war; a once-in-a-generation Underworld leadership spill, *Battle Royale* style.

A fucking heads-up would've been nice.

My brows immediately dip at that, the scowl tugging down my mask with the movement. Although I'm still not convinced it was for one hundred percent altruistic reasons, I guess that's exactly what Winters *was* trying to do back there.

Despite how my brothers and I feel about how things went down between us, if what she claims is true, that would be considered her doing us a favor. And she was right: she didn't owe us a thing.

Even if the sullen voice of my pre-teen self disagrees.

That Callum insists she owes us *everything*.

This Callum would settle for just exactly why the fuck she's been hiding from us all these years.

I really shouldn't care whether or not she's wrapped up in this Underworld shit. The way she had her pet Suits hovering all around her, she's clearly already made her bed, all nice and fucking cosy—right?

Like I said: *not our fucking circus.*

The hostess pulls up beside an empty table, and I almost run into the back of Atlas, so lost in my thoughts. I bristle, pissed at myself for losing focus while walking through the middle of a room full of snakes, and flex my fingers against my thighs.

I have to stop when I feel the shoulders of my suit pull tight.

"Gentlemen," she gestures.

From the quick glance I take around us, I can see that it's definitely one of the smaller and more intimate place settings. It looks like some of the tables could seat a dozen or more people. I wonder if that's because of the size of our party, or if it's based on hierarchy.

Probably both.

The card on the table reads:

Northern Sovereignty:
The Rox Boys
Sponsored by: The Alessi Family

I grimace as I drop into a seat to Tristan's left, re-reading the fancy script. Twice.

The Rox Boys. A stupid fucking name that someone at the Academy coined once, years ago, and for some reason it's stuck. But for once, my irritation is not with the name itself.

Just how much do these mafia fuckers know about our everyday lives?

"Refreshments and menus will be along shortly," the woman chirps before she's bustling back toward the dining hall's massive double doors.

Lake takes a seat with Atlas across from us, leaving two seats empty on opposite sides of the circular table. "Good, I'm fucking *starving*," he complains, rubbing his fingers across his barely-concealed stomach. Warm light from the giant chandeliers above bounces off the bare skin across his chest.

My mouth pulls down as I watch him flick open the lid on his Zippo a few times. He's so agitated, he's almost feverish. His eyes haven't stopped scanning the tables.

When was the last time he took his meds?

Atlas is also taking a moment before the server comes back to absorb everything he can about our immediate surroundings. I follow the path of his watchful glower.

Everything about the room is huge. It's a large, uninterrupted antechamber that's attached directly to the main foyer. Almost like a ballroom of sorts. The wall behind me is made from more of that cold, red stone. I'm assuming that's where the building gets its name.

There's a service area set up at the back for the waitstaff, along with a well-stocked dry bar. A sea of round tables fills the rest of the space, with the three factions seemingly zoned by the color of their tablecloth. The large section of seating we've been assigned to is covered by gold linens. A smaller number of tables positioned closer to the entrance have white coverings instead. The rest are black.

And directly across from us in that black section are several tables whose diners are all wearing black feathered masks. My stomach inverts when I catch sight of white-blonde hair, a visual confirmation that Sabine Winters is indeed tied to a Southern syndicate.

Fuck.

"One o'clock, black table, far corner," I mutter,

keeping my volume low enough that only Tristan will catch my words. As much as we love Lake, I know I need to keep our hyped-up, golden-haired puppy from drawing even more attention by spinning around and seeking her out.

Tristan's eyes zero in on where Sabine sits beside a solitary figure at one of the tables.

"Do you think that's him?" he mutters back, again, for my ears alone. Two fingers pluck absently at a set of silverware. I run my eyes across what I can see of his face. He looks composed but he must be feeling off-kilter if he's openly fidgeting like this.

"The Mayor's tall, dark hair, yeah? Could be him," I shrug. I don't really pay all that much attention to the comings and goings on the other side of the Tethys. We've got more than enough bullshit keeping us occupied in Rox City as it is.

"The fucking *Gray Man*, Callum. And she was dancing with *Midas*, of all fucking people."

Yeah, I'm still reeling from that little tidbit myself. Tristan had been giving us a rundown about seeing the *King of the fucking North* and Sabine when the woman herself had shown up, boy toys in tow.

"I still think maybe he just saw a pretty piece of ass," I hedge. But seeing her now—sitting down to dinner directly beside who we can only assume is the Gray Man —I'm starting to see the growing unlikelihood of that assumption.

Tristan flicks his chin in frustration. "No, they sounded way too chummy for that. He was asking her all sorts of questions. About Rox Academy. Basically threatened to take her home with him."

The fuck?

He hadn't mentioned that earlier. At the look of confusion wrinkling the corners of my mouth, he lifts a shoulder, dropping it heavily. "I don't fucking know, and that's what we need to find out. As soon as possible."

"She's staying at our hotel. Cyber security there isn't very slick for an Underworld outfit," Lake smugly supplies, but there's still an uncharacteristically pinched edge to his expression. "It wasn't even a challenge to pull her room number."

My eyes snap up, jaw clenching. The little shit was eavesdropping, after all. "Why would you need her room number?" I ask, carefully.

He doesn't even look at me, just spins the empty glass in front of him.

"Stay away from her," Tristan snaps. "The hotel's security might be shit, but you won't get anywhere near her. She's surrounded by Enforcers."

Unfortunately, there's no missing the dangerous glint in Lake's eye, even behind the modest gold half-mask. And I'm *very* familiar with that look. It's a look of challenge, and it always appears right before something reckless follows. "I'm going to go see her," he announces in a waspish tone.

Tristan's jaw pops.

"We need a plan first," I insist, hoping to defuse them, at least long enough to get through this fucking meal. We can't have the two of them at odds in case Sabine was right—and the Suits *do* ambush us.

His hands come down, fingers digging into the edge of the table.

"*No*," I mouth at him, but my warning only makes his face harden further.

Goddamnit.

I'm not going to be able to let him out of my sight for the rest of the night. Otherwise, he's going to find himself on the end of Blondie's chokehold and for once, I don't think it's going to be the kind of one he'll enjoy.

"Menus," Atlas interrupts, tone low and urgent.

My mouth snaps shut, waiting impatiently for the server to get through double-checking our orders. He taps each of our food requests into his tablet, making a special note to follow up on Tristan's celiac requirements. His partner leaves both a crystal decanter of whiskey and a carafe of water sitting in the center of the table.

But the moment they finally leave, I sense someone else approaching out of the corner of my eye. This annoying fucking mask blocks most of my peripheral, but I'm so keyed up tonight that anyone moving in the general proximity of my brothers has me glancing around defensively.

My already twisted-to-fuck guts somehow squeeze themselves more tightly when I turn my head and clock the identical pair of assholes sauntering right up to our table.

Just five minutes.

That's all I'd wanted. A breather from all the games and the bullshit.

Five lousy fucking minutes.

"Look, they even saved us a seat," one of the Donato twins sings out, his gravelly tone rough on my eardrums.

Raphael. The white stripe at the front of his hair is a dead giveaway.

"Honored, boys, really," Gabriel snarks in his equally grating accent, circling around to take the empty spot between Lake and Tristan.

Raphael slaps a rough hand down on my shoulder, dragging out the last empty seat to my left. Atlas visibly stiffens as he makes a show of settling in between us, stretching his arms out over the backs of our chairs.

"So, what's good, Rox City?" he asks, flagging down a passing server with a lazy flick of a hand at my shoulder.

"We're here, we wore the masks. All deliveries have been made. What else do you need?" Tristan's tone remains dismissive, but there's a pulsing tick of agitation along his temple. I bump my thigh against his.

"We're friends, aren't we?" Gabriel smirks, ordering both himself and his brother a gin. "Can't a group of friends just sit down and enjoy a nice meal together?"

No. We sure as fuck *weren't* friends.

The nicest way to put it would be to say these two Northern clowns were our handlers. They told us whenever our boss said to jump, and we jumped. We didn't ask questions. We just *jumped* and hoped to hell it was fucking high enough.

In reality, the Donato brothers held our leashes, and

they knew it. If they wanted to, they could whisper in Sandro Alessi's ear that we weren't pulling our weight and our hard-fought Underworld meal ticket would be no more.

"Ah, fuck, *incoming*," Raphael mutters darkly, running a hand through his oddly bisected hair. He's looking over in the direction of the Southern tables as he says it, and when my eyes cautiously follow his, I see there's a large man now bearing down on us.

A large man whose craggy face is partially covered by black feathers.

You can't trust any of them.

Gabriel flicks a look back over his shoulder. "Well, that's our cue," he chuckles, rising back to his feet. He buttons his jacket closed with one hand.

"Yeah, it's been fun, boys," Raphael rasps, viciously squeezing both mine and Atlas's shoulders before he too slips from his seat.

"I think you know we'll be in touch," Gabriel adds with a pointed look, startling the server who just appeared by scooping their matching gin orders off the tray himself.

"Be good now." His twin salutes us with his glass and a final mocking smile.

The two of them then turn and stalk away right as the Suit arrives. He glares at their backs, watching their leisurely retreat toward the exit.

"Can we help you?" Tristan asks imperiously.

The man's eyes swing back to our table, assessing my brother's straightened posture and folded hands. Not exactly sure what it is he's looking for, but Tristan only gazes back at him expectantly.

He grunts. "The four of you will be having dinner with the Gray Man tonight," he declares in a no-nonsense tone. His voice sounds like he chews rocks for a living.

Tristan tips his head, subjecting the Suit to his own inspection. "I'm sorry? Are you sure you have the right table?"

The Suit's weatherbeaten features finally crack with a smirk. "Yeah, kid, I've got the right table."

THE MAN, who didn't bother to introduce himself, leads us straight to the last section of the hall any of us want to be sitting at right now.

How the fuck do we pretend we have no idea who either of them are?

Tristan and Atlas might have professional poker faces, but I'm always told I wear my mood out for everyone to see. And Lake is a single glance from Sabine away from climbing these red walls.

"The Rox Boys, sir," our escort says as he starts assigning us to our seats. He puts Atlas on his boss's left, while Tristan is placed directly across the rounded table from him. A pouting Lake is given the spot to Tristan's right, and I'm left acting as a human buffer between him and Sabine.

Just fucking great.

"I've been hearing good things coming out of

Roxborough about you boys," the Gray Man says languidly by way of greeting. He's leaning back in his chair, a leg crossed over the other and a glass balanced on his knee.

Sabine is picking idly at a plate of sushi. Her back is straight, but her face is ghost-white.

I'm trying not to stare at her and give our connection away when the Gray Man beats me to it. "I believe you have already met my daughter," he continues cooly, lifting two fingers in her direction, and if it hadn't been for Sabine's offhanded remark about Midas earlier, I think my eyes would have bugged out of my head.

He thinks I'm Sebastian's daughter rather than a ward.

As it is, I still have to work to keep my jaw hinged shut. Tristan clears his throat in surprise. He offers a polite shake of his head. "I don't believe so, sir."

"She's just started at your Academy," Grayson prompts, with a feline smile.

"Ah yes, that's right. *Sabine.* The mask threw me," Tristan amends while waving a contrite hand in front of his face. "We're honored by the invitation, Mr Winters, but we're unsure why we're here."

The bark of laughter that his answer pulls from Grayson immediately flares all the hairs on the back of my neck.

"Mr Winters, yes, well done," he drawls, taking a sip of a whiskey that probably costs more than my monthly paycheck at the garage. "But no names here. You understand."

"Apologies, sir. How can we help you?" I croak when Tristan's mouth only thins.

His eyes gleam. "My organization is always on the lookout for up-and-coming talent. I've found that the sister academies in our Twin Cities tend to produce some of the brightest young minds in the state, especially in the business, politics, and science domains." He takes another measured sip of his drink before returning it to rest on his knee. "I like to persuade as many as I can to come and work for me before they are plucked up by someone else."

My own gaze desperately wants to slide back to Sabine in accusation, but I keep it fixed on the Gray Man.

I'm only at your Academy to do a job.

Is that what a 'librarian' was for? Finding these kids before they were snatched up by one of the out-of-state Ivy Leagues or a Fortune 500 company?

"And I think the four of you are headed for great things," he finishes, lifting his glass once more. He watches us from over its rim.

"You want us to come work for you?" Tristan asks, injecting just enough incredulity into his voice.

"You already hold quite an advantage over most graduates. They might hear the rumors and tales, but not many come to me with any real working knowledge of our world."

"Yes, because we already have an employer," Tristan says carefully.

I watch as Sabine pulls a subtle face in warning, hiding it from her boss by placing a small piece of sashimi in her mouth. I have to drag my focus away from her lips and force myself to examine the rest of her posture instead. She looks like she's in pain with how stiffly she's holding herself.

"I gathered as much from your presence here tonight. They sat you with the *Northern* Sovereignty," Grayson seethes, the temperature of his voice dropping further with each word. The disappointment seeps from him like ice frosting across the tabletop.

My hackles only rise further.

Shit.

My eyes flick back to Sabine as understanding dawns. *She's not in pain. She's....afraid of him.*

"We needed to get the Aces off our backs," I throw out quickly, hoping to appeal to his ego. Everyone knows how much the Suits and the Rox City bikers despise each other. "We didn't know the Gray Men were an option. We just took the best offer."

Grayson hums, deep in his throat. His gaze somehow feels both freezing cold and searing hot as it brushes over me, leaving my skin tight and clammy beneath my collar. "I suppose you couldn't have known better," he finally concedes.

I didn't even realize how tensely I was holding myself until his dismissal has my shoulders dropping in what feels suspiciously like relief.

He sniffs. "It's probably best if you get that sorted then, what with tonight's announcement."

"Sir?"

"You're not going to want to be living in a Southern

City without the protection of the South once these Labors begin," he explains casually, and if we didn't now know better, it might have sounded sincere. "Sabine holds a wealth of knowledge about our world and has agreed to guide you on my behalf. Her team is stationed in Roxborough for the foreseeable future. I urge you to connect with them before the roster is sent out and targets become set," he finishes vaguely.

Sabine keeps her eyes fixed on the table before her, but I'm watching her so closely I see the way they flare once behind her mask.

And it's all the confirmation I need that despite the fact he still hasn't revealed his relationship to him—*or even his name*—this man has every intention of dropping Tristan head-fucking-first into this sanctioned shitfight for the Crown.

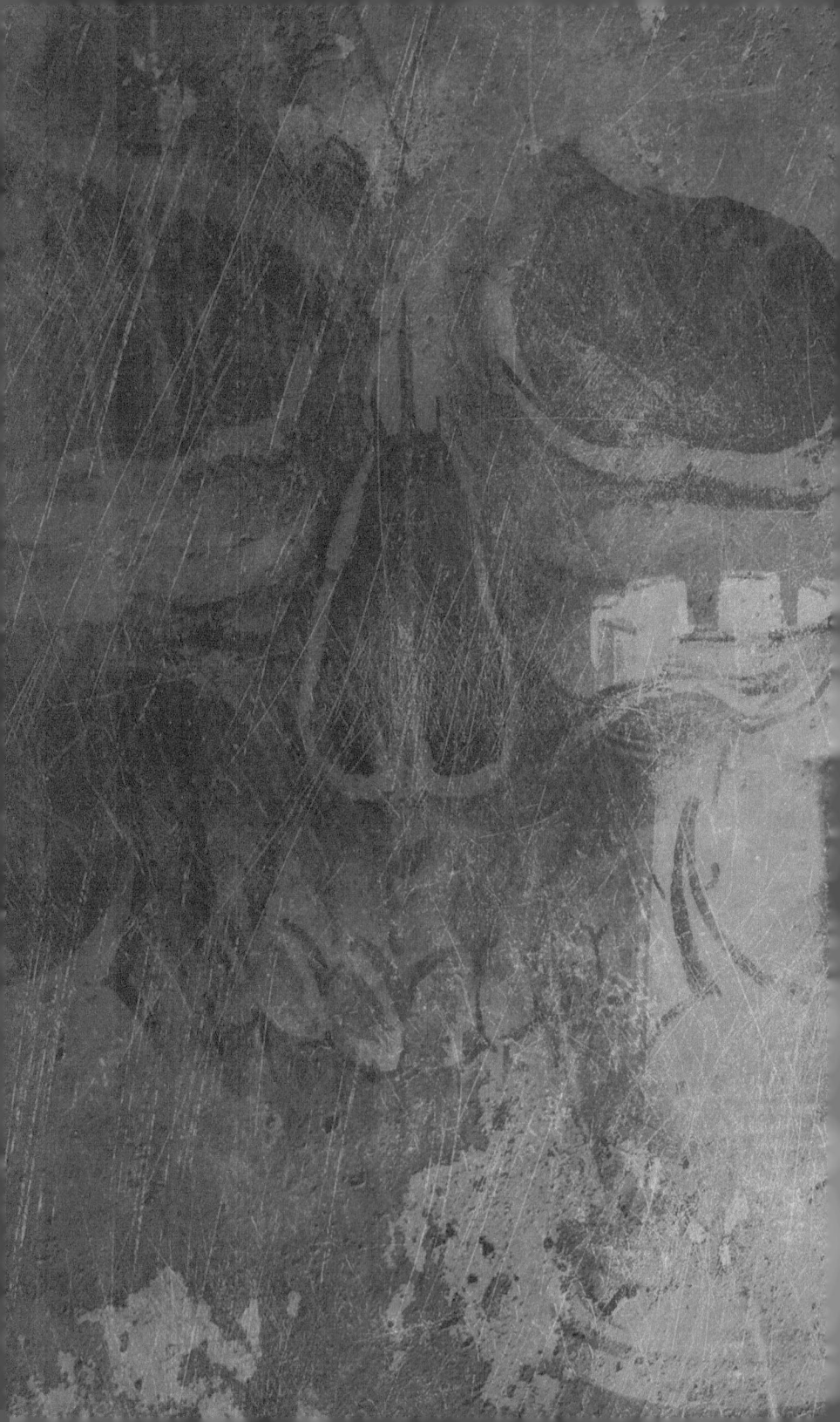

CHAPTER XIII

SABINE

A HEAVY, rhythmic thumping snatches me from dreamless sleep.

At first, what I think I'm hearing is just my neighbors getting busy putting the *bang* in *gangbanger*—but then my cumulonimbus-filled brain registers the sound as the door.

As soon as the last of the painfully tense dinner courses with Sebastian and the Rox Boys had ended, Zeus had kept his promise—whisking me away while the after-dinner *digestifs* were still being served.

Surprisingly, I'd been permitted to leave both the table *and* the Symposium with nothing more than a clipped reminder that Dominic would be in touch regarding my report. I might've treated that too-easy dismissal with a lot more suspicion, had it not been for the Little Drummer Boy headlining his own rock concert from behind my temporal lobe.

As it were, Dio had practically needed to carry me back to my room at the Delphi—a neutrally-owned and operated Underworld hotel whose Symposium guests were shielded by the law of *Hospitium* until checkout time on Monday morning.

Six mini-bar bottles of vodka. Apply head directly to pillow. Do not pass go. Do not collect $200.

Now, for some reason, I'm being forced unwillingly into consciousness. All while I still have both an information hangover *and* an actual hangover.

With a pained groan, I roll over and reach to wake my phone.

10:51pm.

Uggh. The fuck?

I'm still dry swallowing a handful of Tylenol when the pounding sounds out again, only louder. This time, the noise is obnoxious enough that it whips those last lingering brain clouds into a full-blown cell system.

I swear to *fuck* it better not be Dionysus. Not when the man has key access and strict instructions that include no booty calls before midnight.

Snatching up my copy of the room key with a muttered curse, I stomp over, ready to scan open the secure door and gift whoever's interrupting my battery recharge with a striking new asshole.

I'm not exactly sure who I *was* expecting when I yank back the handle, but it most certainly wasn't the guy I so brutally hit and quit just yesterday.

Yet there he is—blond surfer curtains falling across a troubled brow as he white-knuckles the top of the doorframe. There's an oddly disquiet air about him, like the taste of ozone on your tongue right before a storm.

And *fuck*.

Me.

His mask is gone but he's still wearing that fucking corset.

"Hermes," I breathe, trying to whip my features back into something resembling blatant disinterest. Then he leans forward, and suddenly 'disinterest' is the last thing on my mind.

The move stretches every one of his visible muscles in the most obscene ways possible, bringing him so close that we're practically sharing breath.

It would be *so* fucking easy just to give in and meet him all the way. Dig my nails into his shoulders. Run my tongue over that small cluster of violets tattooed over his heart. Bite those candy nipples until they're red and swollen.

But what I see lurking behind his freckled, hazel eyes gives me pause.

It's the same thing I've been seeing there all night.

Something *wild*.

And *hurt*.

This is the third time in only twenty-four hours I've been faced with this haunted look of his. Trying to banish the image doesn't seem to help either; it only seems to pinch at something else instead. Somewhere deep behind my sternum, and with cold, probing fingers that remind me of Sebastian.

Talk to me about the Rox Boys.

"You left me," he states in an unnervingly flat tone.

I forcibly swallow, trying my best to ignore the ache in my skull.

And my chest.

"At the beach? Yes, and I did try to warn you." The words feel paper-thin as they leave my mouth and I push my tongue against the inside of my cheek, trying to stave off the weird ache of it.

He must have known the likelihood that his coming here would end in rejection. And still, he hunted down my location and sought me out.

"That you don't do feelings?" Hermes prompts, more defensively this time.

The echo of Midas's poison joins Sebastian's frost. *Made any new friends?*

"Don't," I lift my shoulders in an exaggerated shrug, "won't."

Can't.

Uncertainty still crowds his expression, but there's a ghost of a crooked smile when he insists impishly, "But you already broke one of your rules."

"What rule?"

"About high school boys."

This guy.

I need to remember that he's just a mission. That he was just about to have dinner with the Donato twins before being swept in by Sebastian's bullshit. That in reality, I barely fucking know him—him or his friends.

But there's just something so innately...*familiar* about him. Like when a song comes on the radio that the DJ insists is new, but the melody is one you just *know* in your bones that you've heard somewhere before.

I've been convincing myself it's just because he's got

the same easygoing personality as Dio, but that niggling itch in the back of my head has got me wanting to ignore all the warnings.

And to keep digging deeper.

So, instead of doing the most logical thing and closing the door right in Hermes's face, I step back, opening it wide in silent invitation.

At first, he lingers at the threshold, his fingers curling against the doorframe like claws as narrowed eyes bounce between mine. His wickedly handsome face is still painted with all the same misgivings he arrived with. But then I see the moment he makes his decision, and as his resolve begins to solidify, it drives out that lost look completely.

When his arms finally drop back to his sides, his face splits with one of those devilish grins that I'm much more accustomed to seeing there.

It's almost like watching the sun breaking through the clouds…or some shit.

Oh my god. Who the fuck even am I right now?

It's just a stupid face on a stupid boy.

A stupidly pretty face that I *maybe* enjoyed having trapped between my thighs yesterday.

That's *all.*

I need to get a fucking grip.

With his mind made up and confidence restored, Hermes shoulders straight past me, sauntering inside my hotel suite like an insouciant prince and throwing himself down in the middle of my hotel bed. It looks as though his jacket and shoes didn't make it back with him from the Symposium either.

Lacing his fingers behind his head, the cheeky fucker smirks up at me like he's won something. He sighs dramatically. "Don't you ever get tired of always fighting the inevitable, Wifey?"

His words have me bristling, but I'm not even *touching* that pet name right now.

One battle at a time.

I scowl at him as I stalk back over to the bedside table. It's ridiculous how fucking hot he looks right now, and he clearly knows it. He takes the opportunity to flex his lower abdomen, sending an answering shudder through my pelvis.

"Move the fuck over," I grouse, trading my keycard in for my phone. He proceeds to make a show of inching back, deliberately leaving me with only enough room to fit up against him. He crooks his arm and pats the meager space he made just for me.

Asshole.

When he still refuses to move, I'm left with no choice but to lay shoulder-to-shoulder with him on the narrow mattress. As I drop down beside him, Hermes immediately curls himself around me like a cat, nuzzling into my neck.

"*Dude,*" I huff.

"You love it," he purrs. Actually fucking *purrs*.

Dio had helped me Houdini my way out of the gown and into one of his huge tees before I shooed him out the door. Now my exposed skin feels volcanic wherever it connects with Miller's. The velvety ribs of his corset are molded against the forearm that's trapped between us.

He is right though. I don't...*totally* hate it.

"Whatever," I frown at him, trying to stave off the amused smile that's threatening my mouth with its violent uprising. I busy myself with pulling up my unread messages.

THE CHAMBER OF SECRETS

8:33PM ME

Don't plan on me being conscious anytime before sunrise

8:33PM ME

PEACE

9:01PM KNOX

9pm check-in

Apparently Boss knows about your off-book cleanup @ RA. Z about ready to go over the table

9:02PM KNOX

Boys left 10 min ago

9:03PM DIONYSUS

9pm Check. All clear. Cutest sleep face ever

9:04PM KNOX

Man, Rhett

I can't be your pallbearer

I just got my nails done

9:06PM DIONYSUS

Lies. You'll cover me because I got all
the Zaddy tea 🌙

9:06PM KNOX

...

8in? Were you fr?

9:07PM DIONYSUS

Easily

9:08PM DADDY ZEUS

Nope, my 🍆 is now off limits.

9:08PM DIONYSUS

Cut the man some slack. Blue balls are
no joke.

9:10PM KNOX

Exactly!

I'm just demanding reparations, Boss

10:00PM KNOX

10pm check-in

2IC will be @ RA on Wed re: 12 Labors

10:01PM DIONYSUS

10pm Check. All clear.

As I finish reading my Crew's ridiculous text exchange, I can't help but grimace. *Dominic will be at Rox Academy as early as Wednesday.*

But then I catch the time, and snort, realizing that it's almost the top of the hour. Time for the Enforcers to check in again.

Perfect.

Dio answers my video call with a disconcerted look on his face. "You're awake already?"

"Yes, no thanks to you," I chide, angling the screen so he can't miss the Hermes-shaped leech currently plastered to my side. "All clear, my ass, D-man."

The call instantly drops.

"I waited until he left to piss," Hermes confesses against the side of my throat, and a hiccuping giggle bubbles through my nose, burning my nostrils with anticipation. I lay frozen then, ignoring the urge to card my fingers through the curls that tickle my cheek, until not two minutes later—when there's a telltale *beep* followed by a *schnick* as my so-called Enforcer lets himself in.

I sit up to meet him, my six-foot, human-sized poncho lazily following my lead.

Dionysus's face holds nothing but wicked satisfaction as he comes through the door, duty weapon out and trained directly on the tattoo over Hermes's heart. To his credit, Miller doesn't so much as bat an eyelash.

"I already told Apollo this shit wouldn't fly." He toes the door shut behind him, his smile wide and mocking as he adds, "She kicked you to the curb just yesterday, and you're here pestering her again already?"

"*Jesus Christ*," I hiss, rising from the bed to play referee, but Orbison only sidesteps me, keeping us both in his line of sight. Exasperated, I step closer and smack the barrel down, angling it toward the floor.

"Such a fucking flirt," I scold him.

His smirk only deepens.

"Pretty sure there are rules against this sort of thing," Hermes says airily.

After another intense staredown, D grunts once before flicking the safety on and slotting his handgun back into its holster. "*Fucking Hospitium*," he mutters as he begins shouldering the whole kit off, but it's without heat.

At the sound of Hermes moving across the bed behind us, I turn back around—only to catch sight of him mid-crawl, blond locks falling haphazardly over his face and taut ass high in the air.

Dio and I groan in stereo.

"Have you two been formally introduced yet?" I ask my bodyguard, who's now heading over to the weapons safe in the corner of the room. Partygoers may not be able to enter the Symposium itself armed, but no such rules apply outside its doors. We just can't readily *maim* the other guests.

No matter how annoying.

"Not...officially," Hermes answers for him, cocking his head as he eyes the older man with interest. He's now perched at the end of the mattress, sitting back on his bare feet.

That has my brows rising.

When would they have met...*un*officially?

Wait.

Who's the guy from the warehouse? Hermes had asked me last night. I'd assumed he was just talking about following us out from the diner that day. Dionysus had clocked their GT slinking after his Lambo right as we left the school.

"Did you enjoy the show?" D asks him cryptically, and smug as fuck.

"The hell does *that* mean?" I demand, eyebrows now right at my hairline.

Neither man seems inclined to elaborate, and in the interest of keeping things moving, I decide it's time to channel my inner game show hostess instead.

"Well, then—Dionysus, *this* is Hermes," I begin with a flourish of my hands in the direction of my recently acquired bed guest. "He's also a professional chaos pansexual. The two of you will get along quite famously, I'm sure."

"Oh, I'm *sure*," D agrees with a throaty chuckle between the sounds of velcro tearing and magazine catches releasing.

"And *this* here is Dionysus," I say, watching with satisfaction as they run equally hot eyes over one another, "he'll be your ruin today."

Those unruly, golden curls flare like a halo as Hermes's head snaps back in my direction.

"*If* you're a good boy," I add, pointedly.

Dio chokes before covering it with a barked laugh.

"I'll be the best fucking boy you've ever had," Hermes moans in agreement, hands steepling before his naked chest like a supplicant.

Eager and ready to worship.

And we're ready to help him find his religion.

"Strip," I bark and he leaps up to obey like I just shot him in the ass with a TASER.

Dionysus makes a sound of approval, moving to stand with me by the foot of the bed. "These first," he instructs, hooking a finger into the waist of Hermes's ass-hugging pants. He snaps the band. "Fuck, look at that ass. They look painted on."

Again, Hermes doesn't hesitate, peeling them straight down his long legs with practiced grace. To no one's surprise, he's gone commando—leaving him naked but for that goddamn corset, its curved edges following the defined lines of his hips.

He's painfully hard already; the glistening head points eagerly toward his belly button.

"*Naughty*," I tsk loudly, taking a moment to circle him and admire the way the muscles across his back dance beneath my hot attention. Inspection completed, I slide my palms around his trim waist, pressing myself right up against the pert ass I was just admiring. "I thought you said you were a good boy, but you're already making such a mess," I scold him.

Hermes sucks in an excited breath at the contact, his abdomen contracting sharply when my hands begin to explore. The right takes a leisurely journey northwards, fingers tiptoeing up the corset's soft velvet boning before tracing along the length of his sternum. Meanwhile, the left is busy mapping the dusting of hair still partially hidden by his waist trainer—and then across each sharp angle of his pelvis.

Stroking. Caressing.

By the time one palm settles against the strained cords of his throat, the other around the base of his leaking cock, he's an absolute quivering mess: skin hot, breaths short, pulse hammering beneath my fingertips.

"Beg for it, baby, and we may just make you into that sandwich, after all," I murmur against his jaw.

And then, with both hands—I *squeeze*.

Hermes immediately arches against me.

"Oh, *fuck. Yes.* Yes, *please*," he whimpers, Adam's apple vibrating against my palm with each desperate word. "I'll clean up every last drop. From *both* of you. I *promise*. So clean, no one will even know I was here."

"We'll see about that," I hum. "Now *this*," I continue, tugging at the corset. "As much as I love this on you, I need you out of it. Completely."

Hermes preens at my praise, tracking me closely as I move to face him again. Tanned fingers stroke the length of fasteners, before carefully revealing the taut muscles of his abdomen—one popped fixture at a time.

The trainer drops to the floor.

"Dio, get rid of that penguin suit and find the lube."

"*Yes*, ma'am," he rasps, immediately stripping off the jacket and getting to work on his shirt.

"And you—you're going to put that talented tongue of yours back to work," I tell Hermes as I prepare to undress myself.

I pause with my fingers teasing the hem of my sleep shirt. The shower I had before crawling into bed had already washed away my concealer. If I take this off now, all my tattoos will be on display.

Dionysus must read the conflict on my face. "Cat's already out of the bag, doll," he says softly, down to only his dress pants.

I mean, he's not wrong. They saw our masks tonight. They witnessed me at Sebastian's side. If they didn't believe my claims before, it's only a matter of time before they'll be forced to. I nod, lifting it over my head and rolling my shoulders back.

Hermes's gaze immediately roams over what he can see of my tattoos, wrapping around my upper arms and peeking over my shoulders. It remains assessing until it snags on my dual nipple piercings and his lips part. "Where have *those* been hiding?"

I let out a small, strained laugh. "Needed to keep everything above the waist covered to stay incognito," I offer, cutting my eyes to Dio, who tilts his chin down. "But like he said, cat's out of the bag."

Hermes nods, but then his eyes drop further, zeroing in on the matching patterns Zeus left along my lower hips. "Are those...bruises?" he asks. There's nothing but curiosity in his voice, but for some strange reason, I find myself covering the marks with my hands.

I feel oddly protective of them.

"Okay, no more shop talk," Dio growls, kicking away his boxers. His cock bobs aggressively when he straightens up to his full, keenly muscled, and heavily tattooed height.

I have to bite my lip at the strangled whimper Hermes lets slip at his first eyeful of a completely naked Rhett Orbison. "See? Ruin and damnation, six ways to Sunday."

For once, D doesn't stop to indulge my playful teasing. "Alright babygirl, get your cute little ass on the bed. Need you soaking my face."

Sounds like a plan to me.

"Hey, no, wait! She said *I* could go down on her," Hermes protests with a whine that I really shouldn't find so fucking cute.

"I don't think so, little boy. You can wait your fucking turn, maybe even pick up a few pointers."

"I don't need any fucking pointers, I had her screaming on m—"

"Boys!" I interject loudly with a sharp clap, earning myself a matching pair of sheepish looks. The apples of Hermes's cheeks are now an adorable shade of pink. Dio scratches the back of his neck. "There is no reason for the two of you to be bickering about something so *easily* resolved."

I mean, the solution really is that simple. I wait for the lightbulbs to go off.

"Gonna a flip a coin?" Dio jeers. "Fuck that, I'm calling seniority."

"Honestly, D, I'm disappointed in you," I chastise. "Use your *other* head."

His scowl only deepens, so, with a wide sweep of my hands—and all the airs of an Underworld *imperatrix*—I generously propose: "You can *both* lick my pussy."

"*Fuck. Yes,*" Hermes moans, at the same time as Dionysus grunts, "Works for me." Without warning, the Enforcer scoops me up and throws me back onto the bed. I let out a wheeze as I bounce twice, and as soon as I manage to settle back against the pillows—I sigh, happily.

Work smarter, not harder.

The guys follow closely behind, each of them stalking up the length of my legs like two big cats. When they both reach my thighs, I let them fall open. Two sets of eyes glue themselves to the finger now tracing the neatly trimmed strip leading down to my pussy.

"Hungry?"

"Always said your cunt should count as one of the essential food groups," Dio muses, propping a cheek onto his fist. He runs his tongue along his lower lip.

"I feel like I should be saying grace first," Hermes adds, in perfect sync with the eternally charming, shit-talking asshole lying across from him.

Fuck, there's two of them.

I roll my eyes at them both, but Dionysus isn't even close to dissuaded. "*Amen,*" he breathes against my clit before licking a languid stripe over puffy lips—adding to the prominent wetness that's already in real danger of becoming a permanent state of affairs.

To all the lingerie I've loved before.

Before his tongue can even manage a full circuit, it's joined by Hermes's eager strokes. At first, he seems happy to follow Dio's lead, helpfully teasing and caressing. However, it's not long before the two of them fall into an oral battle for dominance. Their tongues begin to war, each of them expertly slashing and dancing and tangling.

"Don't fight, boys, there's plenty to share," I think I say, but my eyes cross and I don't even know if the words quite make it out of my mouth. Any headache I might've woken up with is now nothing but a distant memory.

Undeterred, they clash with my clit.

With the inside of my cunt.

With each other.

Finally, the two of them take their skirmish south to the rim of my ass.

My hands shoot out, spearing through two sets of equally thick, sun-kissed hair. Gripping on for dear life, I do my best to absorb every blessed detail of the sights and sounds before me.

Two blond heads working in tandem.

Their names on my lips—hovering there like a whispered benediction.

A vision.

A fantasy.

A new addiction.

The orgasm their antics wrestle from me is of the type that rearranges the psyche. A molten heat floods my pelvis, causing every muscle in my thighs and abdomen to seize at once; jackknifing my spine like a damn stomach crunch.

It's aggressive, raw, and all-consuming.

And it's one thing I definitely won't mind reliving over and over again.

Amen, in-fucking-deed.

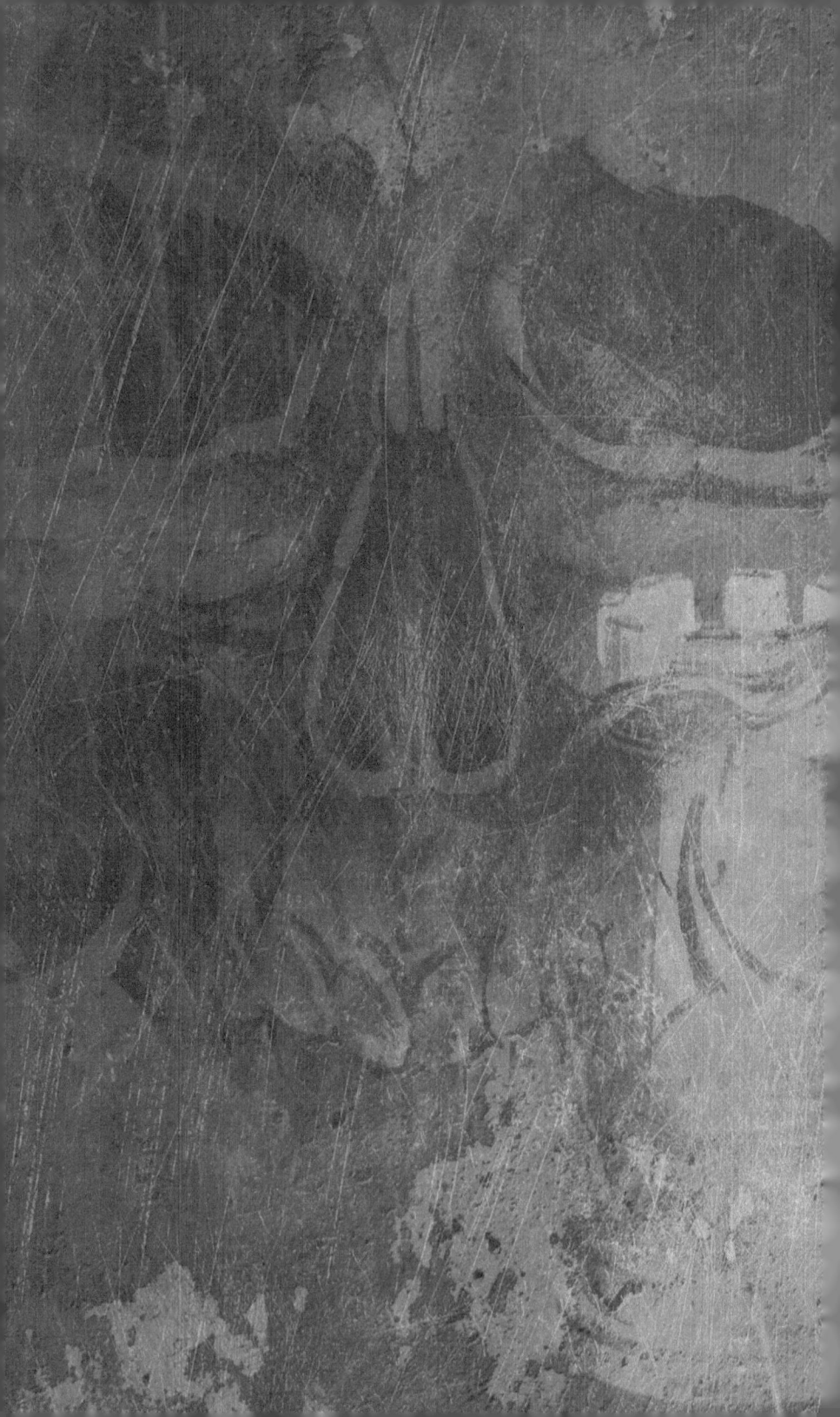

CHAPTER XIV

RHETT · DIONYSUS

AS MUCH AS I'm digging the sweet tang of Sabine's ass—and Hermes's adorable efforts to top from the bottom with nothing but his tongue—I think I'm going to enjoy the little prick's submission even more.

I know my dick definitely will.

The moment Sabine's thighs stop shuddering and her hips release, I'm rising to my knees. Her fingers slip free from my hair with the movement, and already I'm missing the vicious scrape of her nails across my scalp.

"*Fuck*," she exclaims, tits heaving.

My own chest throbs while I steal the moment to drink her in. I'm so fucking greedy for more of *this*, right here: Sabine, with flushed cheeks and her damp hair plastered to her forehead. Her glazed, gray-blue gaze fixed on the hotel's coffered ceiling, full lips parted slightly as she breathes through the comedown.

Sabine, with all of her guards down and her face soft, too busy basking in her afterglow to overthink.

It's the only time I ever get to see this much fucking *life* in her eyes—after she's come so hard, they cross.

I've known since the beginning that what she wanted —no, *needed*—was something easy and uncomplicated. No strings attached. I knew it was the only way she could shut down all that Gray Man bullshit from swirling around her pretty little head. Even if it was only ever just for a few hours at a time.

And well, fuck, it's not like *uncomplicated*'s ever been a real hardship for me.

Uncomplicated's my middle fucking name.

But this routine of hers—pulling away the second I pull out, getting dressed like her ass's on fire, then slipping out the door like I'm just some random john in a seedy, backwater hotel?

I wasn't lying when I told Zeus it's no longer just about sex for me.

No strings attached? *Uncomplicated*?

Nah, babygirl.

See, you and I?

We're a whole fucking String Theory's worth of *very much* complicated.

And the only thing in this cursed world that makes a lick of fucking sense.

I know the timing's all wrong, but I'm fucking done waiting. No more sitting on the sidelines, content with casual scraps of affection.

It's time she knew I'm all in.

That I've *always* been all in.

I'll make her see how good strings can be.

A flash of golden hair—brighter than Sabine's cool, platinum blonde—has my chin dropping to my chest. Hermes's focus is fixed on her face as he pushes up on his forearms.

Oh no, you don't.

"And where do you think *you're* going?" I growl, snatching him away from her with my own fistful of curls. His warm back lands against my chest with a clammy kiss of skin-to-skin. "Not done with you yet."

The startled noise he makes in the back of his throat has my cock flexing eagerly against his pert ass. Tilting his head so I can admire the strong, tanned lines of his neck, I grin as his Adam's apple visibly jumps. "I'd love to see my cock stretching out this pretty, little throat— right *here*," I murmur, giving the slight bulge there a gentle stroke.

A shiver rocks his shoulders.

Pleased, I give his locks another firm tug, this time angling him back so I can better see his face. My other hand drops to grip his straining dick, loving how hot the tattoos look as my fingers move along the length of him.

"Would you like that?" I ask him.

His eyes flare wide as they meet my narrowed gaze, and he couldn't hide his excitement, even if he wanted to. He's already leaking all over my hand. *"Please."*

"Not today," I say with a press of my lips against his pulse point, feeling him sag against me with disappointment. "I want to see my cock stretching out that hot little ass instead."

I chuckle as he immediately rallies. *Fuck,* but I do love the desperation.

When I check in with Sabine, I find her silently

observing the two of us through half-lidded eyes. I flash her my best bedroom smirk, my lips still glistening with her cum. "This should be another one to mark off your *fuck-it* list, babygirl."

Her answering laugh is all husk. It strokes its way along my sternum in the same teasing manner that my fingers lazily stroke Hermes's dick.

She needs this—to chase this next bigger, better high, and I'll always help give her what she needs.

Hunt her, tie her up.

Share her.

Just so long as the list of things she needs always includes *me*.

She shuffles up the pillows then, the glinting bars through each one of her nipples inviting eye contact with her pert tits. She's sweat-slicked and still a little shaky as she joins me on her knees.

So fucking beautiful.

The opening *pop* of the lube bottle's cap sends Hermes's hips bucking back against me.

"He's an eager one, isn't he?" Sabine purrs, moving closer. "So eager to please."

"*Yes*," he breathes. His head also tries to bob in enthusiastic agreement, but it's pulled up short by the unrelenting hold I have on his hair.

Sabine's teeth sink into her bottom lip while she watches my tattooed fist working his cock for another minute.

"Spread him for me, D," she finally instructs, voice

raspy as she gets to work drizzling lube all over the fingers and palm of one hand.

"You heard her," I whisper in Hermes's ear, shifting so that one of my wide thighs can fit between his, my knee pressing forward until he's forced to shuffle them further apart. I tug his cock harshly toward his abdomen, feeling his balls draw up beneath my pinky.

When Sabine joins me at his back, I reluctantly withdraw my hold.

Hermes wheezes with the loss.

"I've got you," she assures him, pressing between his shoulder blades. "That's it," she coaxes again when he tips forward, landing on his hands.

Without another word, I seize his ass cheeks, opening him wide for her.

As soon as I've granted her access, Sabine slides her palm up from beneath his balls, mapping a slick path along his taint. Two fingers circle the tight entrance there, teasing. Another generous drizzle and her probing finger sinks in easily.

"Gorgeous," I murmur, transfixed as she gently works the lube inside. A second finger quickly joins the first, scissoring, stretching.

"Good?" Sabine asks, lowly.

"*So good,*" Hermes replies thickly, the pleasure practically dripping from his voice, just like the cock now leaking steadily onto the bed covers below him.

Without losing her rhythm, Sabine leans over him, squeezing the bottle over the head of my own swollen shaft. She catches my eye as I begin spreading it liberally, all the way down to the base. My fingers graze idly over the cold rungs of my Jacob's Ladder as she studies me.

"I've already fucked him," she finally says when I don't say anything. Her tone is even, but there's a subtle hint of a question at the end.

I knew this, obviously. I *was* the one who drove her back to her dorm when she ditched him, after all.

It's what she's *not* saying—or rather, asking—out loud. She wants to know if I'll willingly go in raw, like I do for her.

Only ever for her.

"Seems like a bad move, babygirl," I mutter.

Sabine smirks and it's a challenge if I've ever seen one. "But bad moves are my favorite."

I swallow, because—*fuck*. "Okay."

Guess we're doing this.

Grabbing another handful of blond curls, I pull Miller roughly back up and out of the way. With my focus still locked on her, I nod in the direction of the headboard. "On your back then, babygirl. Need to be able to see your face for this."

She doesn't hesitate, and as soon as her shoulders hit the pillows again, her tattooed thighs are naturally bracketing my larger ones.

I'm still kneeling with Hermes's back to my front, anticipation boiling in every muscle, and as soon as I press my weight forward, he folds just as easily as the first time. He lands with a hand on either side of Sabine's shoulders, and I follow him down, my hard-on nestled snuggly between his cheeks.

Then, with a strained breath, I line him up—ready to feed him into her still wet, still greedy cunt. As I push forward with my pelvis, Hermes slides in just as easily as her fingers slipped inside his eager ass.

"Look at you filling her up so well," I tell him, and it's not a lie. He's got the perfect-sized cock, spreading her just so. "How does she feel?"

"Should be. *Illegal*," he chokes out with the first experimental pump of his hips. His tight ass flexes with the movement. "Death grip. Gotta be. Assault. With a deadly. *Weapon*," he pants along with each new stroke, voice high and strangled with need.

"Your pussy-drunk ramblings are adorable," Sabine moans out, face lit with amusement. There's a small, rare smile that's trying to creep its way across her face and I fucking eat that shit up.

I plan on giving her plenty of reasons to practice that smile.

Zeus and I just need to finish getting her free and clear first.

Hermes groans again, glancing down to watch himself as he works in and out from between her pussy's swollen lips.

But then his chin lifts, damp hair hanging wildly over his forehead as his focus travels back up to her face. His biceps flex as he tenses, like he's readying himself. He's hesitant now, nervous.

Why?

Ah, shit.

I brace myself.

"Can I kiss you this time?" he asks her, ever so gently. Like he's trying not to spook her. But it's too late— Sabine's expression has already blanked.

He freezes while still inside her.

That's my cue.

I lean back, giving myself just enough room that I can line myself up properly. Then, grabbing a hold of Miller's slender hips, I squeeze once. "Breathe," I bark, and it's the only warning he gets as I punch straight into his ass, driving us both forward with the motion.

Hermes squeals as he takes me to the root, at the same time as he bottoms back out inside Sabine. There's nothing gentle about the way I take control of him then— but the noises he makes each time I pound my way back into him tell me he's not a stranger to hard and fast.

I grunt as each of my cold piercings drags over every hot ridge and valley of him.

Hot *and* tight.

Just like her.

Fuck. Why does he feel so fucking good?

Sabine's tongue darts out to wet her lips, watching the shapes we make as we move over her together. The rising tide of her release seems to have swept away her moment of trepidation; her face is relaxed once more, eyes heavy and full of lust as she focuses on Hermes's sweetly tortured features.

"You take him so well," she praises him from below. Hermes's response is babbled and incoherent, completely and utterly lost to the divine pleasure of her cunt.

My gaze collides with Sabine's, sharing a heated look

together over his shoulder before I drop down against his dewy back. And when my hands land over his, his long fingers instinctively curl between mine.

Each vicious snap of my hips feels like it forces him deeper and deeper inside her—until I'm not entirely sure whether it's Hermes and me sharing Sabine, or if it's me and Sabine who are sharing the little blond fucker. But it feels good either way; my using him to pleasure her like he's our own personal sex toy.

No, not just good.

Right.

"Fuck, *right there*," Sabine's moaning now, and from the way Hermes's ass clamps down in response, I know he's got to be close as well. The color is high in both their cheeks, sweat dotting their hairlines.

Thank *Christ*, because I'm about ready to go over the edge here, myself.

"Babygirl, you gonna soak his cock while I flood this tight little ass?" I smirk down at her, loving that spark of extra heat my words always seem to light up in her eyes.

"I'm almost there," she pants, eyelashes fluttering.

My pace ramps up. "You gonna come too? Fill that pussy up like the good boy I know you are?" I grit out against Hermes's ear.

"Can I?" he practically whimpers back.

Fuck.

"Yes, you earned it, *come for us*," I urge, my voice coming out with an extra sharp, domineering rasp.

Sabine's eyes roll back with my words—right before the two of them lock up, gasping and groaning together through each of their joint orgasms like it was choreographed.

The unrelenting pressure on my cock is more than enough to tip me over, but it's the sights and sounds that finally do me in. Before I know it, I'm violently unloading, filling Hermes to the absolute fucking brim.

Just as I promised him.

Toes curled and biceps stinging, there's a second where I think I could stay right here, like this, forever. Instead, I force myself to pull out and roll away so I don't collapse and crush them both.

But not before I catch sight of the decadent fucking cream pie I made of Hermes's hole.

"*Fuck*, that's a beautiful mess. Wrecked that ass *so good*," I groan, like I'm in pain. "Made him into a Twinkie, babygirl. All full of cream."

"I fucking love Twinkies," Sabine breathes out, voice thick and features slack with what could only be described as pure satiation.

Hermes is still sunk deep inside her, face tucked up against her throat. "You make the best fuckboy sandwiches, *ever*," he slurs adorably before his shaggy head shoots up to look between us. "Respectfully," he adds with a crooked grin.

Shit, that's cute.

My laugh is throaty as I take him in. Wild curls, pink cheeks, and a set of shiny hazel irises. Too pretty for his own good, and the two of them together? A fucking sight for sore eyes. "Hell no, disrespect us, Miller. Hard. And repeatedly."

"Repeatedly?" His shy expression brightens and then *fuck*—it's like watching a train wreck happening in real-time as Sabine's cool voice slices straight through that post-coital high.

"Okay," she announces, bodily rolling Hermes's prone form away from her own. "I need another shower. You've both got ten minutes to make yourselves scarce." And then she's up and off the bed in a flurry of sandalwood and sharp hips.

The sound of the bathroom door clicking shut behind her sounds like a gunshot in the silence that follows. The answering ache in my gut has me scrubbing at my face in frustration, and after a final, aggrieved huff, I throw an arm across my eyes.

Anything so I don't have to look Miller in the eye for this conversation.

Because I didn't miss the spark of devastation that she lit the moment she filed him right back into that box of hers that's labeled *Casual Encounters*.

Know that fucking feeling better than anyone.

"Better go, man. She'll see you back in Rox City."

And I really can't offer him anything more than that. As much as he deserves some semblance of aftercare, he's not going to find any cuddles or sleepovers here.

In fact, the longer he stays, the harder it'll be on him later.

Speaking from experience.

There's a rustle of sheets and the whisper of leather as he slips himself back into that criminally tight pair of pants.

"Will you be there?" he asks, after a pause.

Fuck. Kid sounds like a kicked puppy. Something pinches deep in my chest. "Yeah, I'll be around."

He lets out a shaky sigh, before giving a single, jerky nod toward the door.

Yeah.

Then, without another word, he too is gone, and an otherwise empty hotel suite never sounded so loud.

CHAPTER XV

SABINE

AS PROMISED, Dominic appears outside my dorm's building on the Wednesday immediately following our trip to Themis. I'm not sure how long he waited here just to accost me after class, but his gravelly voice once again drifts out from a corner of the shadowed portico the moment I step past its threshold.

"Librarian."

My spine snaps straight.

"Dominic," I reply saccharinely. "Please call me Sabine while I'm on school grounds."

When he moves into the low light, he throws me a pointed look that tells me exactly where I can politely store my request. That has me sighing through my nose because who am I to argue the finer points of endangering my closely protected identity with the Gray Man's Second-in-command?

"How can I help you?"

And why couldn't this have been a phone call?

Or better yet, an email.

"Haven't received the Symposium report yet," he

grits, sucking on his teeth in consternation. His expression—*as always*—is hard and cold like a sheet of granite. I wouldn't be at all surprised to find him moonlighting as one of the gargoyles that line the buttresses of some of the Academy's older buildings.

My eyebrows jump before I can catch them. "Because it's only been *three days*, Dominic. There were over 2800 people to sort through."

As soon as the words pass my lips, I purse them, knowing I should probably retry that. He may not hold a candle to Sebastian's cruelty, but he *is* the only person with a direct line to our boss. Even his fellow Councillors must go through him first. If I piss *him* off, there's every chance he'll shoot me straight to the top of the shitpile for punishment.

Wouldn't be the first time, either.

"Sorry," I amend, attempting to at least *sound* contrite. "He's always given me as much time as I needed. I usually need at least a couple of months to collate and crosscheck, and this year, I have to juggle schoolwork, recruiting, and now training up the Rox Boys on top of that."

Casually slipping his hands into his pockets, he tilts his head, staring me down for a long minute. Dominic Licata could hold a master class on carving expressions into stone, and the look he shoots me this time is also just as plain to read. *Because you were still in his good books then,* the look says.

"You were told I was coming today. The Labors are about to begin. We need those names and details."

"I understand," I reply, so sweetly my teeth hurt. "But I thought you were coming to discuss the Labors themselves. I need more time for the report. He needs me free for the trials, doesn't he? Give me two months, please."

"One month."

"Six weeks for the full report. And as soon as they announce the Crown contenders, I'll prepare a preliminary workup of their attendance on the night."

It's an edge the other participants won't have. If a Southern member managed to score an invitation to the exclusive party, chances are they'll be involved with the Labors in some capacity. It might give us clues about possible trades and alliances based on who they each spent time with over the course of the evening.

My mind flashes with images of Smiley making nice with his rival Irishmen, and Trick chatting with one of the Four Horsemen.

It's a tangled fucking web, with hundreds of possible connections. A mess I could rightfully be sifting through for years. But I don't have years. Not even months. *Weeks*, if I'm lucky.

He clucks his tongue, but then reluctantly, he nods. Once. "Six weeks. Jackson has our skeleton plan for the Labors."

I do my best to keep my expression nonchalant. "He's staying in Roxborough?"

"He'll be staying with the rest of the Juniors for the duration of the Labors. Easier to have you all in one place for Herald broadcasts."

Translation: Easier to keep an eye on you all.

Not that I doubted for a second that the Suits would be throwing their name in the hat, but I guess that's my actual confirmation. It almost seems a little unreal, though. After so much time spent scheming behind the scenes, hoping to clear the Southern chessboard for himself, Sebastian now has to execute his bid for the Crown through official channels instead.

I'd say it's *kismet*, but we all know that none of us are *that* lucky.

"Okay, I'll get myself caught up."

"Herald said the First Labor goes out after the roster, so anticipate starting Sunday evening."

I nod.

"Six weeks, and get the Southern challengers to me as soon as possible. I'll go through Jackson for handling each of the trials as they come in."

"Yep, of course," I agree evenly. You won't ever catch me arguing against having Zeus as another Gray Man buffer.

"And remember, Librarian, you do still need to sort out the Academy before the end of the school year." His voice grates against my eardrums.

"Yep." *Like I could fucking forget.* They'll be needing fresh meat more than ever now. I ignore the deliberate use of my designation this time.

And then, without another word, he slips back under the shadowed cover of the building and is gone. I stand frozen in place for at least another five minutes, listening for returning footsteps. When I'm satisfied he's not coming back, I yank out my phone.

"Are you alright?" Zeus's soothing baritone floats through the receiver and wraps around my tense shoulders like a warm blanket. I haven't seen him since Monday morning, since we were unceremoniously shipped back to Roxborough via private jet escort. But just the knowledge that he's still here cleanses some of the horrid taste that Dominic's visit left in my mouth.

No, I thought your father was going to change his mind and have Dominic dump you back in Lexington, after all.

Or at the bottom of the Tethys River.

"Dominic just left," I say instead.

"I told him I was running point, that *I* would handle the trials," he grinds out.

"I know, but he wanted my report from Sunday. Like, yesterday."

"*Jesus,*" he mutters under his breath. "Those lists take months to put together."

"I know! I told him I would try and at least get the bigger players done once we knew more about the contenders," I continue, my gaze following a rather large crack that's spidering through one of the bricks at my eye level.

"Sabe—" Zeus starts, almost hesitantly.

My skin prickles in warning. "What?"

He sighs. "There won't be an official roster until Sunday when the seven days are up...but Dominic has informed me Sinclair *was* nominated to enter on behalf of the Gray Men. As one of two formally sanctioned heirs."

"What?" I suck in a breath. Foreign wisps of protectiveness lick around my ribs. "Just like that?"

"Just like that."

"Wait, *Dominic* informed you?"

"Dominic," he confirms, a bitterness creeping into the fringes of his voice. "I've not heard a single word from Sebastian since Sunday's dinner. Apparently, informing your only known heir that you fathered a secret child eighteen years ago was a task so beneath the Gray Man that it was best left to his Second."

I rub a knuckle across my sternum, feeling a sudden kinship with the fissured wall in front of me.

Because what do you even say to that?

"I'm...sorry, Jax. He didn't mention anything just now."

"Probably figured you'd just hear it from me," he grouses. "Didn't offer any proof either, just informed me that we'd be expected to work together and that my Crew had to *cover him like we would the Codex.*"

Wow. I love that's what we've both been reduced to: the disposable son and a useful tool. Whose worth only extends as far as their submission.

"Always such an ego boost," I mutter, some of the same bitterness threatening to ruin the sharp lines of my sarcasm. "Does Apollo know yet?"

"I don't know, sweetheart. Did Miller say anything to you?"

"Miller?" I choke out.

Fuck, did D—

"He tells me everything. You should really know that

by now," comes Zeus's terse reply. I can't read that particular tone of his, though.

Is he disappointed?

"Go and find him. We need to prepare for Sunday."

ROOM ASSIGNMENTS for the upcoming academic year aren't locked in until the very night before the September semester begins. That meant starting my first day at Rox Academy with a few small holes in my student data, and so when I passed Apollo in the hallway that first morning, I'd mistakenly assumed it was because he was one of my new neighbors.

When we did get a hold of the finalized dorm numbers, and I was able to update each of the student dossiers with their assigned rooms, I discovered that Tristan Sinclair did, in fact, *not* live on that floor.

He didn't even live in the *building*.

Turns out the Rox Boys all share a communal apartment only available in the cluster of carefully restored buildings across campus. One of the larger buildings that Foster had unfortunately been unable to work his magic on and have me assigned to.

But I'm totally, completely *not* green-eyed over the gorgeous Gothic mansion in which they get to lay their heads at night—*or* the fact the doorframe I'd seen him leaning against had actually belonged to one *Sloane Walker*.

Jealousy?

Nope.

Never met her.

Hypocrisy, on the other hand—that's a witch I know well, as any *Imperium* woman does. Like Apollo calling me out for my 'overnight guest' while in the middle of his own walk of shame?

Men.

They're just as good at getting on my nerves as these *motherfucking* pins in this *motherfucking* lock.

Christ, do I hate the new mechanisms on these fancy modern doors. Why would anyone upgrade a heritage building's perfectly beautiful, perfectly pickable, vintage hardware?

Knowing every single one of the Boys had a free period right now, I'd expected at least *one* of them to be in. But after my knocking went unanswered, I'd decided I wasn't going to pass up a perfectly good opportunity to snoop on my new teammates.

Unfortunately, it looks as though they've had a custom lock put in because my duped master key hadn't worked at all. Hence the heavy make-out session that's been happening between my toolkit and the Boy's front door.

"Haven't already spent enough time on your knees for the Rox Boys, Winters?" a masculine voice sneers from somewhere directly behind me.

Leo.

My picks dig into my palms as I spin in place. Fuck him for sneaking up on me, but also *fuck him* if he thinks I'm going to sit here and let him slut shame me. "Jesus,

Baker, put a bell on that pretty little Aces collar of yours, would you?"

The thundercloud covering the handsome footballer's face darkens even further. "What the fuck are you talking about?"

"You don't think I clocked you with those two Clubs back at the Guardhouse?" I smirk up at him, watching as his lip curls. He looks freshly showered, wet hair combed back and his gym bag still slung over his shoulder. The Titans would have just finished practice.

"Is *that* why you've been avoiding me?"

Leo shifts so he can cross his arms. He could really take some notes from Ares, though; the move isn't as intimidating as he thinks it is. But where in the hell did this new backbone come from? Surely not from being what equates to a Strange Aces errand boy.

Maybe I just added a little too much chocolate syrup to that vanilla milkshake of his.

"Huh, *nope*," I drawl, turning back around to my task. "I just don't double dip."

"You know Sinclair's not as perfect as he likes everybody to think. There's going to be hell to pay for breaking into their room," he grits out.

My eyebrows rise, as I pretend to study the lock. "Oh, I'm counting on it. Are you going to be the one to tell him, Leon?"

"You should have taken my help," he spits, the frustration when all he gets is more of my back so evident that it has a small grin tugging up the side of my lips.

"Still think I'm going to have to pass on that," I say.

My tools stay poised against the strike plate, making no moves to go further. I don't want to risk the linebacker trying to follow me inside if I somehow manage to conquer these pins while he's standing in my blind spot.

There's a beat of silence. *"Fine,* guess I'll just thank you for popping my slum cherry, then," he snickers cruelly.

Oh, because what's more important to the student elite than their reputation? And how *devastating* to be not only labeled a whore, but a *low-class* whore.

Lucifer should really save on an eternity of whips and chains and just send everybody back to high school.

"Nice. So your game's weak both on *and* off the field," I observe, blithely.

"Fucking bitch," he hisses under his breath, prompting me to turn back to him with lips slightly parted. Before I can respond, he spins around and shoves a key into the door behind him. The second it gives way, he shoulders angrily through the doorframe, taking great pains to slam it shut so loudly it rattles.

I then spend several more frustrating minutes—both trying to brute force my way inside and to reconcile the sinister promise in Leo's flashing brown eyes with the shy golden retriever I seduced last week. When I'm finally able to stagger to my feet and push open the door, it's with bruised kneecaps and a throbbing headache at the base of my skull.

From the floor plan, I know that each bedroom occupies one corner of a long, rectangular space, opening directly into a large communal living area. The kitchen and lounge themselves are similar in design to my own; both clean and rigid in their industrial minimalism.

Running a finger along the top of the massive TV screen, I snort when it comes away clean. It's completely spotless in here, and I can't help but wonder who exactly's to thank for that. What it must be like for the pristinely pressed Head Prefect of Rox Academy to share a space with Hermes, who moves through life like his only mode is *Mayhem*.

Standing in the middle of the living area, I study each of the closed doors. What the floor plan couldn't tell me, of course, was who slept *where*.

Behind *Door Number One* is a basic Rox Academy dorm setup of double bed, standing closet, and desk. One wall is taken up entirely by a large window seat that overlooks the Academy grounds. The opposite wall houses another closed door, which—from its positioning —should lead to one of the Jack-and-Jill style bathrooms that bridge each pair of rooms.

This particular bedroom is utilitarian in its decor; sparse, with only a few soft blues and dove grays among the charcoals for color. The bed's been made with painful, military precision, and the desk is almost completely bare of objects.

My eyes snag on the stack of pre-med textbooks.

Apollo.

"*Yahtzee*," I crow, striding quickly across to the desk. Even before this paternity bombshell, he was their self-appointed leader. If they kept any records pertaining to their alliance in the Underworld—his room would be the perfect place to start.

I slide open the top drawer as carefully as I can, so as not to shift the contents inside. I doubt the Boys would go so far as to dust for prints, but they'd certainly noticed their shit being moved around. Inside are the usual homework suspects. Notebooks, stationary. A printed copy of this semester's timetable.

But at the very back of the drawer, tucked behind a leather pencil case, sits a nondescript ring box.

My neck prickles as I reach for it.

A ring? For who?

Sloane?

Just as my fingers brush its velvet sides, however, I'm frozen by the distinct sound of a key turning in the front door lock. My eyes dart toward the bedroom door that's now sitting ajar.

Fuck. Maybe I should have sent a text after they didn't answer the door.

"Does this look like it's been tampered with to you?" Apollo's voice filters through the open floor apartment, a frown evident in his tone.

My fingers fly back to the sides of the open drawer, trying to lift it just slightly off its tracks, the goal being to slide it home as silently as possible. I curse inwardly when it doesn't budge.

It's Hermes's voice that answers back, but it sounds forced with false humor. "Hmm, maybe? I was pretty wasted getting back on Saturday, I could have scratched it up then. You had to come let me in, remember?"

I pause, hearing that. I'd already come face-to-face with the aftereffects of my dumping him—when he'd turned up at my door at the Delphi. But the knowledge that he went out and got wasted because of it drops down like a jagged stone in the pit of my stomach.

"Don't remind me," Apollo replies darkly. "I was the one who had to clean the bathroom."

My eyes slide over to the ensuite, wondering briefly if that means the two of them share. Swallowing, they slide back to the open drawer in front of me. He sounds *pissed*, and that's someone he practically considers a brother. Something tells me he's not about to roll out the red carpet for the veritable stranger who's broken into his room with the express purpose of touching all his things.

"Yeah, because you're always *so good to me*," Hermes's voice teases again, only this time in *much* more honeyed tones. "Always cleaning up after us, and solving all our problems."

My lips part. *Woah.*

There's a pause, and my ears strain desperately.

"How about you let me solve at least *this* problem for you?"

A muffled grunt, and then, *"Mmm."*

Holy shit.

Slipping off my heels, I tiptoe as quickly as I can on socked feet toward the entrance to Apollo's bedroom. I ease my phone out, opening up the selfie camera. And when I crouch down and angle it carefully around the bottom of the door, it gives me an inverted but unobstructed view of the source of those heated sounds.

A shirtless Hermes in profile—as he kneels between Apollo's splayed thighs, his hand stroking lovingly over the sizable bulge in his best friend's sweatpants.

Oh, good. God. *Damn.*

Voyeurism kink activated.

The two look as though they've come straight home from an intense workout, deliciously rumpled with their matching Academy track clothes and sweat-slicked hair.

Apollo lounges back against a single armchair like a dark king upon his throne, and I watch with fascination as a distinct tug-o-war of emotions takes place across his Romanesque features.

Lust wars with anger, wars with frustration, wars with desire.

Battling between an obvious preference to stay in control—and a *need* to let go.

Please let go.

Hermes's tongue peeks from between rosy lips as he meets Apollo's glower head on; both waiting for permission and challenging his resolve. Apollo's fingers curl into the padded armrests of the chair and his nostrils flare. And like the quintessential brat that he is, Miller's hand never stops stroking.

Please.

Minutes tick by.

Guys, I'm literally begging you here.

Please just take his fucking dick out of his pants.

Just as I swear I'm about to expire from the anticipation alone, Apollo looks down his aquiline nose at Hermes.

"Take it out," he commands.

YES.

Hermes leans straight in, long fingers tugging down Apollo's waistband in an eager bid to free his erection. When it springs forth, the head kisses Hermes's cheek and leaves behind a thick trail of pre-cum.

Without another word, Apollo spears his hand through the golden locks that hover over his lap, guiding their owner roughly down. The entire length of him then disappears down Hermes's throat in a move so hot it has me clenching down on absolutely nothing—like my pussy's trying to telegraph an emergency message back to Dionysus:

LAKE MILLER STOP
NO GAG REFLEX STOP

"So *good* for me," Apollo grinds out.

I nod in enthusiastic agreement. *So good.*

"I'm sorry," he suddenly laments in a ragged voice, and I suck in a breath.

But it's not an apology.

It's a *warning.*

Because Apollo's now holding Hermes's head hostage and fucking up into his mouth with absolutely *zero* mercy.

I realize then, that *this* is him: raw and uncut.

Without the crisp uniform and equally crisp sneer.

This is Tristan Sinclair finally *giving in.*

And he's unleashing more and more tension with each violent thrust.

Hermes takes every bit of the abuse; happily, if the consenting groans and the tent in his own sweatpants are anything to judge by. It makes me wonder just how often he lets him use him like this—like his throat's nothing more than a therapeutic speed bag.

"So *good*," Apollo pants a second time.

Christ. Just the *sounds* coming from the pair of them, let alone the picture they make. These two are going to be *la petite mort* of me.

When I can no longer ignore the SOS call my clit's transmitting, I slowly ease my weight forward and onto my knees, the hardwood floor now blessedly cool against my heated skin. My fingers snake beneath my skirt, seeking to grant any kind of relief they can. Thankfully, I'm already *right there*, thanks to their unintentional edging.

The wet slaps of Apollo's hips slowly start to bleed into the sights and sounds of another night.

Of the cold press of tiles lining a blue-lit nightclub restroom floor.

Of the distant thump of industrial bass.

Of nails clawing into powerfully corded thighs while the same thickly veined cock bruises my eager throat in much the same way.

Just try and forget us twice, I fucking dare you.

Our orgasms crest at the exact same moment.

Eyes wide, I clamp a palm across my mouth, catching the desperate, straining wheeze before it can betray me.

Right as Apollo's hips stutter and he shoves Hermes's nose flush against his pelvis with a grunted, "*Swallow.*"

The entire *tableau vivant* is now so deeply burned into my retinas that it's earned its rightful place as one of the single hottest things I've ever witnessed. It'll be damn near impossible to top this moment.

I'm still kneeling, my fingers still buried two knuckles deep, when the next low, raspy words I hear are—"Find what you were looking for?"

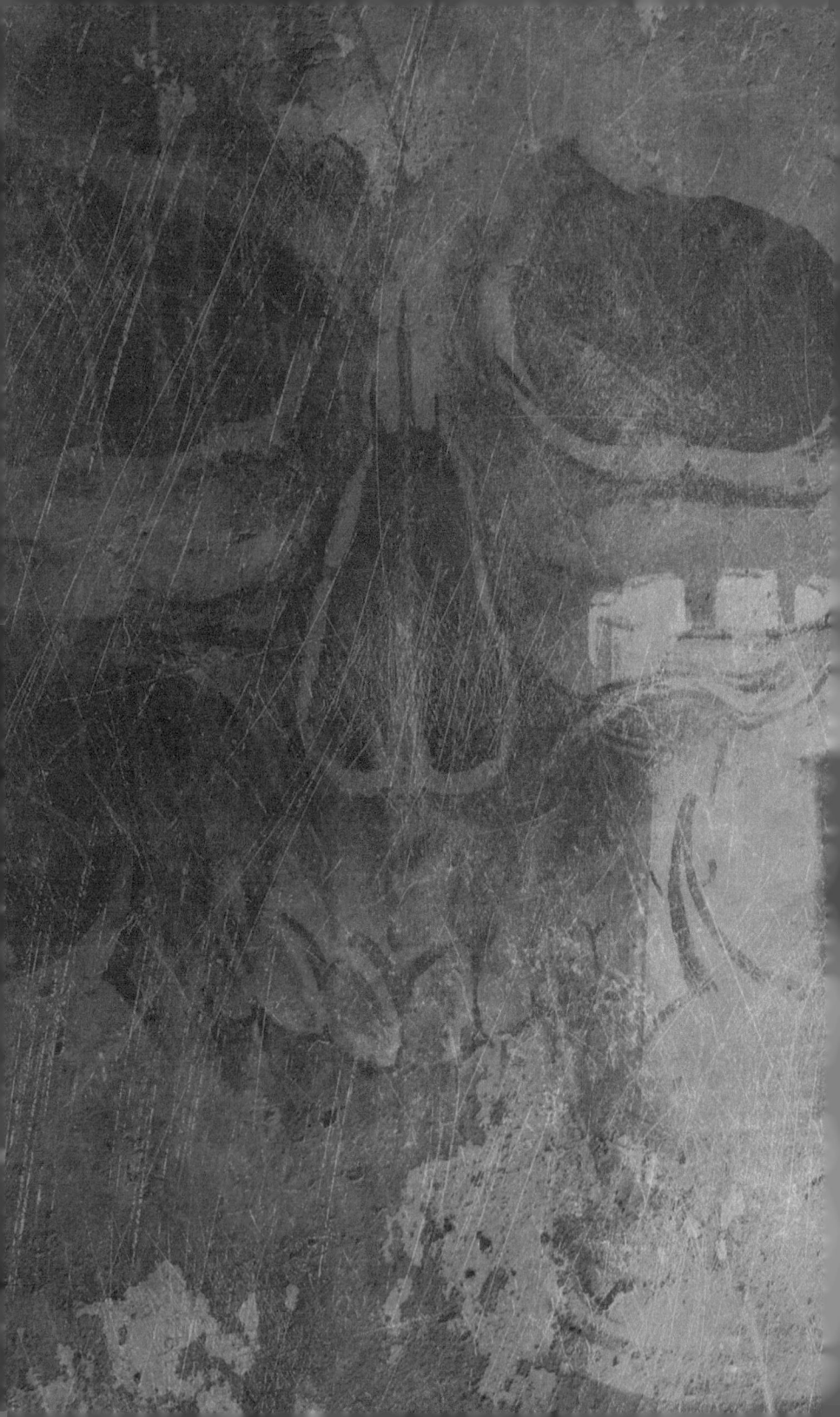

CHAPTER XVI

LAKE · HERMES

WELL, *well, well.*

If it isn't our naughty little Goldilocks, caught sneaking in to play in our beds while the cats were away.

Wait—are we the cats, or the bears?

No, *cats. Definitely cats.* I know she likes it when I purr for her. Or when I *lick* her. And I thought for sure when she kicked me out of her bed in Themis, that was going to be the last time I ever did.

Yet here she is, kneeling for us at Hades's feet.

But *why* is she here?

Whose bed were you trying to steal, Goldilocks?

I didn't even hear Hades come in, too busy getting my shit scrambled by an Apollo in all-out berserker mode. It doesn't happen too often, and really on when he's stressed, but it's a sword I will always happily fall on. And one of these days, I'll manage to convince him to drive that sword home *somewhere else.*

Regardless, I haven't had a chance to come, and now my dick's trying to stage a furious escape and I'm leaking like a sieve.

I narrow my eyes at Sabine, pressing down against the raging hard-on with the heel of my hand.

If it was a bed she was after, all she had to do was ask. I'd happily share mine with her. *Any day of the week.* Just not sure about how much 'sleeping' we'd get done, though.

My bed is juuuust right. Just like my dick, remember?

The problem right now is the bedroom she happens to be kneeling in front of is *Apollo's*—and he doesn't let anyone into his room.

Ever.

I'm not sure even his long-lost Jelly Bean here could get that man to give up access to his zillion-thread-count sheets.

I know, I've tried.

Hades is still glaring down at her, all doom and gloom like his godly namesake, like she's the last person on the planet he'd ever want in his space. Not that she seems bothered by him in the slightest. In fact, she's been steadfastly ignoring him, opting to continue eye-fucking Apollo and me instead.

Finally, Sabine looks back up at him, meeting his glower head on.

"No. But I did enjoy the show," the vixen snarks, holding up two glistening fingers without an ounce of shame.

Oh, man, that's so goddamn hot.

I fucking *love* that Apollo and I were the reason she got herself off. But I also don't know whether or not I should be disappointed that she didn't try to join in on the fun.

"How the fuck did you even get in?" Apollo growls from above me, tucking himself back into his sweats.

Shit.

Also love a growly Apollo.

I press down harder, stifling a groan.

"No outfit's complete without them," she replies airily, pulling a small leather case from her pleated skirt and flipping it open.

Lock picks.

Fuck. Gonna need to start updating our wedding vision boards again soon.

As soon as he takes in her kit, Apollo immediately pushes to his feet, eating up the distance between them in just a few careful strides. He takes a moment to match Hades's glare, staring her down.

Then he's grabbing her by the ponytail and yanking her to her feet.

No claws come out. All I see is a pair of pursed lips and the answering flare of arousal in her eyes. The latter has me biting down hard on my lip in excitement, though it doesn't surprise me in the least.

We already knew she liked being hunted down like prey and fucked into the dirt—why *wouldn't* she enjoy a little manhandling?

I'm fully expecting Apollo to start bodily dragging her to the front door, so imagine my delight when he continues on through the doorway to his bedroom instead.

I yelp, scrambling to my feet and chasing after them.

Apollo. Bedroom. Sheets. Cannot *fucking miss this.*

As soon as I'm safely past the threshold, Hades steps in behind me, pulling the door shut. He makes a beeline toward the mostly empty desk, gingerly taking a seat on its surface.

I blink.

Today's just full of fucking surprises.

I'm still wondering if I shouldn't be finding my phone and texting Ares to get his ass straight home, when Apollo shoves our girl directly onto the pristinely made bed. She drops down on her ass, bouncing a little and raising her eyebrows.

"What do you have in mind?" she asks, voice husky. She doesn't skip a beat and that's another thing I love. When it comes to hooking up, she doesn't seem to balk—she'll go in blindly.

Just got to get her to go all in on the rest of it, too.

"Lie down on your back, head off the end," Apollo twirls his finger, instructing her into place like the bedroom drill sergeant he is. His expression is slightly pinched, and I swear he's trying not to glare at all the new creases in his duvet.

Sabine immediately lifts her legs, spinning around to get into position, and only further roughing up the bedclothes. Luckily, his attention's quickly diverted by a flash of emerald green lace from beneath her uniform's hemline.

And now that I'm looking for it, I see there's the hint of a matching bra underneath her white Academy-issued blouse.

Know what shiny goodies that's *been hiding now, too.*

Apollo doesn't turn from the bed, just holds his hand out behind him, gesturing me forward. "I think it's Lake's turn to punish that mouth, don't you?"

I jerk forward like someone's yanked on my strings.

"I'm almost sorry I'm not wearing any lipstick today," she says with a wink, a mocking tilt to her lips now.

Her words manage to tease out a low, amused grunt from my brother and a muttered curse from me. Just when I thought I couldn't get any fucking harder—now I'm conjuring up another image of her leaving that cherry-red lipstick kiss at the base of Apollo's dick.

Fuck.

When Sabine flicks her eyes across to the desk, her brows pulling together at something that she sees there, Apollo immediately sidesteps, shielding Hades from her line of sight.

I completely get *why* Apollo feels the urge to protect him, but for me, the fact Hades entered the room *willingly* speaks volumes. Beneath that thorny shell, he wants her just as badly as the rest of us.

He's just not ready.

"No. He won't be joining us," Apollo starts, defensively. "He—" he pauses then, cutting his gaze toward the silent figure still perched on the desk. Choosing his next words carefully, so as not to expose those deep, invisible scars. "He prefers to watch."

We're all frozen, waiting for some biting response to that, instead she only gives a single, upside-down nod in understanding. Considering her own weird kissing hang-up, I'd be surprised if the two of them don't have more in common than we know.

Just not exactly sure how well trauma bonding with the source of your own trauma ever goes, though.

"Lake," Apollo urges.

I've already lost my shirt some time between walking in the front door and my best friend impaling my mouth on his dick. My Academy sweats are equally quick to find the floor.

Then I'm standing over Sabine's prone form, admiring the long column of her neck as it arches back and over the foot of the bed. Now ponytail-free, her pale hair cascades in a sheet down the front edge of the mattress. Holding my gaze like a challenge, she tilts her head back even further, parting her full lips in invitation.

Daring me to make my move.

Joke's on her, though. I always choose dare.

"*Shit,*" I hiss the moment I slide across her tongue and the hot heat of her throat engulfs me.

"Won't last long, Wifey," I add through gritted teeth. I was already halfway to coming when Hades found our Goldilocks hiding behind the door.

I concentrate on keeping my strokes even, trying my best to stave it off as long as humanly possible, but Sabine's torturing me by doing fucking Kegels with her esophagus. "*Shit,* maybe don't do that. *Yeeees! Fuck.* No. Wait, yes, *do that again,*" I babble, eyes squeezing shut in bliss.

The muscles of my back dance reflexively when I feel a warm hand skim down my spine. I twitch, once, and then I'm crying out my release. As soon as I unload the first rope, Sabine sweeps her tongue over the head like she's playing catch with my load.

Fuuuuck.

I figure I must've blacked out at some point, because suddenly hands are grabbing my biceps and I'm pitching forward. My back hits the mattress as we roll—and then I'm left blinking dumbly up at a victorious Sabine as she kneels over me.

The sight of her straddling my torso—lips red and swollen and gray eyes glittering—has my spent dick rallying in response.

But then she leans in, and my entire body freezes.

She grips my chin, tugging downwards so my jaw pops open.

My eyes flare wide as her lips begin to part.

But not so she can drop a kiss on my mouth—but so she can hand off a mouthful of my own cum, instead.

"Did you just fucking snowball me?" I wheeze out, chuckling when I've managed to swallow most of it down. My chin definitely took a hit. Maybe even my cheeks.

She smirks down at me. "You look like a glazed donut."

Definitely got my cheeks, then.

But she can turn me into a whole fucking box of them, if it gets her to smile at me like that again.

"Yum," I hum back at her, happily.

The bed dips and I whine as Sabine's snatched away. I struggle up onto my elbows, only to find Sabine on all fours, her head pressed firmly into the mattress as Apollo stands behind her. The fingers of one hand are splayed across a round ass cheek, while the fingers of the other curl inside her.

There's a dark look in his eyes and a determined slash to his mouth.

Oh, fuck. Looks like the beast wasn't put back in its cage, after all.

"What's got you so wet? Was it watching us? Or having your slutty throat used like a cocksleeve?" he croons in a voice like pure sex.

Sabine moans, her response muffled by the blankets now pushed against her face.

"What was that?" he demands.

She lifts her head. "A little of column *A*—" she rasps, before her response cuts off with another cry of pleasure.

Apollo's fingers slip from her then, joining the other hand on her ass. He squeezes roughly, spreading her wide. I only catch a glimpse of his sheathed cock before he steps up closer to the bed and lines himself up.

His hips snap forward, their thighs colliding with an audible slap of skin.

"Not sure why you keep thinking you can get away from us," he taunts, with another hard thrust. "But you'll learn your place.

Christ.

In response to his growl, my dick gives the room another jaunty salute—more than happy to be stroked to the sight and sounds of the object of our obsession being railed into the bed.

Sabine and I share a groan each time her entire body jerks forward with the force of my brother burying himself inside her.

As I tease my shaft, I steal a glance at Hades, hoping to see him with his own cock out—but to my disappointment, he's still sitting in the same exact position. However, his focus *is* completely locked on Sabine's pussy and his knuckles now grip the desk's edge tightly.

I guess this sort of counts as exposure therapy?

Baby steps.

My attention snaps back to Apollo when he grits out, "You're. *Ours,*" followed by, "Need you to come, Winters —*now.*"

I swallow, stroking faster, and as he ruts into her harder, I pretend he's also talking to me.

Nothing hotter than when our orgasms are twinsies.

"Not how it works, *Sinclair,*" Sabine mutters, valiantly trying and failing to serve him attitude before she's gasping all over again.

"*Now,*" he commands once more—and like he's the motherfucking snake charmer for the female orgasm— Sabine's eyes flutter shut, her expression tensing with anticipation. Then she's tumbling right into the bliss she was fighting off, back arching, thighs shaking.

Her low, eager moan fills the room, and like good little soldiers, the two of us follow her over that cliff and into oblivion; Apollo emptying himself inside the condom, and me turning my abdomen into a prize-winning Pollock.

Panting, I stare up at the ceiling and marvel at the fact I just came so hard I lost vision.

Twice.

But as my beautifully sated brain begins to reboot, slowly clawing its way back online, I notice Hades slipping from the room, and my thoughts are quick to sober.

Instead of enjoying the high, I find myself bracing for what inevitably comes next.

Sabine rolling off the bed, getting dressed, my guts doing their best impression of a constrictor knot. That familiar itch beneath my skin.

All feeding into that heaving black hole that lives in my chest.

Maybe I should be getting used to seeing her turn her back on us by now, but I just *can't.*

But before anyone even has a chance to move, Apollo's terse instruction cuts through the room.

"Get dressed. We need to talk."

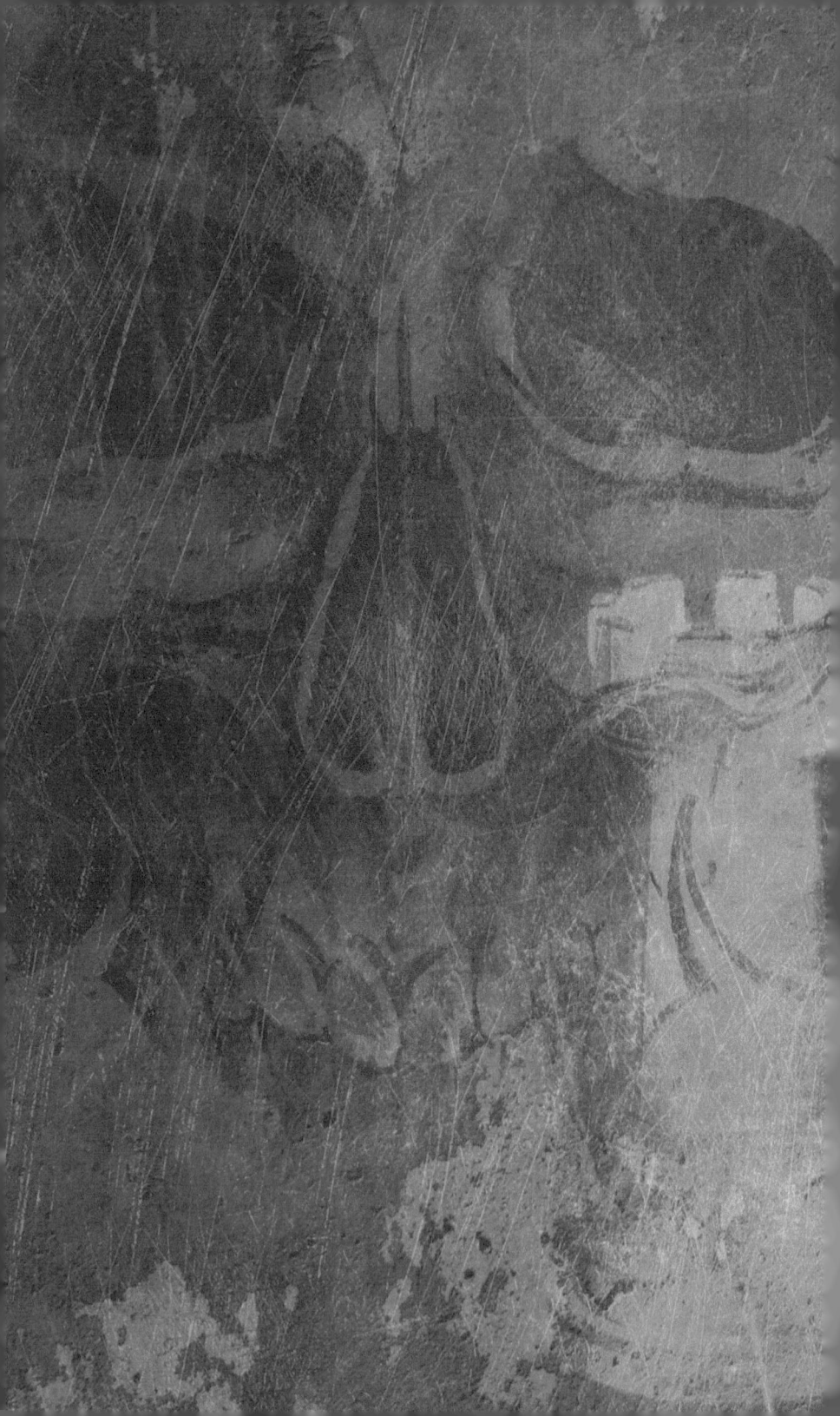

CHAPTER XVII

SABINE

THIS CONVERSATION IS EXACTLY why Zeus sent me to track down the Boys in the first place. It's also exactly what I promised to give them as soon as we got back to Rox City.

So why am I still holed up in Apollo's ensuite some twenty minutes later, dragging out my post-fuck routine and only succeeding in delaying the inevitable?

And why do I no longer recognize this woman staring back at me?

I've seen her face before: sex-tousled hair, swollen lips, and raccoon eyes. I've seen it a thousand times, in a thousand different mirrors. But never, ever quite like this —with this pinch of concern at the corners of her eyes, or the disturbed creases that bracket her mouth.

Somewhere around here was a line that I never should've approached, let alone crossed.

And now it's too fucking late.

Because they're already at my door, and they've come armed with battering rams.

Emotional castle invaders.

Slowly working through my defenses, one by one. Leaving their hairline fractures all over the lead casing around my heart, alongside the two small fissures that both Zeus and Dio were already determinedly working on.

With an audible sigh, I let my shoulders drop and allow my head to fall forward.

God.

I am so fucked.

When I finally emerge from Apollo's ensuite, it's to find the man himself, also freshly showered and wearing a new track into the hardwood floors of their living area.

Hermes is sitting bundled up on the same armchair the two of them just gave their performance from. The only thing visible over the fluffy red blanket is a shock of curls and a pair of solemn hazel eyes.

I clear my throat. "Where's Hades?" I ask, still a little hoarse from screaming into Apollo's mattress.

"Checking the cameras while we wait for Cal to get back."

"Cameras? You've got access to the Academy's servers?"

Good luck getting anything useful there. I'd already set up Foster with timestamps to wipe from outside both of our dorm buildings. There's no longer any record of Dominic, my embarrassing tango with the Boy's front door, or Leo's confrontation out in the hallway.

"*His* cameras," Apollo says, pointedly.

Oh shit.

Hades is notoriously private—and there hasn't been a

firewall that Hermes couldn't sweet talk the pants off—so of course, they'd have their own secure network setup.

I just hope there are no cameras *inside* their dorm.

As soon as that thought forms, the image of a brooding Atlas Rhodes fills my mind.

Find what you were looking for?

Fuck. He *does* have cameras inside their dorm.

And for the first time since they came home, I'm grateful they interrupted me when they did. Apollo and Hermes's arrival unintentionally saved me from getting into a proper sweep and some *real* trouble.

But now I'm curious what Apollo's *'hell to pay'* might look like. Whether or not he would have happily 'punished' me for it.

He certainly has the filthy mouth for it.

The front door swings open with a crash and Ares barrels inside their apartment. His auburn locks look like he's been tugging at the longer pieces on top.

"What happened?" he demands, his deep voice rough with anxiety.

Apollo's brows knit together as he takes him in.

"Text made it sound like it was an emergency," Ares clarifies, gym bag dropping heavily to the floor as he moves around the couch. Apollo frowns at it with consternation.

That's when Ares finally clocks my presence.

His whole body goes on alert, shoulders bunching and the muscles in his jaw launching into their favorite jazzercise routine.

"Why is *she* here?" he growls out, and I *know* I

shouldn't enjoy it so much because clearly he doesn't like me—but *goddamn*, it's got some *heat* to it. I feel that growl in *all* my places way down low.

Stop it, you hussy, I just fed you.

"I said *important family meeting,* and she's here already because she broke in," Apollo says, side-eyeing me. "I think it's time we all sat down and had that talk. Laid some of those cards out on the table."

I don't miss the way he doesn't specify *whose* cards— or the way he only said *some*—but who would I be to press for more? I honestly would have no leg to stand on there. I also have no desire to feel like the biggest hypocrite in the room.

Hades chooses that moment to finally re-emerge from one of the bedrooms, this one at the opposite end of the suite. He prowls over to stand shoulder-to-shoulder with Ares.

Great.

Now that they're all here—and we're not trying to beat the clock or dodge a bunch of Suits—I'm all out of reasons to keep stalling.

I pull in a long breath and take a step toward Apollo, wincing as I feel the pull of a wet silk gusset against my sore cunt. I had to choose between putting my saturated lingerie back on or going commando under my pleated skirt.

Ares instantly bristles, side-stepping to block my approach, inked fists curling at his sides.

"I'm not armed with anything but a few tumbler picks," I offer him with a slanted smile, "and this." I hold up a folded document between two fingers like it's poisonous.

And in all the ways that count, it is. That insidious report is the reason nobody I care about has slept in almost five days.

Our fingers brush as he reaches for it, a dubious frown pulling down on his handsome face.

As he unfolds it and takes in the laboratory logo at the top of the first page, that frown morphs into one of concern. He takes a moment to scan the tabled data there before flipping over to the second sheet, where I know the interpretation of the results is printed. Then he reads it again.

"Tris," he calls, lowly.

Apollo immediately moves to his side, Hades a silent ghost at his other shoulder. Hermes, however, is still doing his best impression of an armchair burrito, watching us over the edge of his blanket.

Ares hands the paperwork to his best friend. "I don't know man, it looks legit, but who knows if it's been faked."

I don't think Apollo's regal face has ever looked more like a statue's than it does right now. Fine marble features freeze; his pale cheeks hollow, and his strong jawline set in place as he, too, scans the document.

But just like those already threatening the hard shell of my resolve, I can see the tiny cracks forming along the stone walls of his composure.

His eyes flick up to mine.

Ocean blue Grayson eyes.

Not as crystalline as his brother's, and not as dark as his father's, either. But a stunning compromise between the two.

"It's verified?"

I nod. "Your brother had our tech guy quadruple-check. It was a legitimate test and the results reported don't show signs of tampering."

"What about the sample itself?" Apollo asks with another frown.

I pull a face. "It's a private laboratory, they're not required to store samples indefinitely. They destroy all material after three years."

"So, there's a ch—"

I sigh, waving off Ares's skepticism. "Look, I know it'd be nice and easy if the test was faked. But Sebastian is *obsessed* with his legacy and keeping it in his bloodline. Why would he go to the trouble of falsifying DNA when he could just create his heir and spares the old-fashioned way?" I spread my hands. "For all we know, he went out and knocked up a bunch of women, and you just happened to win the birth race."

My stomach fizzes at the thought of that. We already had *one* heir whose life was in danger of being made forfeit. We didn't need another.

"Besides, have you guys ever seen a picture of Lexington's Mayor? *Both* of his biological sons are the spitting image of him." Crossing my arms, I turn to look directly at Apollo. "You're a Grayson, Tristan."

Ares doesn't say anything, just stares down at the

papers in Apollo's hands. "Maybe we should go see your mom, Tris."

Apollo's cheek jumps, but he still hasn't looked away from me. By the looks of it, his mind is attempting to fill in the most likely series of events that would've led to Rosaline Porter-Sinclair being forced to carry, birth, and raise the child of the fucking Gray Man.

He shutters those thoughts and smoothes his face.

"And the Labors?" he asks, deliberately pushing the conversation away from his mother.

"That's mostly why I came here to speak to you," I reply, doing my best to plaster on my most abashed look. I can't help the chuckle, though. "When nobody answered, I couldn't resist a little snooping."

Ares glares at me. "Try harder next time, Winters."

"Don't pretend you wouldn't have done the same, knowing my connections," I snark back at him. I bet he'd be the first to toss my room, given half a chance. And he wouldn't bother to hide the mess, either.

His eyes dart to the armchair where Hermes sits, giving him right away.

"I knew it!" I crow. "I bet he had my file pulled the moment I stepped foot on campus."

Ares has the grace to look a little sheepish at that. "At least I didn't come to your room to "talk" with a B&E toolkit in my fucking pocket," he mutters.

"I told you I don't go anywhere without them."

"The Labors?" Apollo's firm voice prompts again, effectively ending our bickering.

"Right," I sigh, arms dropping back to my side. I move over to take a seat, dropping down and sinking into the plush cushions with my eyes closed. That tension headache is back, digging its claws in all around the base of my skull.

When I open them, Apollo is sitting opposite me. Ares and Hades hover behind his couch. Hermes is now perched forward on the armchair. His blanket cocoon has fallen, pooling forgotten around his elbows.

I have to grit my teeth and drag my eyes away from the view that gives me of his naked chest.

Focus, Sabine.

"Your father's Second-in-command, Dominic, informed us today that you *have* been formally nominated as a participant."

Apollo gives me his best impression of a living marble sculpture, while Ares scowls, digging his fingers into the back of the couch above his best friend's shoulder. "Are you saying Tristan could be the next Southern King?"

"It's a sovereignty, not a monarchy. The two sides are still beholden to the rules and treaties of the *Imperium in Imperio*," I correct him.

"Whatever," he grouses. "Sovereign, then."

"No. The point of the Labors is to settle the Southern succession issue, yes, but it's also being used by the Arbiter as penance for all the months of infighting." My hands rub up and down my thighs, as I continue. "The heirs must compete and win the Crown on *behalf* of their factions."

"So they just get to sit back and let us duke it out for

them, and then whoever wins it just hands it over?" Ares asks, still grumbling.

"Yeah. That's what she meant when she said they'd be *carrying the burden of their father's debts.*" I grimace.

"How is that punishing anybody but the heirs?"

"It is bullshit," I agree, then shrug, knowing while it's not fair on them at all, it's not so cut and dry for their sires either. "But she's still forcing them to decide whether they want that potential power badly enough— and exactly what they're willing to pay for it. Remember, it's a race to complete the tasks *or* it's the last man standing."

"Risk versus reward," Hades grits out.

I nod. "Exactly. They could win the Crown *or* they could lose their entire bloodline in the process."

"But how do you know all this? That's the real question," Ares spits. He turns away, cursing under his breath. The trap muscles across his upper back pull his Academy shirt tight when he lifts his arms to scrub his face. "None of this makes fucking sense."

My palms slide along my thighs to my knees as I sit forward. The skin is dry but I still feel a flicker of unease, right behind my sternum.

"When I was fourteen, Sebastian Grayson took me from the streets of Lexington and made me a ward of his organization. He then spent almost two years having me pulled apart, turned inside out, and put back together."

The room is silent. The looks that have been ranging between doubtful to outraged have all now been replaced by varying degrees of intrepid.

Apollo shifts. "What does that mean, exactly? Pulled apart and put back together?"

A spiderweb of discomfort spreads across my neck and shoulders at the reminder of my time with the Belgian. I pull in a fortifying breath, nostrils flaring.

"Exactly what it sounds like. Intensely physical cognitive and psychomotor training designed to create the perfect archivist for his information empire." Shoving each one of those memories back down with a sharp, bile-filled swallow, I add, "One that was unfeeling, uncaring, and most importantly—*unbreakable*."

Apollo's eyes look remarkably like his father's dark, icy ones when he asks cautiously, "Is that what you meant about someone being able to make you *'feel fear'*?"

I nod. "He had them train my fear to always take a backseat—so that if someone were to get a hold of me, I wouldn't break just because I was scared."

"But—*why*?" Apollo grounds out. His cool tone is heating back up again with the warmth of his repressed anger.

"Because of the information I hold for him."

"Which is *what*?" he prompts.

"Everything. Every piece of information that Sebastian has ever gathered and wanted to keep a secure record of. Every detail of every person important enough to have ever lived and ranked in the Underworld. Every known birth, every death, every marriage, every deal, every trade in the *Imperium*. All his contracts, all details of his holdings and fiscal reports. All the meeting minutes. Anything he needs recorded. I keep a record of all of it for him."

"The Librarian," Hades rasps.

"Yes. The keeper of every last, little dirty secret of his."

I squeeze my hands around my kneecaps, holding my breath through the tense silence that ensues. Bracing for their next question about my past.

Sabine Winters is dead.

But instead of demanding I explain to them why I seem to be wearing a dead girl's name, Apollo sits forward, elbows propped on taut thighs. "You said at the Symposium that he sent you here to do a job? What was his endgame?"

I tilt my chin, relaxing just a margin. "He sent me in to recruit for the next generation of Gray Men, with strict instructions to return with at least 300 new potential Suits by the end of the academic year. You four...you were non-negotiable."

"All four of us? Not just me?"

I lift a shoulder. "I guess he assumed you came as a package deal."

Ares grips the couch again. "What did he want so many recruits for?"

I scratch a finger along my brow, considering where to start.

"He's had designs on this half of the Sovereignty for years—way before the Green Knight's death left the Crown up for grabs," I say. "But while the Suits were busy icing out all the other Southern gangs, Mobs,

Bratva, Mafia families, Triads, syndicates, cartels...the one-percenters were busy setting up chapters in every state. The Strange Aces didn't have half the connections or reputation that the Gray Men had, but they *did* have the numbers."

I purse my lips, knowing full well that was behind Sebastian hunting me down on that icy morning in Lexington five years ago. "He was pissed at the oversight, and it rankled him that Patrick Mahoney chose to set up his MC's HQ right across the river. Like a giant *fuck you*. Before all this, Sebastian had been hellbent on making a run for Governor, just so he could do the most damage to Roxborough at the local level before he went after the Senate."

"So he's just using the Academy to make up the numbers?" Ares says, working his jaw. "Was all the talk about the '*brightest young minds*' more bullshit?"

"Even if he managed to *fiscally* run this city into the ground, it all comes down to a basic manner of manpower, yeah. He's outgunned. But he wasn't lying about wanting to poach potential politicians and moguls and scientists. He's built his empire on puppet strings and insider knowledge; he still needs fodder for his information machine."

"That's a lot of trade secrets you just so willingly handed over," he sneers. By the sound of his roughened voice, he's still very much questioning my motives. "Are you also the reason we've got dead girls showing up in the Academy bathrooms all of a sudden?"

I blatantly ignore that last jab. They don't need to

know all the ways I've fucked up, just the basics of why I'm here. "Sebastian asked me to, remember?" I remind him. "But that's not the only reason."

I push to stand and Ares straightens with a scowl. Apollo just watches me carefully from beneath dark lashes when I take a step forward.

"The Gray Men used to value discretion and shadow work above all else. But greed *always* wins, and even before this announcement, my Crewmates and I saw the writing on the wall. The Suits are desperate for the Crown—Labors or no—and they're heading down a path that we don't want to follow. Your father has started picking up on that resistance, and it's only a matter of time before the Gray Man starts cleaning house."

"So what's next, then?" Apollo asks, spreading his hands before him.

I have to bite my lip to hide the little rush of excitement the idea of having their full cooperation gives me.

Clearing my throat, I pull my phone out, opening up a new group chat with the four of them. "Come to this address on Sunday afternoon."

"What's there?" Apollo frowns down at his own screen as I make my way to their dorm's front door.

"We need to prepare for the release of the roster and the announcement of the first Labor." I pause with my hand on the handle. "And you can meet your older half-brother properly this time."

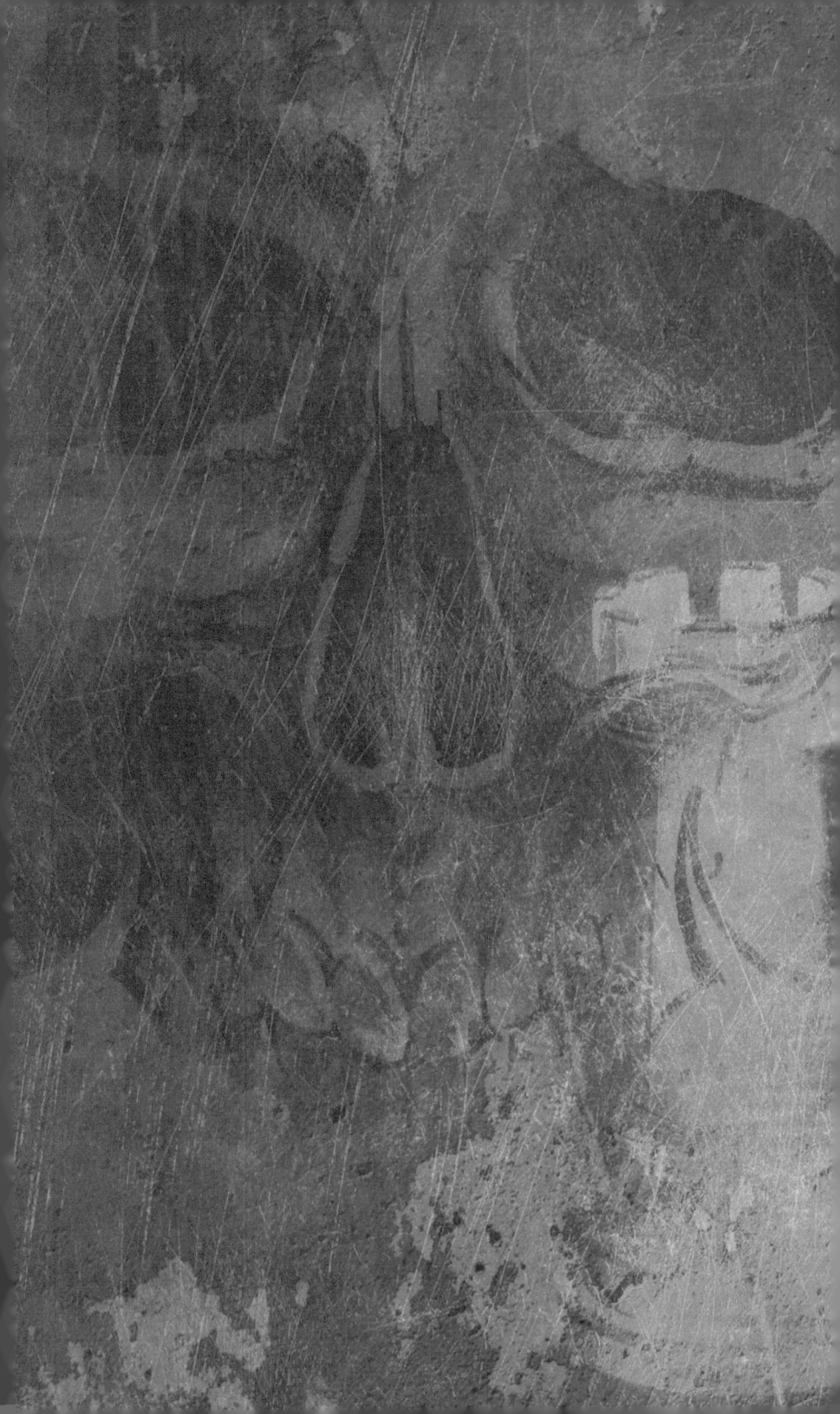

CHAPTER XVIII
CALLUM · ARES

"HEY MAN, I thought Brick was on the schedule tonight. You got me down for the first round with a... *Dionysus*?" I call to Oz as I round the doorway into his office.

Tristan hates that he's an Ace, but the guy doesn't seem to care much for the Club's dealings outside of his little haven down here in the Underground—the fighting pit hidden beneath the Guardhouse. He only cares about filling his cage with bodies each week.

And how many rounds they can last.

I'm his top earner.

"Nah, Brick called in last minute, said his 'Ma was in the hospital'," Oz replies with air quotes from where he's lazily reclining in his beat-up swivel chair. He follows by throwing his pair of ancient shitkickers up onto the desk and crossing them at the ankle.

"Smells like bullshit," I offer. The aptly named meathead hasn't turned a single match down since he signed on over the summer. I would have thought he'd miss his Ma's own *funeral* if the price was right.

"Mm, I think this new guy was just hungry for a spot," he bobs his head in agreement, a cigarette defying gravity as it dangles precariously from his mouth. "Must be a helluva sweet talker."

"Have you seen him yet?"

"Yeah, big blond fucker," he muses, lips twitching. "Might give you a run for your money, actually."

"You mean *your* money," I say, rolling my eyes.

I don't do this for the cash. Though every dollar I do earn, Atlas immediately invests for us—and in turn, I manage to rest a little easier at night. The only real currency worth earning here is the cold, hard satisfaction of my fist connecting with an opponent's jaw. Blood pounding in my ears and a crowd so loud that it drowns out the sound of the angry hornets living inside my chest.

The nest of hornets *she* keeps fucking kicking over every time she walks into the fucking room.

Fuck.

Oz shrugs, oblivious to my internal war. "It'll be a good fight." Then he waves me off, reminding me I still need to get ready.

"Alright man, thanks," I throw back at him as I turn and head out to claim my locker for the night. Just as I make it down the makeshift hallway outside the organizer's office, however, I catch a glimpse of that increasingly familiar long, ash-blonde hair, and the furious buzzing starts up all over again.

Because I'm here tonight for one reason, and that

reason *isn't* to see my 5'10", sass-mouthed ghost of my childhood past.

It's to beat the memory of her out of my head using my cage rival's face.

What I need to do is just head straight to the bathroom—tape up, stretch, and get myself into the mindset needed to walk out of that bloody arena as nothing but the victor.

Instead, I'm striding straight toward our specter like a man possessed, pulled like our chests are linked by one of those fucking red ribbons of fate, or some shit.

She's not looking at me and I have to force down what feels like a growl. Her head snaps up from her phone only after my boots stride into view.

"Ares," she greets warily, tipping her chin at me. No doubt trying to gauge my reception to her following all the messy bombshells she's been dropping on my family this week.

Ares.

Definitely still getting my head around the fact she went to the trouble of giving us all codenames—though now I know a little more about her connections, the *why* makes a little more sense.

But I must not secretly hate it too much because my chest puffs right the fuck up at the sound of it.

And considering where we are, it's pretty fucking fitting, actually.

"Winters," I grunt. "You're here."

Of course, she's fucking here, you idiot.

"Yeah," she huffs, turning to elbow someone in the ribs. "Although *Fight Night at the Underground* wasn't exactly what I had in mind for my Friday evening when I said I wanted to go out."

Fucking tunnel vision. I was so focused on Sabine, I hadn't even noticed the other man standing directly beside her.

"But D's sick of being stuck in Rox City with only Knox to spar with, so I agreed to tag along. Thought I could also suss it out for recruiting potential," she continues, eyes roaming over the rowdy, red-faced patrons slowly filling up the stands.

I grunt. Finding out Sabine Winters is now a headhunter for a corrupt criminal organization might just edge out this bullshit with Tristan's paternity for its level of weirdness.

She's wasting her time, though. Most of this crowd are Aces or Ace groupies.

"I guarantee you *will* get all hot and bothered, though," the guy with her purrs. He gives her a sultry eyebrow waggle, earning a playful slap to the chest with the back of her hand.

My teeth click as he glances up and I lock eyes with him.

Fantastic.

It's the blond fucker from the diner.

The one we followed out to the middle of nowhere and had to watch play cat and mouse with our girl.

The lighting was shit, and he'd been wearing a mask,

but I assume that was also him hovering behind her like an overgrown bulldog at the Symposium.

"*Ow*, fuck," Sabine grouses, flexing out her fingers. "Are your pecs filled with fucking concrete?"

My own fists flex in response to their playful banter, seeing how relaxed their exchange is. *Easy.*

"*Au naturale*, babygirl," he grins, lifting her knuckles and pretending to inspect them for damage. He smirks up at me and then makes a show of leaning down and running his tongue along them with a single, languid lick.

All while holding my gaze.

What the fuck.

"Why the fuck are you even here?" I blurt, taking a step forward before I catch myself. That angry swarm in my chest is vibrating louder; the reins I try to keep in place on my temper in real danger of slipping away.

"I'm the guy you're about to tap out for, sweetheart," he taunts right back with a dangerous grin. One that has all sorts of memories swirling forth—his wicked laughter, his large body caging Sabine's up against the door of his car.

Pinning her body to the floor.

If this really is my opponent—then for the first time since I stepped foot inside the Underground's cage, I'm not one hundred percent confident about the match's outcome.

"*You're* Dionysus?"

D. That's what she'd called him. I should have fucking put two and two together.

"In the flesh," he winks, but then follows it up with a pout. "I see that little fucker Hermes didn't mention me, then."

"D," Sabine cuts in like a warning.

I shoot a searching look between them, now thoroughly confused. Hermes is what she was dubbing Miller that night after the Guardhouse shooting, right? But how would *this* guy know that? That was after he'd seen us at the warehouse.

"Lake?"

"Blond, yay high, likes being turned into a Double Stuff Oreo?"

"*Orbison*," Sabine hisses again, her eyes flashing toward mine.

With the cautious look she now assesses me with, coupled with the smug expression on Dionysus's face, it doesn't take a genius to guess exactly what happened.

I feel dizzy. "What, all three of you?"

When my brother had managed to drag himself home —smelling like sex and sea salt and on the edge of a manic episode—I tried to ignore the fact it was because he'd hooked up with her.

After hearing that he *and* Tristan had both fucked her —together, and in Tris's bed, no less—those same feelings of trepidation had only deepened.

Not because I'm jealous of my brothers.

The idea of my sharing her with them isn't a new one.

Sabine's always been ours.

But because I'm afraid she's not the same girl we lost six, almost seven years ago.

That she's apparently got this whole other life—one that we'd also have to learn to share her with. I'm afraid that if we let her worm her way back in and we start playing house with her, that we'd just be packing all of these unresolved feelings down inside the cracks of our foundation like a bunch of C-4.

At which point, we may as well hand her the match so she can skip straight to lighting the cord and blowing our hearts to fucking pieces.

Again.

And I know Lake's not as discerning as the rest of us with his bed partners, but hooking up with *this* guy? It almost feels like a betrayal. Like he's been sleeping with the enemy.

"Ares—" she starts, and for once, it seems she's unsure about her next words.

To be honest, I don't know what she could say in this moment that wouldn't make me want to crack a tooth. Luckily for her, she's saved by Oz's grizzled voice coming over the tinny PA system to announce last bets on round one.

"That's our cue, babygirl," Dionysus declares, slapping her on the ass.

"*Asshole*, I'm going to do a lap of the crowd," she chides, but the scowl she gives him is playful. She's not exactly short, but *fuck*, in comparison, he makes her look almost...delicate.

Yeah, not liking my odds tonight.

"C'mon, the thought of watching the two of us—

shirtless, sweaty, and getting our bloody punch on–*isn't* tickling your kitty's fancy?" Dionysus teases. "Not even a little?"

Jesus Christ, it's like this guy's dial is permanently stuck on *seduction*.

"Go warm up, or whatever the fuck you need to do," she gripes this time, shoving him in the direction of the mini locker rooms they have set up for the fighters. He finally relents, sauntering off with a last wink at us both.

"Look—" she tries as soon as he's out of sight.

My boots squeak against the damp concrete floor as I immediately turn, ready to head in the same direction as my opponent.

"*Wait*," she calls to my retreating back.

It's all I can do not to turn back at the hint of a plaintive lilt in her voice, but I can't deal with any of that right now; I'm just about out of time to get myself fight-ready.

"Come find me after," I growl over my shoulder. "We'll talk then."

DAMN, he can move fast for being such a large motherfucker.

I might have several inches on him, but this Dionysus guy's built like a powerhouse—all broad, solid muscle mass.

I pivot, his knuckles only grazing my cheekbone

instead of the hard jab behind them finding its connection.

Trap muscles ache sharply as I bring a wrist up to swipe across my forehead, matching rivulets of blood and perspiration inching down my face. There's a tiny amount of satisfaction when I see Dionysus do the same; forced to squint against a small but aggressive bleeder that's now dissecting one of his brows.

A tiny amount because absolutely none of it's slowing this fucker down. *At all.* And I've already lost track of how long the match has lasted, thus far.

Even still, I can't help the manic grin I'm wearing. I always feel at home in the cage. The adrenaline of the fight loves to hold me hostage on the canvas, and it's been so long since someone managed to put me through my paces.

Dionysus returns the wide smile with one of his own —lips and teeth equally as bloody as mine. He runs a sweat-slicked palm down the line of his obliques. "Not slacking on me, are you, *Ares*?"

Asshole.

I'm starting to flag, and he knows it. I can see him sizing up the condition of each of my weak spots.

Sees I'm tight around the lats, that my range of motion isn't all there.

Clocks the knee I'm slightly favoring.

I don't fall for his taunt though. Instead, I crack my neck and slide my feet back apart. Bringing the weight forward onto the balls of my feet. Waiting on tenterhooks, hoping to catch any hint of his next plan of attack, all while trying not to lock any of my aching joints into place.

He nods in approval at my show of resolve, knowing I'm not going to be the one to go on the offensive this time. Not in my state. So it's only another slow blink of heavy eyelids before he makes the first move, feet gliding across the cage floor like he was born to dance, not bare-knuckle fight.

My eyes are hooded, but they still eat up every vibration of muscle, every rise of his chest, until—

Right there.

There's a split second between heartbeats when I telegraph the subtle drop in his torso, and I finally realize he's about to try ending this thing in a grapple, not a strike.

I brace my weight then, pitched forward to meet him; slick, tattooed muscles slipping and sliding when we collide in the middle.

The sides of my ribs pinch as I haul one arm up and under, snagging him before he can manage to readjust his axis. The clinch is fucking messy; there's just too much sweat and blood and fibrous tremors to pull it off with any sort of finesse.

But it works.

It fucking works.

I know it does the moment I feel his pelvis flex forward and his knee rotate inwards, shifting his center of gravity just past the stable point needed for a guy his size.

And I know for sure it works the moment we crash to the floor and the takedown is mine.

Fuck.

It's done.

"*Shit*, I really fucking needed that," Dionysus gasps out from beneath my chest. He's staring up at me intensely, something like pride in his olive-green eyes.

I hum before clambering gingerly to my feet, feeling like every blood vessel in my body is trying to fill itself all at once. I glance down at him, mind blank of anything but a cloud of endorphins, before finally offering out my hand. He takes it with a cheerful slap of his palm to mine, letting me haul him to his feet. My ribs and thighs bark with the effort.

Another enthusiastic slap—to my upper back this time—and I don't protest at all when he uses the hand to steer us toward the gate. I can barely even hear the roar of the crowd right now; my head still feels like it's underwater with the rush of the win and the throb of my injuries.

"Can't wait to work with you, man," Dionysus is saying against the shell of my ear. "You're gonna be dangerous once we finish polishing you up."

"We?" I croak.

"Knox and I will train you, fit you out. I'm sure Zeus will be happy to jump in on marksmanship. You any good with long-range weapons?"

"Uh, only ever run with handguns. A few blades."

"All good, we'll sort it," he says with a grin.

I blink, twice, when I'm suddenly deposited in front

of Sabine. Somehow, we'd made it all the way out of the cage and back onto the Underground floor.

"Babygirl! Ares for the *win*," Dionysus crows, cuffing my head and giving it a gentle shake while I sway in place. "Alright, I'm hitting the showers, our girl will take care of you," he adds with a final slap to my shoulder. I nearly groan out loud when my abused delts scream in response.

But then my eyes land on *her* and all the pain takes a backseat and the familiar buzz starts back up behind my sternum.

"C'mon, big guy," her mouth says, and all I can think is *that fucking mouth.*

I realize, rather belatedly, that she's started gently herding me in what I think is the direction of the locker room. She has one arm wrapped around my waist, the other held gently against my abdomen. And I'm struck by just how *non*-Sabine the gesture seems.

Because there's nothing *gentle* about Sabine Winters.

She also doesn't shrug off the arm I settle around her shoulder, and for just a moment, the droning din of the hornets lowers—just a little.

I can make out the doors to the improvised bathrooms when our path is darkened by one of the absolute last motherfuckers I want to be dealing with when I'm still coming off a fight that intense.

Or ever.

"*Baker*," I grit out.

"First Sinclair, now Jameson, Winters?" the prick says, dragging his eyes down her body, the disdain clear in his voice. "Do they know you broke into their place yet?"

"Le-*on*," Sabine greets him, enunciating his full name in a way that, for some reason, has the sneering linebacker flinching. *Interesting.* "If it isn't the consequences of my own actions. Again."

The fact these two hooked up is not news to me, but it still torques the fuck out of my guts just thinking about him being with her.

Inside her.

My eyes burn.

This fucker's days are numbered.

"Rich coming from you, Baker. Why don't you fuck off back to your little biker clubhouse?" I growl, very casually pressing her closer to my side. His eyes flick down at the movement before he redirects his sneer to me.

"Says the wannabe gangster. Don't hate because you and your boys passed on an opportunity," Baker mocks, spreading his hands.

"Not sure if wiping Club asses is anything to brag about, but you do you, I guess," Sabine shrugs, trying to tug me forward.

"We passed for a reason, dumbass. Enjoy our scraps," I jeer.

"Enjoy *mine*," he spits right back, with another pointedly aggressive rake of his eyes over Sabine's slender form. His smile is oily.

Just before I can lunge at him, Sabine yanks me sideways so suddenly I almost pitch over. She uses my momentum to turn us and then bodily steer us away from the smug fucking Titan.

"Raincheck," is all she says, staring straight ahead.

Looking forward to it.

Because I didn't miss the look of dark fury that flashed across Baker's face the moment she turned her back on him.

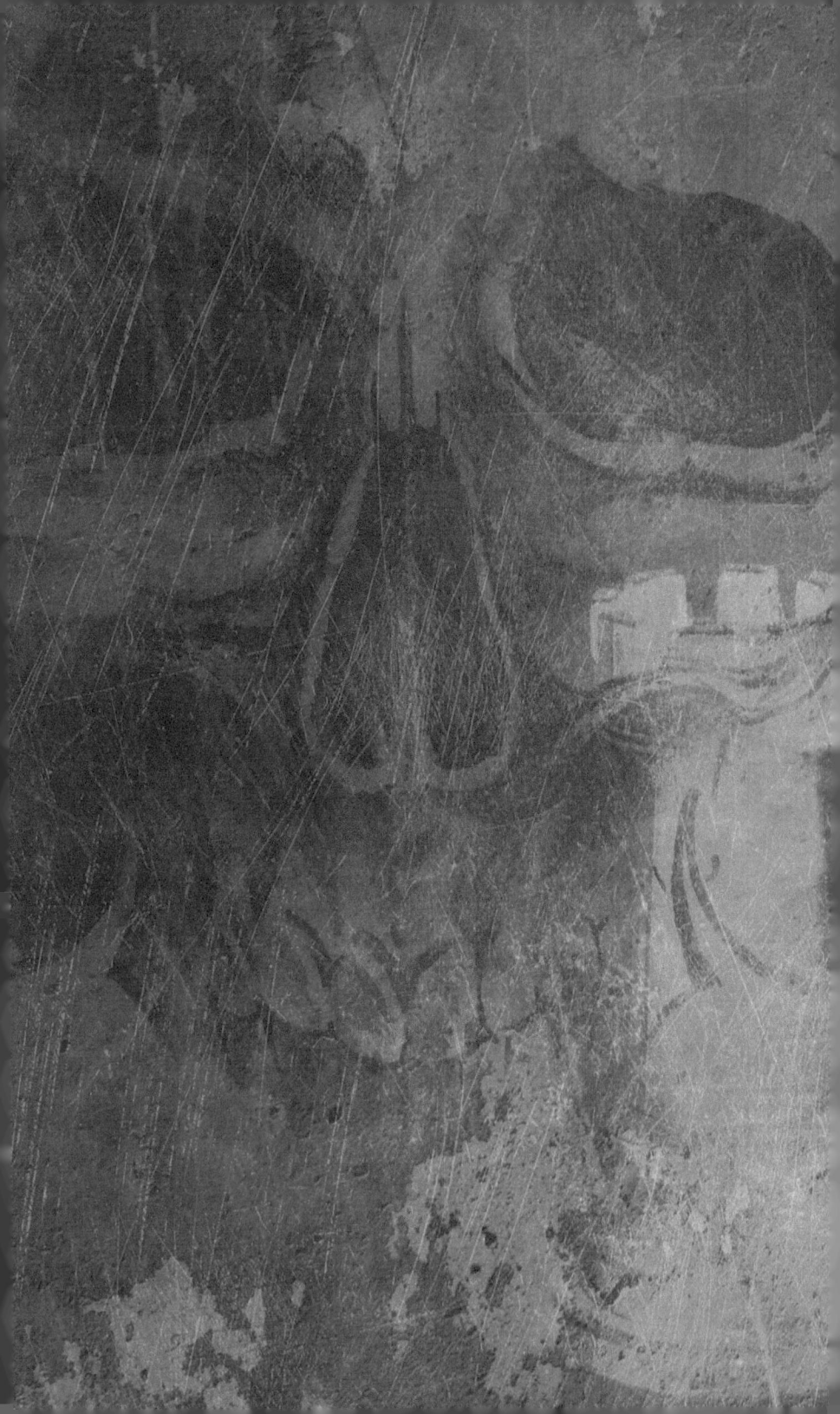

CHAPTER XIX

SABINE

I DON'T NORMALLY REGRET my one-night stands. It's hard to regret something if you never spare it a second thought. But Leo Baker is starting to haunt me like the motherfucking *Ghost of Hookups Past*, and I'm wondering what it's going to take to finally exorcise his ass.

"Still can't believe you *actually fucked him*," Ares snarls the moment we're alone in the designated champion's locker room.

When all he gets from me is a considering hum in the back of my throat, he starts making an angry beeline toward his belongings.

Ares's gear sits waiting for him on a low-set bench in the middle of the makeshift tiled floor. Instead of starting his warm-down, however, he deliberately positions his back to me, shoulders set and hands hovering over the small duffle.

Perhaps it was meant to antagonize—but all his cold shoulder really does is treat me to an unobstructed view of some disgustingly defined back muscles and their sprawling artwork. The abstracted skull piece is stunning; spliced through with wilted roses, and various broken timepieces and heavy on the black ink. It stretches down his spine in a massive void of yawning jawbones and harsh, aggressive lines, before eventually crumbling back to dust somewhere below his waistline. The haunting imagery continues down both muscled arm sleeves, across his torso, and all the way up to his chiseled jawline—every single inch dark and aggressive, just like him.

As I observe him silently, the only sounds between us are the steady drip from a nearby shower stall, and Ares's labored breathing. Every movement of his is stiff with both pain and frustration. His bloodied fists clench in time with the sharp rise and fall of his shoulders.

I've personally never seen Dio lose in one-on-one, hand-to-hand combat before tonight, and I'm sure the victory must have tasted sweet despite the mouth full of blood the Enforcer left him with. There's none of that elation now, though. Instead, he's poised on a knife's edge, straddling that adrenaline and the frustration about Leo.

But something about all of that unbridled rage trapped beneath his skin beckons to me like a siren call, and I suddenly want him to give me something— *anything*—other than his back.

What would it take to tip him over?

"Because he works for the enemy...or because he wasn't one of *you*?" I finally decide to toss back at him like a taunting grenade, hoping like hell he'll bite.

The man in question doesn't turn, only scoffs loudly, the echo like a sudden whip crack against the tiled room.

He can't hide the small shiver that judders down his spine though, not with the way each of the taut muscles ripple along its path.

"What makes you think you have any right to chime in on who I fuck?" I take a quiet sidestep, hoping to get a better view of his side profile as I continue to needle him. "Any right to *care*? If I want to fuck a Titan—hell, if I want to fuck an *Ace*—I'd have every right to."

Right there. A muscle along the side of his jaw pops, but all he does is shake his head as he tears open the zipper and begins rifling through the bag's contents.

"It's your world, Winters, we're all just living in it."

His voice is a wounded growl and it yanks at something unnamed—deep inside my chest cavity—and for once, I don't think, I just move; desperate to close the distance between us.

"What is it exactly that you're so afraid of?" I ask when I'm standing at his back.

The answering flinch is subtle, but on a man Ares's size, that small, involuntary jump of his shoulders may as well've been a bellow. But for whatever reason—that jab is the hook that reels him, and he finally turns, slowly. Almost as if he expects his movements to spook me.

I already told you I don't scare easily, Jameson.

And when he finally *does* face me—the sight of all that blood, sweat, and hostile ink, all covering such an obscenely ripped torso, has me biting down so hard that I taste copper on my tongue.

Jesus. Fucking. Wept.

To add insult to injury, those training shorts of his hang so criminally low that they leave absolutely nothing to the imagination. A dark treasure trail beckons me south, down to where a set of Adonis grooves carve inward on narrow hips like a tattooed air traffic controller directing me in for the landing.

There is no fucking way he's real.

"You," he says, lowly. But now that gravel edge sounds a lot less *hurt*—making that single-word delivery sound more like a threat than anything else.

And well, let's just say my libido responds *very* well to threats. So it's a good few seconds before my brain kicks back into gear and I even register what he said.

"Me?" I prompt ever so innocently, shrugging off my leather jacket as I recover my wits. I throw it towards the bench, where it lands beside his opened bag.

"I just know you're gonna break us," he practically whispers in response. Honey-brown eyes bore into my gray ones. The silver nose ring he must have slipped back in post-fight winks beneath the fluorescents.

"Why is that?"

"I've killed for you," he sneers at me, instead of answering my question. A flash of surprise lights up his sharp features—*there and gone*—as if he didn't actually mean to voice that sobering fact out loud.

I tilt my head, considering his body language.

I don't *think* it's the fact he shot those men in cold blood that's bothering him, necessarily. With the way he handled himself, I'm sure he's defended his brothers numerous times. No, I think it's more likely an issue of how easily he found himself coming to *my* aid—someone who was supposedly a complete stranger to him.

My fitted baby tee slithers up and over my arms on its way to join the jacket. Ares's gaze immediately drops to my chest, taking in the meshed bralette that does absolutely nothing to hide my piercings. Going by the growing bulge in that tiny pair of athletic shorts, I'd wager I'm not the only person in this room who's a fan of that fact.

"Why?" I prompt again, fingers slipping into the band of my leather leggings and quickly working them down my thighs.

When I'm left standing in nothing but a matching set of sheer lingerie, Ares's nostrils flare in frustration. My lips quirk as he continues his grapple for restraint. The expression he wears as he stands frozen before me is giving both doubt and desire equal stage time.

Eventually, Ares must decide to turn the dial on whatever's been eating at him straight to *'fuck it'*—because his eyes suddenly snap up to mine, full of resolve.

And they're fucking *twinkling* with it.

"You're lucky I'm an ass man, Winters," he chuckles then, and it's *dark*; all traces of that earlier vulnerability now well and truly under lock and key.

With a choked laugh, my hands fly to my chest, giving the modest endowments there a single, protective squeeze. Lifting my chin, I shoot him my best attempt at an imperious look.

"Oh, so you've chosen violence then, big guy?" I demand with all the faux indignation I can muster. But it's an epic battle just to maintain a straight face.

Because no one told me Callum Jameson had jokes.

My mocking challenge, of course, is only met with a further teasing smirk. A lazy lift of those impossibly broad, stone-cut shoulders.

"God of War, remember?"

Oh no. Have I created a monster?

I narrow my eyes. "I suppose peace was never an option, then, huh?"

Ares doesn't answer my low taunt with words, but by bursting forth with all the delicious power and aggression of an apex predator denied their prey for far too long. Giant, tattooed hands scoop around my naked thighs, the motion jerking my ass up high and forcing my legs to wrap around his hips.

Then he's moving us until we're colliding roughly with the nearest vertical surface.

The corrugated wall of the makeshift structure groans on impact.

Ares's face instantly buries between those tiny, offensive mounds of mine while one hand is busy desperately tearing down his shorts. The hot length of him slaps against my covered mound the moment it's free and—*fuck me*—he's definitely working with something *thick*.

Strangely, I find the fact he hasn't even attempted to kiss me during this whole sordid process exactly one part comforting, one part insulting.

Oblivious to my wandering thoughts, and without a shred of warning—he grabs a hold of my thong and tears completely through it.

Okay, then.

"You clean?" he rasps against my collarbone, spearing two large fingers inside as he does. They enter with no resistance, of course; not with the absolute carnage going on down there.

"Clean. Covered," I gasp back.

He withdraws them without a word, but I'm too distracted by the sharp, punishing nip of his mouth over one of my nipples, tugging the piercing there between his teeth. The flimsy material of the bralette gives about as much pushback as my pussy did his questing fingers.

Exactly zero.

"*Good,*" he growls, and with a bend of his knees, he lines himself up and then he's driving into me so hard the wall rattles again.

"Fuck!" My eyes disappear into the back of my skull with the combined surge of pleasure and pain at his unapologetic breach. There's also the extra pressure and drag of a large ring I wasn't expecting, but considering the rest of his canvas, shouldn't at all be surprised by.

"*Shit,*" he curses against my neck as he straightens, "can't fucking believe it."

Neither can I, big guy.

And then Ares is rutting into me like this is both the first and last time; all the building frustration and tension between us translated into each violent thrust. I can't breathe, let alone form coherent words. I just let the clench of my cunt and his desperate, answering strokes speak them for the both of us.

Hard, fast, and punishing.

Just the way I prefer it.

By the time I feel the orgasm building...burning...and finally *bursting*, the locker room wall is very much in danger of coming down around us.

"Fuck, Winters, *yes*," Ares pants out, a bead of sweat winging its way down his temple, "I'm right there. Are you there?"

"Ah, fuck, *now*," I cry my response into the sweat-slicked, auburn mess of his crown.

With my words, he grunts once against my skin, rough hands yanking my hips tight against him as he spills inside me.

Our twin breaths are unnaturally loud in the silence that follows, chests heaving in sync. He takes his time slipping out of me, easing me back down to the ground with uncharacteristic gentleness. With Ares no longer inside me, our combined mess gleefully coats the inside of my wobbly thighs.

"Not bad, Winters," he barks, tucking himself back into his shorts with a nod.

Be still my heart. "Ah, you say such sweet things, Jameson," I quip back, with absolutely no heat. I feel sore and achy and yet so incredibly light.

I watch with further amusement as he reaches down and snatches up the shredded remains of my underwear. I only raise my brow at him, silently saluting another fallen comrade. But now, I wish I was still on good terms with our Accountants—I kind of want to know whether or not I can claim ongoing lingerie replacement as a work expense.

"Spoils of war," he declares with another smug shrug, before tucking them safely into the band of his shorts.

I can't help but grin at his caveman antics, but he doesn't return it. His expression quickly sobers instead. Simmering amber eyes hold me hostage with their intensity. "Don't fucking break us, Winters."

And as he turns his back, I could swear he adds a muttered, *"Not again."*

Then I'm once again left with the empty, accusing stare of a giant, rotting skull.

WHEN I FINALLY EMERGE, Dionysus is ready and waiting, having already showered in the opponent's locker room while I was busy *assisting* Ares. His dirty blond hair is now wet and neatly combed, and there's a fresh Steri-Strip over his brow.

"Slick little setup they got down here," he says with an appreciative whistle.

I'd been expecting innuendo the moment I stepped out, but his gaze as he takes in the massive fighting cage and its tiered seating actually *is* admiring.

"You'll have to build me one of these once we're all settled," he sighs in that way he always does when he's daydreaming about our mythical life after the Gray Man.

If only a happy ending was in the cards for me.

"The Aces do love their fight clubs," I cajole, weaving my way through the bloodthirsty throng and trying not to roll my eyes at his happy delusions.

"So," Dio says as he jogs back to my side, rubbing his hands together. "Is he as big as he looks? Pretty sure I got a good hint of what he's working with during that last takedown."

Aaand there it is.

I shoot him a careful side-eye, trying to gauge his thoughts about Ares and me. The two of us have never claimed to be exclusive, but does that automatically translate into him being on board with my fucking around with the *rest* of the Pantheon?

"Uh, yeah, you called it. My fingertips wouldn't have been able to touch, that's for sure." I give him a strained chuckle.

D's brows raise expectantly. "You don't know?"

"I didn't exactly get to test that theory; it was just a quickie."

His eyes jump between mine, assessing, before he prompts more seriously, "But you wanted it, yeah?"

"What's not to want?" I laugh again, this time a little more genuinely.

"*Baby,* don't do that," Dionysus scolds me. He blows out a breath, measuring his next words. "I think it's different, with them. *You're* different."

My forehead wrinkles and I shoot him a dirty look. *What bullshit is he on about now?* "Different, how?"

D moves in closer, bumping his shoulder against mine.

"You've been back for seconds *and* thirds with Hermes," he says pointedly. "And Apollo's hit that, what —twice now? Right?" He punctuates that particular observation with an appreciative and not-at-all-subtle glance back at my ass.

*I mean...*he's not wrong.

Before the Boys, Dio *had* been the only one I'd ever allowed a repeat performance.

Why?

Because he never questions *why*.

And he understands me well enough that he doesn't need to.

I might even go so far as to say he understands me better than anyone.

The way Ares and I had come together was brutal. Animalistic. *So fucking hot.*

And perhaps, somewhere underneath the surface of all that raw physical chemistry, there'd been a flash of something else.

But that doesn't mean he's right. Right?

"When was the last time you got high?" he asks suddenly.

I blink.

"High? Um. Day before the Symposium." *Blunts in an abandoned lifeguard hut with a certain curly-haired trickster.*

"Seriously?"

Am I?

Maybe I've thrown back a few Xannies here and there...but nothing even close to the usual amount.

The realization is like soft prickles across my scalp,

and I *really* don't like scalp prickles. They usually precede either a need for self-preservation or a need for self-reflection, and right now?

A little of column A, a little of column B.

"Maybe I should pump the breaks then, especially if we're going to all be working together," I offer, half-heartedly.

That has D instantly slamming to a stop and choking out a laugh. "Did you seriously just imply you shouldn't shit where you eat?!" His huge body bends at the waist with his mirth.

"*Fuck.* No, what I meant was—" I start to grumble, and if I could still blush, I think my face would be hot enough to land me a bed in the burns ward.

Kill me now.

I pick up my pace.

"I think we're a little past that, don't you?" the shithead continues in the same teasing tone as he dogs my steps. "Because, I mean, *I've* definitely eaten where y—"

"Don't even think about finishing that fucking sentence, Orbison," I groan like I've been shot. "What I *meant*, was: I've already got you and Zeus, right? I don't need *that* much free-range dick to get through the day."

"Wow," Dio murmurs, his steps stuttering for a moment.

I glance at him with a frown. "What? You *can* have too much of a good thing, you know," my stupid mouth says. "Haven't you ever accidentally killed a plant by overwatering it before?"

"Wow," he breathes again, massive shoulders pulling up around his neck as he looks away.

The oddly defensive posture is a completely foreign one, and it's answered by a sharp *crack*, deep within the core of my chest.

Suddenly, I can't even *look* at the man I've let consensually violate me in a hundred different ways.

I surge forward, ignoring as Dio calls my name.

Can't a girl just have a crisis of conscience in peace?

All he gets is my back as I push through the Underground's heaving crowd. With the second round only just concluding, the place is packed to the brim with milling pundits, most of them now reeking of sweat and cheap booze.

The only way in or out of the hidden arena is through a decommissioned fire door that leads out onto a branch of subterranean tunnels beneath the Guardhouse.

Dio doesn't call my name again as I push through it, just lets his heavy footsteps rattle the rusty metal catwalk as he shadows me.

As soon as I reach the central walkway, I plunge in the opposite direction to the way we came in, not exactly sure where I'm even headed. I've only been down here once before, and that was when I was half out of my mind, thanks to Sloane's hotshot of *Asphodel*.

I stomp along in silence until finally, I spot a familiar fire exit through the semi-darkness.

And when I shove through it, I find myself standing at the bottom of the same alley again. With the same putrid-smelling dumpster. The same fenced dead-end, still littered with cigarettes, and the same steep incline back to street level.

I let out a strangled wheeze at the irony.

Because it's also the same place I first stepped across that invisible line with The Rox Boys.

I think it's different, with them. You're different.

The place the first of these cursed fucking dominos had begun to fall.

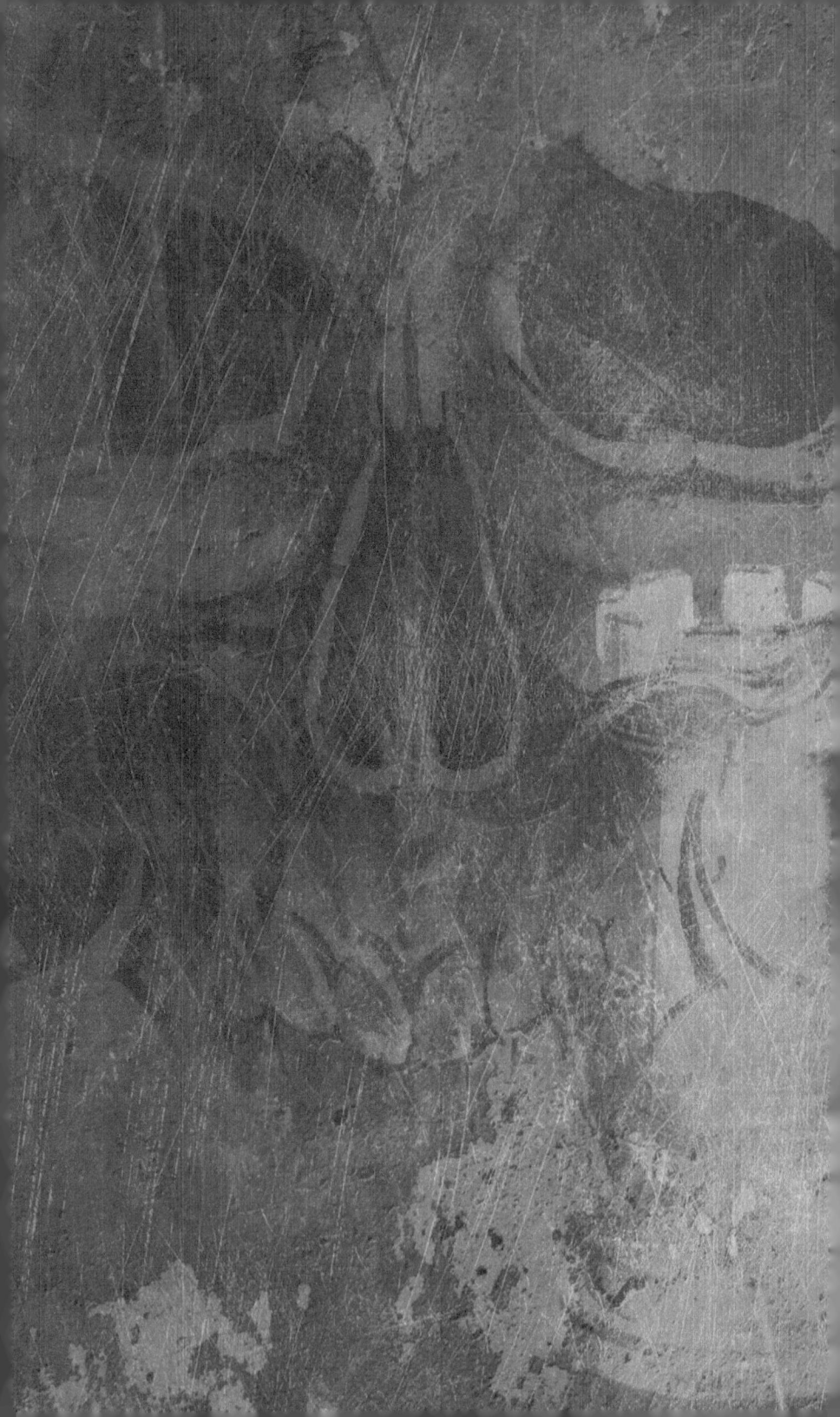

CHAPTER XX

JAX · ZEUS

I NOW UNDERSTAND the real reason my father insisted on keeping me isolated from the Roxborough mission for so long.

I'd blindly assumed it to be some combination of Sebastian needing to keep my presence from tipping off the Aces—and wanting to punish Sabine by removing one of her main crutches: *me*.

But now that Tristan Sinclair is standing in front of me, without the interference of a masquerade disguise, I can see how laughably wrong I was.

Because Tristan Sinclair is the *spitting fucking image* of my younger self.

Had Sabine known me in my teens, perhaps she would have connected the dots for us much, much earlier. Even Rhett had only met me for the first time after I was already well into my twenties. I'd also kept my facial hair for as long as either of them could remember.

Rhett squints, handsome face scrunched in faux concentration. "I can definitely see it now."

A fucking blind person could see it.

These eerily similar faces carry exactly none of our mothers.

They're purely *Grayson.*

I hold out my hand, ignoring both Orbison's levity and the veiled scorn Sinclair shoots him. There's definite animosity there.

But that's something I'll have to get to the bottom of another day.

"Jackson," I offer gruffly. "And I'm sorry that we're meeting like this. I'm sorry you're being dragged into our mess at all."

There are dark circles under Sinclair's eyes, and his expression remains guarded as he takes in the scattered positions of my Crew. But he stands tall in a well-pressed button-down and slacks, holding himself steady with that perfect composure borne of a natural leader.

When he slips the palm of his hand firmly into mine, I take it as a good sign. As much as the revelation of our shared DNA has thrown our entire future into uncertainty, I also can't move forward with him on my team while still holding my father's sins over his head.

He didn't ask to be born to a monster any more than I did.

In that, he's completely innocent.

There's just the matter of Sabine.

Even shaking my hand, Apollo doesn't fully take his focus off her.

In fact, all four of the Boys are unabashedly tracking

Sabine's movements as she putters around behind me in the kitchen of our Rox City homebase.

Jameson hovers right behind Sinclair's shoulder. The plain black tank he's wearing covers a hell of a lot less ink than his tuxedo did. I can now see that the tattoos run over every visible inch of his neck, chest, shoulders, arms, and down to the backs of his hands. His jaw looks about ready to come off its hinge with how tightly he holds it.

Miller is perched on top of the couch in a faded Hawaiian shirt that he's left open, feet propped on the back seat cushion. His mop of blond curls looks wild today, hanging over his eyes as he leans forward, intently watching Sabine cut slices of provolone.

Rhodes—dressed head to toe in black—has his back pressed to the wall furthest from the kitchen, as if he hopes his molecules might somehow find the right frequency and vibrate him straight through it.

One might think that after sharing her with my best friend the idea of Apollo and his friends as potential partners of hers would be an easier pill to swallow.

The problem is that when I made the decision to break protocol and head to Rox City, I was drunk, angry, and desperate to lay eyes on her. I convinced myself that I was only going in there to see her as her Team Leader, and while the beast may have arrived collared and leashed, I'd forgotten to bring its muzzle.

Now that it's had a taste of freedom, I've not been able to re-collar it.

So, although just the thought of her and Orbison no

longer makes me want to put my fist through the nearest drywall, I'm still grappling with the possibility of my needing to further expand that concession.

Sinclair finally drags his eyes away from Sabine and dips his chin at me.

"I guess it's as much my mess now, as it is yours," he replies, with as much signature Grayson confidence in his voice as his carriage.

How did we ever miss this?

His hand slips back into his pocket while he takes a moment to more closely inspect my features. I wonder if this feels as much like a spectacle to him as it does for me.

"So we don't have the same mother?"

I shake my head. "No. My mother was a European crime princess. She died shortly after my birth, and I've never been able to find out much more than that. Sebastian had all traces of her scrubbed."

He nods, considering his next words.

"And the Labors. They have to nominate every heir?"

I sigh, rubbing the bridge of my nose. "Eh, no. Technically, they can nominate *up to three*. They just have to weigh up the risk of not using their strongest candidates against the risk of losing their best potential legacies."

"He didn't even *need* to nominate Tris?" The angry question comes from Jameson. He's guarding Sinclair's back as carefully as any seasoned mob Enforcer, and as much as the circumstances that have brought us all together pain me, what I've seen of them so far looks promising.

"Only entering one name means whoever it is has to live long enough for Sebastian to ascend. A second son doubles his chances. However, we have reason to believe Sebastian already had planned to replace his firstborn heir, and that's the real reason he needs access to his spare."

Sinclair's face hardens at that. "He wants to get rid of you? Why?"

"The Gray Man used to value discretion and shadow work. But greed always wins, and I saw the writing on the wall—well before he started sending the Suits down a path I didn't want to follow," I say, slipping my own hands back into my pockets to hide the fists forming.

"I started working on putting contingencies in place in case our organization reached a point of no return. Unfortunately, he started picking up on my resistance, and now we're almost sure he's going to use the Labors as a cover to start cleaning house. Especially now that you're eighteen." I lick my lips, desperate for some moisture. "His own contingency plan, ready to action," I add, ruefully.

Sinclair's eyes slide back to the kitchen. "Cleaning house?"

I follow his gaze to where Sabine is now floating into the dining area, a grilled cheese sandwich between her lips. She's opted for an oversized cable knit sweater and tight faux leather leggings.

"She's too valuable to him. But the rest of my Crew? Fair game."

His voice drops low with urgency. "But she's in

danger, isn't she? If not from our father, then at least from others. I saw the way Midas was looking at her on Sunday night."

I can't help the dark scowl that takes over my face at his words. Jameson shoots a hand out when I crowd my brother's space, snagging my elbow. I ignore it.

The claws of possession are pulling harder than his grip ever could.

"That's the only reason you're even here. I don't give a single *fuck* about the Crown. But that doesn't change the fact that we're all about to be dropped right in the fucking middle of a civil fucking war, and the only thing I care about is getting *her* out of this in one piece," I hiss, tone harsh and just as low.

"Something we can agree on, then," Sinclair spits back at me, pushing Jameson's hand off my sleeve.

"There are snakes everywhere. You have to stay on your guard, even at your school," I urge him. My jaw clenches at the thought of Sabine having to sleep down the hallway from one of them. "Which reminds me, you should know that after the roster goes out today, there's a good chance Sloane Walker will find out who your biological father is."

His head rears back at that. "Come again?"

"Sloane Walker *née* O'Sullivan. She's actually the daughter of Smiley, one of the Irish Mob bosses who are going after the Crown."

Sinclair's barked laugh is disbelieving. "Are you telling me she's an heir as well?"

"She's a princess, but she's not an heir. It's very rare

for daughters to be named in our lines of succession. They're usually married off instead."

"So she's not competing?" Ares sneers. "Shame. Would've liked the chance to take that bitch out," he adds with an annoyed roll of his shoulders.

My brother only thins his lips. "But she's still likely to hear my name come up as one of the Gray Man heirs."

"Exactly," I say before lowering my voice even further. "She already knows that Sabine's connected to him as well."

That earns me a thunderous look from both of them. "We're not going to lose her a second time," Sinclair hisses between his teeth.

My confusion must be obvious because he waves it off. "That's something we still need to work out with her, but for now, just believe me when I say we're at your disposal."

My shoulders drop just a fraction, and then I take his acquiescence as the opportunity to move over and take a seat in the only armchair. As I settle back, I bring one foot up to rest on my knee, lacing my fingers there.

"Now, I know you've been doing things on your own, so far. You all seemed to fall into a natural set of roles when you're together," I continue, voice rising in volume. "But we don't have time for leadership struggles and power plays. Since I'm already well acquainted with both Sebastian—and his Second, Dominic—I'll be running point going forward."

Every set of eyes in the room is now busy playing tennis between us, waiting to see which side of the net the ball is going to fall. And right now, the ball is in my younger brother's court.

With Foster's mysterious continued absence since the Symposium, our numbers remain evenly split. But either we go into this as a united front—or we're doomed before we even get to the first Labor.

Apollo's jaw works itself as he mulls over my decree. And I can see it for what it is, because it's what I see every day in my own reflection.

A bone deep need for control.

But we don't have time for this. The clock is ticking down on the Herald's first announcements.

I decide to extend a small olive branch. "Ask my Crew. I'm willing to defer when the need arises," I offer, only for my words to be met with a chorus of choked laughter.

My eyes swing over to where both Sabine and Knox are sitting at the dining table, fists pressed against their mouths. Rhett has his fingers laced over his head, eyes shining while he bites down on his lip.

"*What?*" I grouse.

"Sure, *Zeus,*" Sabine gasps, "Because you're so *amazing* at sharing your toys. *Truly.*"

Rhett's shoulders only shake harder.

My brow lowers.

Keep laughing.

Just know that at the earliest opportunity, I will be tanning both *your asses.*

"Enough," I finally bark, distracting my erection by

slipping my phone out and pulling up my encrypted email server.

Still radio silence from Foster.

"Sinclair?" I prompt him without looking up from the screen.

"You mean, *Apollo*," Sabine corrects me.

"Hmm?" I snap out.

When I glance back over to her, I find her sitting with her leg propped up and her chin resting on her knee. Her giant sweatshirt is pooled back around her hips, leaving me with a clear view of the exact way her skin-tight leggings mold to the natural shape of her mound.

And either she's wearing the world's thinnest fucking panties, or she's gone completely bare beneath them.

Fuck.

Her raspy, knowing chuckle sends a wave of gooseflesh down my nape and I'm immediately thankful that my lap is hidden with my legs crossed as they are. Don't need my brother and his friends getting an eyeful of my rapidly hardening cock.

"I just think it's best if we stick to the callsigns, at least during the Labors. It might help give us an edge while communications are being monitored," she says. But her eyebrow is cocked in a challenge.

Between the attitude and the pants, she's quickly racking up marks against her name.

And guess just where those marks will be going, darling?

But my lips thin, considering. She's not wrong.

Without Foster here to guarantee our end-to-end protocols, we need any extra layer of security we can get.

"Fine. *Apollo.* What say you? We have,"—I check my phone again—"two minutes before show time."

Finally, after a long, considering look in Sabine's direction, he gives me a terse nod that again reminds me so much of myself.

"Okay, then let's get ready. It's time for the Labors to begin," I say loudly.

The entire room falls into a hiccuping quiet as everyone finishes converging on the living area of our Rox City suite.

Apollo moves to take the couch, dropping onto the cushion beside Hermes. Knox and Ares choose to spread out behind the seats themselves, keeping their hands in their pockets and careful gazes on the scene before them. Hades doesn't move from his post against the wall opposite me.

I expect Sabine to hesitate, faced with so many choices. Instead, she heads straight for me, perching her pert ass on one of my armrests and I can't help the primal satisfaction that swells in my chest.

Dionysus takes up his usual position at my back. But then he leans in, brushing his lips against the shell of my ear, and whispers, *"Welcome back, Daddy Zeus."*

Christ almighty. My dick is never going down at this rate.

Just then, my phone's digital display rolls over to **7:00pm**, and it chimes out with the familiar dulcet tones of an encrypted announcement from the Herald.

A sound I'll no doubt grow to loathe by the end of this.

Swiping it open, I immediately read through it once—carefully—before reading the contents aloud.

⟩ ⟩ ⟩ **START OF ENCRYPTED MESSAGE**
⟩ ⟩   **THE TWELVE LABORS OF SUCCESSION**
⟩   **FINAL ROSTER**
⊢ **FACTION: THE GRAY MEN //** Grayson, Jackson; Sinclair, Tristan;
⊢ **FACTION: O'SULLIVAN-REILLY FAMILY //** O'Sullivan, Aiden; Reilly, Benjamin;
⊢ **FACTION: THE STRANGE ACES //** Mahoney, Ford;
⊢ **FACTION: ESCONDIDO CARTEL //** De León, Diego; De León, Javier; De León, Luis;

Escondido Cartel.

I see when everybody's postures tighten with the same confusion, and I hold up a hand, begging for silence.

"Wait for it."

Almost immediately, a second message comes through, and I do the same as with the first.

⟩ ⟩ ⟩ ⟩ **START OF ENCRYPTED MESSAGE**
⟩ ⟩ ⟩   **THE TWELVE LABORS OF SUCCESSION**
⟩ ⟩   **TRIAL I**
⟩   *You don't go searching for bones in a lion's den*
⊢ **TASK: NEUTRALIZATION**

╞ **TARGET: SENATOR LEANDROS ADRIAN GEORGIOU, 43**
╞ **AFFILIATIONS: United States Senate, Republican Party, Washington State**
╞ **LAST KNOWN LOCATION: Washington, D.C.**
╞ **DEADLINE: 47 hours, 59 min from digital receipt of message**

My hand lowers, and I let the breath I was holding out with a deep sigh.

CHAPTER XXI
SABINE

"OKAY, so first question—who in the *fuck* are the *Escondido*?" Dionysus growls out from over the opposite shoulder of a very perplexed-looking Zeus. Our team lead is still scrolling back and forth through the Herald's roster announcement as if the answer is right there, waiting to jump out of the screen.

"I've never heard of them," he mutters without looking up. "They must have formally registered their Southern affiliation with the Red Court sometime between the Arbiter's announcement and the deadline for nominations."

I lean in, scanning the whole message for myself, before zeroing in on the line with the unknown nominees.

FACTION: ESCONDIDO CARTEL // De León, Diego; De León, Javier; De León, Luis;

My forehead wrinkles as I parse through what was certainly one of the more stand-out observations of the night for me. The shock of encountering a group of Underworld denizens that I had never seen nor heard of before—*at a Symposium, no less*—is hard to forget.

A group of six, dark-haired men. Unknown faction. Unidentifiable tattoos. Lead candidate standing in second position from left. Particular interest shown toward Chiron.

"I think I may have seen them there," I finally say, with a quick look at Knox. "You said you'd never seen cartel markings like that before."

Our deputy Enforcer nods, shoulders curling forward in thought. His shaggy locks are pulled back in a low bun, while his massive biceps and broad torso are fighting to stay contained within a forest-green Henley.

"The *Hidden* Cartel—*cute*, by the way. But yeah, I guess their ink *would* fit with an outfit from that region," he replies, jaw working in thought.

"Regardless, they've got three guys in the ring. All sharing the same name. Could be sons, but could also be younger brothers, nephews, or cousins," I say, as I continue to mull over the bizarre roster entry out loud. "And, side note—it looks like I was right about the O'Sullivan and Reilly mobs joining forces. Aiden and Benjamin are the nephews of the Mobs' two Skippers. And then Trick's nomination is his eldest son."

Zeus glances up at me from his phone. "They're in your report?"

"They're at the top of the list now, for sure."

"What report?" Apollo cuts in sharply.

I watch Zeus's profile, amused at the jump of his pulse point as he works to iron out the scowl that wants to take over his face. Apparently, he doesn't like his younger brother's demanding tone of voice.

A little too close to home, Capitano?

"Sabine is expected to prepare a report, listing each identifiable patron in attendance Sunday night," he explains evenly.

Four sets of eyes instantly swivel back to me.

"Librarian, remember? That's why I was there in Themis. To take all the data that we've ever compiled about the Underworld—physical descriptions, identifying markers, faction signets, et cetera—and use it to identify each guest. I then report that list back to the Grey Men, along with any particularly significant interactions or conversations."

"But no one was allowed phones or recording devices," Ares insists. His expression is particularly dubious.

"I know," I say with a pained smile.

"Then how would you even remember all of that?"

With a sigh, I push the hair back from my left temple. "I know you've all seen my scar."

It's hard to miss. Even after almost seven years, the scar there is still prominent.

"I was in a car accident when I was twelve. Traumatic brain injury—only it left me with what is basically a supercharged photographic memory."

Apollo leans forward then, the look on his face oddly expectant. He probably has a million questions to test me with. Most people do.

But all he asks quietly is, "When you were twelve?"

I drop my hand back to my lap and offer him a half-hearted shrug. "So I'm told. I have no memories of anything before the accident."

There's an eerie moment of silence while each of the Rox Boys stares at me in mute shock.

Before Apollo can open his mouth again, Hermes whispers brokenly, "You don't remember...anything?"

"Uh—" I start before Ares leans forward to grab the couch behind Apollo.

"Nothing?" he grits and the vicious scowl he shoots me has confusion pinching my own brows together.

My eyes dart over to Hades. My lips roll in when I see the hollow expression on his bladed features. "Nope."

"But—" Hermes tries before his words seem to fail him. His head drops forward, shielding the rest of his face from me.

Was that a...bottom lip wobble?

I jolt when Zeus's warm palm slips over the thin material of my leggings to squeeze my thigh. "Right now, I'm more concerned with the first Labor," he cuts in smoothly, and I could just about fucking kiss him. "We only have forty-eight hours to both locate and engage the target. So what do we know about Senator Georgiou?"

I can still feel the weight of four sets of questioning eyes fixated on the side of my head where my scar is. I keep my eyes trained on the mole on the back of his left hand instead.

"*Senator Leandros Adrian Georgiou, 43. Multi-term Class III Senator for the State of Washington. Staunchly Republican.*

Married for eighteen years, with three children," I recite, drolly.

"And why would *Concordia* want us to quote, unquote *search for bones in the lion's den?"* Zeus throws out to the room. He's got the phone unlocked again and is back to staring accusing holes at it.

"No—it said *not* to go searching in the lion's den," I correct, a small crease lining my forehead.

"Okay, *not* to." Zeus nods. "But it lists this first Labor as a neutralization task—*not* a discovery task. Do we think the search would then be figurative instead of literal?"

My finger rubs along my scar as I consider.

It very specifically says *neutralization*. The word may have multiple connotations in other settings, but in the Underworld, it only means one thing.

If we go by *Occam's razor*, then there's a good fucking chance the Red Court has simply sent us a generic kill order wrapped up with a pretty word puzzle bow.

So if that's the case, we're better off just concentrating on the target itself.

"The last sweep we ran on the House of Representatives and the Senate showed he was likely to be a swing vote on an upcoming bipartisan bill. *If* it passes, the new legislation would grant additional surveillance powers for any agencies involved in federal investigations," I muse out loud.

Dio leans in around the chair and tickles my hip. "Can you translate that into Neanderthal for us, babygirl?"

I shoot him a considering side-eye, knowing he's prompting for the sake of our newly minted teammates.

"In the most basic terms, it would allow the powers that be to use the *claim* of an emerging threat to national security to be able to legally *hack, wiretap, monitor, spy*—you name it—without having to obtain a warrant first," I explain. "An *ask forgiveness* kind of deal. Although, they wouldn't even be expected to provide credibility for the claim, just be able to justify their *suspicions*."

Apollo leans forward, steepling his hands. The movement involuntarily pulls my focus. "When you say powers that be, does that extend to the *Imperium*?"

"If they have enough pull at the Federal level, yes. Imagine being able to run a *carte blanche* tap or trace on a competing faction?" I nod, rolling my wrist.

"Or a Sovereign," Apollo adds, pointedly.

"Or a Sovereign," Zeus agrees, dragging his fingers down the side of his beard.

I'm still watching the stroke of his hand down his cheek when it suddenly dawns on me that while I might have been correct about concentrating on the target—I had the angles *all wrong*.

I shouldn't have been concentrating on who the target *was*, but who they were targeted *by*.

"*Or*...an organization responsible for governing an entire criminal empire," I blurt.

"*Fuck*," comes a chorus of cursing realizations.

"So the Red Court's just using this as an opportunity to protect its own ass?" Dionysus grimaces.

"Does *neutralization* mean literally assassinating an

actual member of the United States Senate?" Apollo asks, carefully holding my eyes now. "Or do they want us to simply remove him from office?"

There's a thoughtful look on his face that's such a mirror to Zeus's that it's almost scary. From our recruitment screening, I already knew he was highly intelligent. He speaks at least three languages, plays several sports and instruments, and is on track for a spot in the pre-med program at the University of Roxborough. Nobody will come close to shaking his spot for Valedictorian, either.

But what the file didn't—or *couldn't*—tell me was how analytical and observant he was under pressure. How detail-oriented and forward-thinking he could be.

"That's still unclear, but my gut feeling says this has to do with the vote," I hum. "Which points to termination."

"The guy must have skeletons in his closet," Ares's roughened baritone cuts in. "Show me a politician who doesn't?"

My fingers dig into the armrest of Zeus's chair. He makes a good point. We could use any leverage to smoke him out.

Before I can voice my agreement, however, a third encrypted chime floats out across the room.

My stomach instantly sinks.

That sound can only mean one thing.

"C'mon, man," D groans, dropping his head back. "I haven't even cleaned my Rugers yet."

"What is it?" Apollo demands imperiously.

Zeus doesn't bat a lash this time, too busy frowning down at his phone. There's a small tremor in his index finger as he slides open a new update from the Herald.

I silently read over his shoulder, confirming my suspicion.

⟩ ⟩ ⟩ ⟩ **START OF ENCRYPTED MESSAGE**
⟩ ⟩ ⟩ THE TWELVE LABORS OF SUCCESSION
⟩ ⟩ TRIAL I
⟩ *NOTICE OF LABOR TASK STATUS UPDATE*
⊢ **STATUS: NEUTRALIZATION COMPLETE**
⊢ **TARGET:** SENATOR LEANDROS ADRIAN GEORGIOU, 43
⊢ **LOCATION:** Fortunate Islands
⊢ **ACHIEVED:** Proof of termination received 21 min from digital receipt of message
⊢ **VICTOR:** ESCONDIDO CARTEL

Jesus fuck.

Less than half an hour has elapsed since the first Labor's task was officially announced.

Twenty minutes for a wholly *new* and wholly *untested* third party to waltz into the Southern trenches and place their finger on the Crown.

When nobody answers Apollo, he tries again, "What does it say?"

Zeus's eyes flick up, his expression now grim. "First Labor's over—the new player already neutralized the target."

"The fuck?!" Ares bellows after Zeus finishes reading out the message for everyone else. "*Already? How?*"

"Yes, the proof of termination was attached. Sabine?" Zeus angles his screen.

The now lifeless brown eyes of Senator Georgiou stare up at me in hi-res, the proof a neat entry wound in the center of his forehead. There are no other signs of trauma, and his olive skin has yet to show signs of lividity, further supporting that the photo was taken immediately after death. Everything about the hit was quick, clean, and professional.

"Clean," Dio echoes my thoughts aloud, leaning down next to my cheek.

I hum my agreement, and confirm, "It's definitely him."

"He was apparently taken down somewhere only referred to as the Fortunate Islands," Zeus continues. "I'm assuming the Red Court would do their due diligence, but I'd still like to double-check the location."

Looking up, he pins Hermes with a considering look. I follow his gaze before I can catch myself, wincing when I see the still-morose look on the other end of it. "If I flick this over to you, can you verify the photo's EXIF data?"

Hermes immediately perks up at that and my chest loosens.

But then I realize there's a much bigger problem here than just verifying whether or not the Labor took place there.

The problem is with the location itself.

Fortunate Islands.

I thought I knew every single territory in both the South *and* the North, neutral or otherwise.

Every territory registered *before* the Symposium, it seems.

"Sabine?" Zeus prompts.

"No, I've never seen the name before," I murmur.

"We'll need the coordinates as well," he says to Hermes, just as the blond in question holds up his phone.

"Time stamp lines up, but without an official record of the place, the location data is useless as verification," he says with something like an apologetic grin. "The GPS does put it off the coast of Virginia, though."

"There's no other information in the message?" Knox asks, his deep voice making me glance up.

I shake my head. "Nope, just confirmation that this completely unknown Cartel outfit managed to somehow complete this task in twenty-one minutes."

"Could've just been a lucky break?" he offers as he runs a large hand along his chin. He's got several days of growth coming in.

"They just happened to have someone on this Island when the text message came, a staff member or guard, who just happened to know who the Senator was on sight?" Apollo scoffs.

"Twenty minutes means the neutralization was always meant to be a kill, not extortion or something more nuanced," Zeus adds.

Everyone in the room shares their murmured agreement.

"So what does this mean for us?" Ares asks, huge

tattooed fingers strangling the life out of the poor couch again. The mood in the room definitely feels deflated in the wake of the Cartel's decisive start to the Labors.

"As anti-climatic as it was, that was only the first task." Zeus leans forward then, phone dangling between his fingers as he runs a steady gaze over our makeshift team. "The next one will be announced next Sunday. And we just have to hope to God we're not walking into a trap."

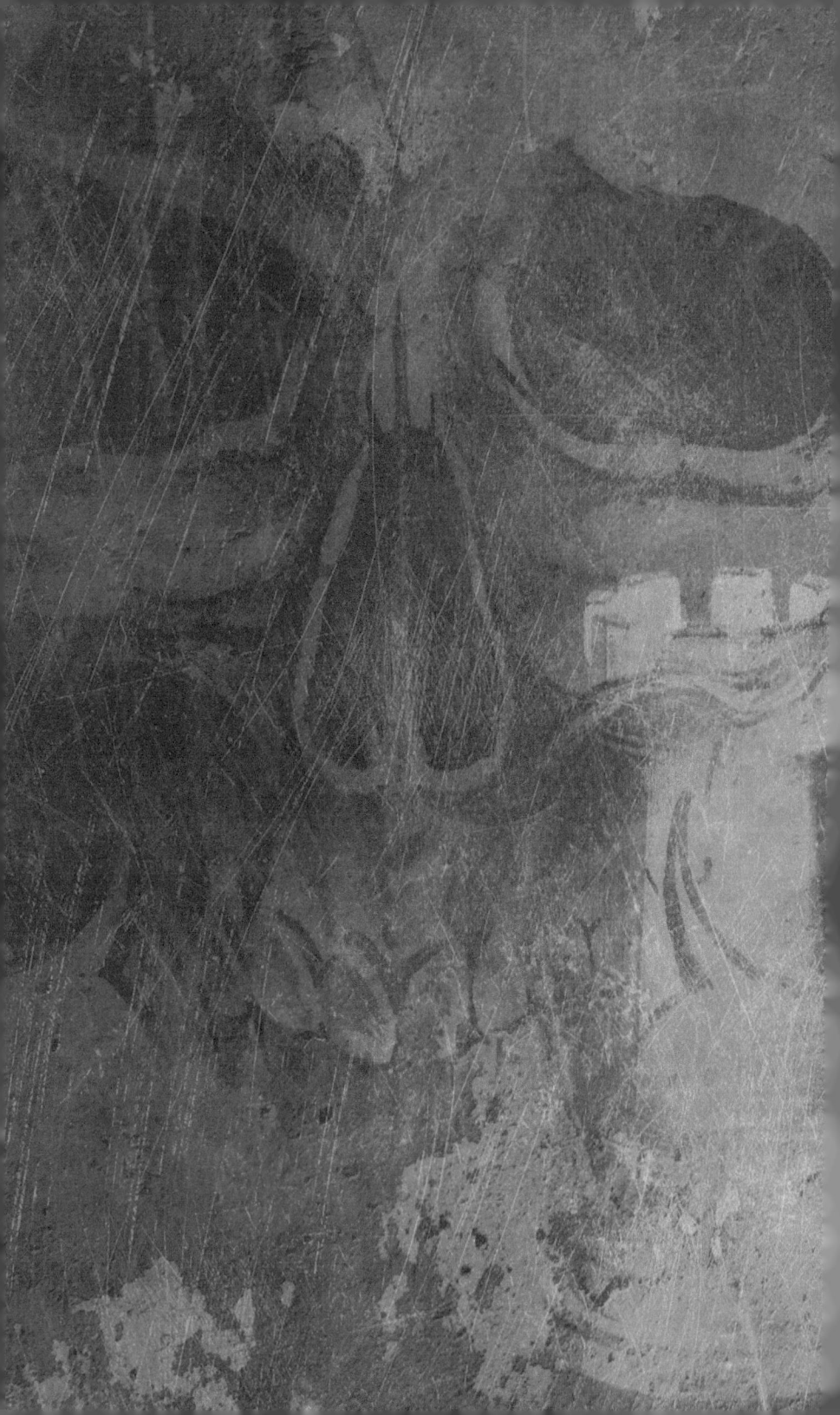

CHAPTER XXII
SABINE

"I DON'T LIKE that you're here by yourself during the week, sweetheart," Zeus mutters as he leans over and pushes open the door to the Briarthorn dorm building. "Especially with the O'Sullivan girl right across from you."

"She wouldn't try anything on campus, especially after today's roster broadcast," I offer.

I just have to make sure I'm not stupid enough to find myself alone with her again *off-campus*. Who knows who the Irish have aligned with? For all we know Trick and Smiley are now drinking buddies.

"There's plenty of room back in the apartment," he presses.

"If I don't live on campus full time, I can't do my job. And if I can't do my job, I may as well just drop out and move to Greenland," I remind him, the resignation thick in my voice. "It's not like I'm here for the education."

"I know, I know," Zeus grumbles, and I'm nowhere near prepared for when he suddenly hooks a muscular arm around my waist, hauling me in. "I just want you close, so sue me," he mutters, burying his nose against my loose hair.

I almost squeak when he takes a long lungful of my scent.

Jesus Christ.

I'm still expecting to wake up from this fever dream, but the hard masculine body pressed against mine feels too solid and too good to *not* be real.

"I'm just enjoying at least sharing a zip code with you again," I murmur warmly. I glance up at him from beneath my lashes and he rewards me with a blinding smile.

"You are, are you? Not quite satisfied with the current bounty on offer from your *Pantheon*, darling?"

His smile is pure Grayson smugness now and it earns him a harsh slap to his chest.

Like I needed the reminder of the messy fucking hole I keep digging for myself. Spending a few hours in the forced proximity of our Crew's apartment, playing *Happy Teammates* was torturous enough.

I think it's different, with them. You're *different.*

"Careful now," he grins down at me, blue eyes bright, "You're already at six."

My eyebrow quirks up in interest as I duck around him to use my room key. "Oh, really?" I drawl as I unlock the door and push inside. "Six what? Six solid hours of uninterrupted sleep? Yes, *please*."

Jesus. Was my voice always that husky?

I don't manage to take even two steps before Zeus is through the doorframe and crowding my back. One arm snakes back around my waist, slamming me back against his chest, while the other slams the door shut behind us.

When the locks slide home, he spins us, shoving my front roughly up against the back of my dorm room door. The entire structure rattles with the impact.

His chest follows, pressing me flush with the wood.

"Six stripes of this bratty fucking ass, that's what," he growls against my hair.

All the oxygen whooshes from my lungs.

Then his body shifts and suddenly I'm airborne.

"*Zeus!*" I manage to choke out—right before my hips slam into the armbar of the couch and I'm pitching forward at the waist. My hands slap down on the cushions, only just breaking the rest of my fall and saving me from a mouthful of soft suede.

Zeus answers me with a hissed curse of his own as he slides his hands under the hem of my sweater and tries to hook my leggings. "Why did you insist on wearing the world's tightest fucking pants?" he mutters darkly. He tugs at the waistband, trying in vain to gain some sort of traction over my hips. "Like *Fort fucking Knox.*"

I laugh into the cushion.

Bite off more than you could chew there?

"C'mon, boss," I snark, "When do I ever make anything easy for you?"

"*Never,*" comes his hissed reply. "But you'll learn to."

My chest empties again at the dark promise in his voice. "*And* you'll learn to love it," he vows, and it sends a shiver dancing along my spine.

There's a rush of cool air across the tops of my cheeks

as he finally manages to wrestle the leather pants over the peach of my ass. He peels them straight down to mid-thigh before he replaces the tight caress of the pants with twin grips of his own.

As he squeezes a handful of each cheek with those large, warm hands, he groans brokenly, *"Fuck,* I was right —you weren't wearing anything underneath."

"I hate the lines," I breathe hoarsely. I've never felt more exposed.

Or turned on.

"Too bad, troublemaker, because as soon as I get you back to my place, I'm leaving some new ones with my crop," he growls. "But looks like I'll have to make do with my belt today."

My intake is sharp and he pauses, taking in the quivering muscles of my thighs.

"Would you like that, darling? Can I mark up your gorgeous cheeks?"

I enthusiastically nod my assent.

"Yes or no?" Zeus asks firmly. "Out loud."

My pulse *swishes* in my ears.

The only two words I want passing your lips are: 'yes' and 'sir'."

"Yes, sir?"

"That's my girl," he grits through his teeth as he yanks my hips up. I squeal out as the movement tips me further forward, bringing both my ass and pussy up even higher. The new angle has my forehead pressing against the backs of my hands.

"Fuck, this *fucking ass.* Do you know how many men

are going to die before this is all over, sweetheart?" This groan is hot against my skin. "How many I'm going to have to kill just for knowing this even exists?"

My eyes hood with his ragged praise. I might be a proud card-carrying member of the *Itty Bitty Titty Committee*, but your girl's got enough cake for a healthy-sized serving.

Zeus straightens and then the opening *clink* of a metal buckle fills the space, followed shortly by the silky *thwhip* of a leather belt being yanked impatiently from its loops.

There's a short pause—right before an experimental *snap*.

I brace.

"How many did I say?" he barks.

"Six?"

"Six, *sir*," comes his firm correction.

I gulp.

"*Six, sir*," I breathe, making a mental note to price a new arm cover for the couch.

Every muscle is poised, frozen in anticipation of his next move.

Everything but my heart—that one's about to beat right the fuck out of my chest.

"Are you ready?"

My fingers curl against the suede cushion beneath them.

"Yes, sir."

"This is for the two months I went without seeing you, hearing you, smelling you," he says, his tone imperious. "Count for me."

The *crack* of his belt colliding with my right cheek is like nothing I've felt before. There's a moment, right at impact, where everything stops—my overthinking, my trepidation, my self-loathing—even my headache.

Everything suspended, for a singular heartbeat—right before the lightning strike.

And then the pain registers and it all rushes back in together at once.

"*One,*" I gasp out, but it's followed quickly by a moan when Zeus's palm caresses the blossoming welt. "More?" he asks, lowly.

"Yes, sir," I choke.

"This is for coming home to me for the first time in two months—covered in another man's seed," he says, his voice like a thunderstorm. It clashes with the sound of blood pulsing everywhere in my skull until it feels like it comes from all directions.

Fuck!

His possessiveness is a tangible thing, and I can feel its weight wrapped around me like a noose.

My chest constricts, but not with discomfort, but rather with the warm, satiated feeling of reciprocation.

Crack.

The second impact, this time on the left, rocks me forward in its ferocity.

And this time the moan comes first.

"Two."

"This is for not trusting me and fighting your need to let go," Zeus continues, still in the same harsh, commanding tones. *Crack.*

"Three."

"For turning my head with your cunt in these pants during the Labor," he hisses. *Crack.*

"*Four,*" I warble in reply. I can feel the slickness over every inch of my bare pussy and inner thighs. All the way down to where the offending pants bracket my knees.

"For wearing nothing underneath them," he barks on his fifth swing.

"Five," I cry out.

My pussy does too. She's weeping real tears.

Zeus growls and everything clenches.

"And this is for the hundred lives I'll have to take so everyone knows exactly who you belong to."

The sixth and final impact of his belt sends me sailing over the edge. Literally and figuratively. My orgasm shudders through my entire pelvis, every muscle and nerve clamping down around nothing at the same time as my entire body pitches forth with the impact.

"*Fuck.*"

I'm not entirely sure which one of us says it, or if we both shouted it—because just as I'm sagging under the weight of boneless limbs, I feel a different impact—the hot stripes of Zeus's cum landing across both my cheeks.

His hands land on the hollow of my waist as he collapses around me, careful not to press his hips against my abused cheeks.

"Maybe one day I'll learn to live with your Boys," he concedes, breath warm against my neck, "but that doesn't change the fact that you are *mine.*"

THE WORST THING about losing out on the First Labor victory?

It wasn't our failure to decipher the full scope of the directive before the rest of the competition. It wasn't even the fact that one of the aforementioned competitors was a complete and total unknown.

It was the absolute radio silence from Sebastian.

The weight of it hung over us all like the Sword of Damocles.

Not even Dominic had uttered a word on how deeply his disappointment ran; he'd simply accepted the first of my Symposium reports in silence before marching straight back home to Lexington.

And not knowing how the Gray Man was going to retaliate burned like hot coals in my stomach. *All hours of the day.* It also didn't help matters that my head was constantly on the verge of splitting right down the middle—and absolutely nothing in my usual repertoire seemed to be helping.

The side effect is a sort of state of involuntary detox, yet I'm still expected to lurk around this school—sussing out and ambushing potential recruitment targets like some kind of criminally-minded charity mugger.

If only I could have Jax come to my dorm every night and work his magic.

Is it possible to get spanking funded as a therapy line item?

My head would live in empty bliss if so.

"Does Papa Grayson know you're hooking up with *both* his sons?"

It's not so much the words themselves as it is the graveled accent that pulls me up short, like someone just yanked on my strings. It's an accent that definitely should *not* exist inside the hallways of Rox Academy and it snaps my head up immediately.

Over to where I find one of the Donato twins leaning casually against the entrance to the senior staff lounge, arms crossed and a dangerous glint in his eye.

The single, white streak bisecting the shock of dark, chestnut hair, marks him as the elder of the two.

And the most ruthless.

"Raphael, what in the *fuck* are you doing here?" I hiss, eyes darting to the staffroom over one of his muscled shoulders.

"Hello to you too, blondie," he laughs roughly and my jaw flexes in irritation.

I'm already fighting nausea and a looming migraine. The last thing I need is to be standing here in a verbal joust with a flirty hitman while my body is forced to purge and my stomach moves through each of the 42 Knots.

To say I was *on edge* would be an understatement.

"Why are you here?" I ask again, more firmly. "The North is forbidden from interfering. I know you know this."

"Not here to cause trouble," he winks. "Maybe I just missed your pretty face, you consider that?"

Jesus Christ.

I drag a hand down my face and then immediately wince. I probably already look like a raccoon with all the sweating I'm doing.

"Rafe, your lungs don't fill themselves without causing trouble," I groan. "Seriously, no one needs you or your brother stirring shit up around here when we're already living in the middle of Ace-controlled territory."

He pushes up off the doorframe, straightening to his full height. Then he drags that unnerving gaze down the length of my body.

"Heard there was an opening in the Art department—and well, y'know how good I am with my hands," he rasps.

I didn't think my muscles could feel any stiffer, but they do. They turn to stone.

There are definitely no staff openings, Art department or otherwise.

Unless he made an opening.

But did Midas send him or is he just here to play his own games? Unfortunately, knowing him—and his brother—both scenarios are just as likely.

I just need to find out if he's here for work...or *ugh*—pleasure.

"Convenient," I hedge, shifting on my feet.

"Very," he smirks as he watches me pull out my phone before tossing me a two-finger salute. "Say hi to Jaxy for me, won't ya? He sounds like he might be just as good with his hands."

And then he kicks off the door's frame, disappearing

back into the faculty lounge with the sinful swagger of an Underworld celebrity.

God fucking damnit.

He's been watching my dorm?

ME

Heads up, there's a Golden Boy in the Rox henhouse

ME

Might want to check if the Herald's announced any new contracts

ZEUS

I'll look into it.

ME

Still no Foster?

ZEUS

Negative.

The last thing I need is to pile more shit on Zeus's plate, but having either of the Donatos sniffing around is never a good sign. And if Gabriel is also playing house in Rox City, then those odds of trouble are literally doubled.

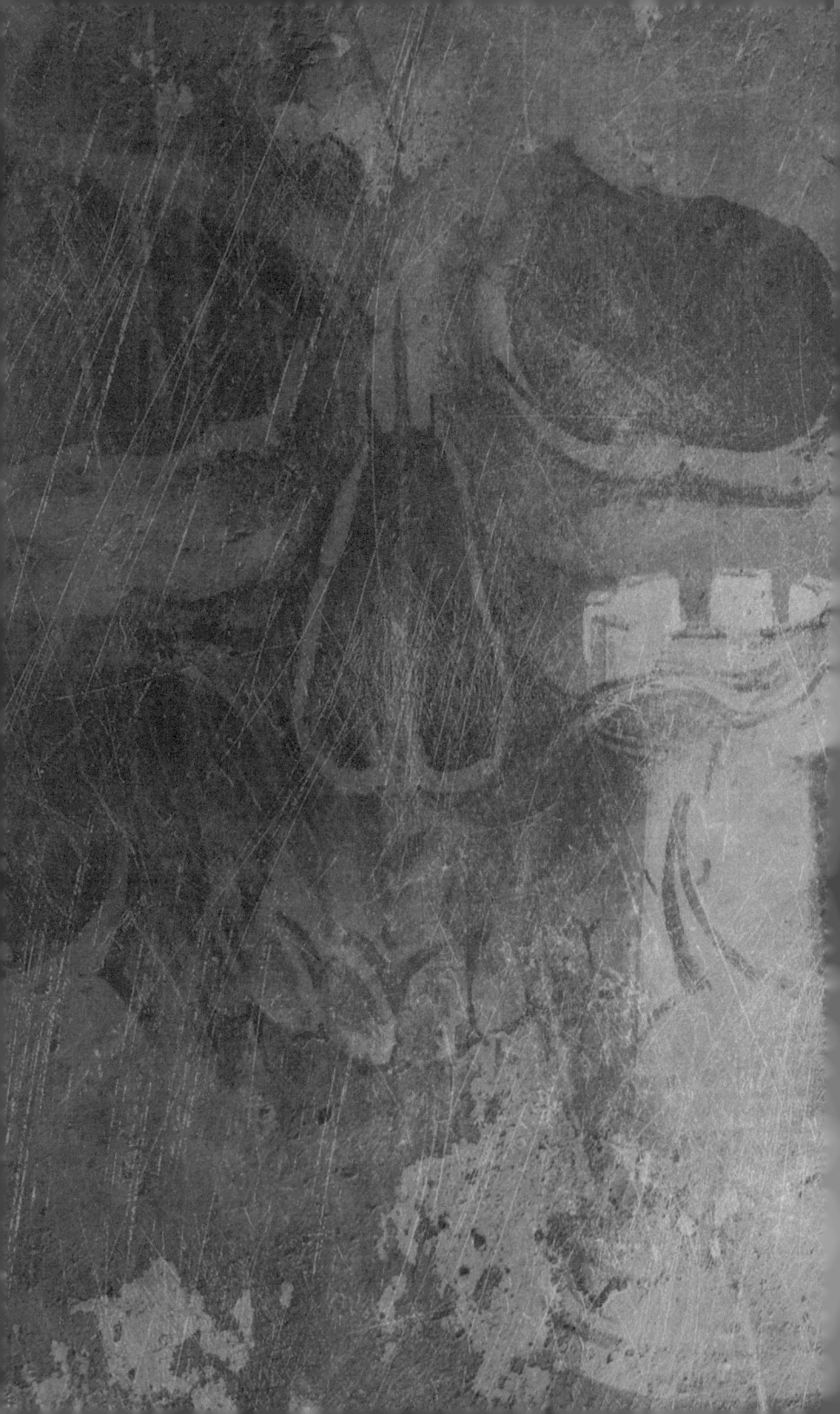

CHAPTER XXIII

ATLAS · HADES

"TEN MINUTES," Jackson warns from his command post at the dining room table. He'd decided that after last week's rocky start, we needed to formally regroup, and somehow that's translated into turning the entire meal area of his apartment into our war room.

By the looks of it, he's also come ready to cauterize some of the more significant bleeders that were causing friction between him and his younger brother.

Because there *Zeus* and *Apollo* sit—shoulder-to-shoulder, identical tablets and glasses of whiskey at the ready.

Something I must try to wrap my head around—both the adopted monikers *and* the biological connection.

The resemblance really is fucking uncanny, though. And not just in the dark swathes of hair, blue eyes, and sharp jawlines—it's in the way they wear their dual mantles of leadership. An echo in the carriage of their shoulders, in the way twin gazes sweep across their team. Checking in and then double-checking again.

Dotting every *I* and crossing every *T*.

And I find having double that steadiness to rely on soothing.

Whatever it was, it's given me the first glimmer of hope that we might make it through this in one piece.

Hermes sits in front of a pair of borrowed monitors, furiously bolstering firewalls and sorting out ping issues for each of our newly encrypted connections to the various *Imperium* networks and databases.

In contrast to Hermes's manic energy is Sabine. Something is off with her today, though I can't quite put my finger on it. Her complexion seems paler, there's a wane pull to her cheeks, as well as a subtle blue bruising below her eyes. Perhaps she hasn't been sleeping well.

Though I don't think many of us have been, to be honest.

Especially after hearing her so blithely explain the story behind her scar.

We had spent almost seven years collectively wondering just what the fuck happened to Sabine Winters. After she had disappeared without a single trace from our lives, one day in December.

I have no memories of anything before the accident.

A passing comment for her, and yet a colossal bombshell for us.

I force my gaze away from her, wrestling with the compulsion to run my knuckles over the phantom pain in my chest.

The only restless members of our group seem to be the three Enforcers—taking turns cleaning their weapons and stalking through the apartment like caged animals.

All in all, there's still a lot of work to be done, with neither party able to rely on the safety net of our employers like we had in the past. But no matter the nature of the next task, we were at least more ready to dive in than we were during our first attempt.

I glance back down to the tablet in my hand, calmly swiping through various camera feeds.

Now that the secret seems to be out between Sloane Walker and my brothers, I've been interested to see what her movements look like around the Academy. So far, either she's gotten really good at detecting my blindspots, or she's been spending an inordinate amount of time off-campus.

Either way, she's become somewhat of a ghost this last week.

"Get ready," Apollo calls, right before Zeus's phone flashes and the Herald's chime fills the space.

The two of them immediately lean their heads together, taking in the announcement.

"Okay, this is what we have," the older Grayson calls out.

I look down at my own screen to find a forwarded copy of the broadcast.

⟩ ⟩ ⟩ ⟩ **START OF ENCRYPTED MESSAGE**
⟩ ⟩ ⟩ THE TWELVE LABORS OF SUCCESSION
⟩ ⟩ TRIAL II
⟩ *The beast with many heads rises with new growth*
├ TASK: DISCOVERY

⊢ **TARGET:** THE LERNA CORPORATION
⊢ **AFFILIATIONS:** Confirmation Required
⊢ **LAST KNOWN LOCATION:** Themis
⊢ **DEADLINE:** 23 hours, 59 min from
digital receipt of message

"Fuck, *yes*," Hermes cheers with an enthusiastic fist pump. "*Team Discovery*," he crows, holding up a palm for me to high-five.

I only quirk an eyebrow at him. While I'm relieved to see a positive trend upward in his mood today, he knows as well as I do that he's not getting any kind of skin from me.

Unperturbed, he turns to address the rest of the room, "Shit's my *jam*," he assures us.

I roll my lips inwards at the heated looks both Sabine and Dionysus shoot in his direction as his narrow hips continue to wiggle in his seat. I also don't miss the way both Graysons pointedly avert their eyes back down to their screens.

"Sabine?" Zeus calls out. Hermes spins back to lock on his screens, fingers poised over his keyboard.

Sabine's head is tipped back against the couch cushion behind her. A small crease forms in her brow as she gathers her thoughts.

"LERNA's a bit of a point of contention for the *Imperium*. The Arbiter likes everyone to live and work happily together, all neatly wrapped up with an affiliation bow," she explains, pulling herself up a little on her seat. "If a citizen or an entity doesn't wish to formally declare for either the North or the South, they can promise to serve both Sovereignties equally—and declare themselves Neutral instead."

"And LERNA's Neutral?" Ares asks, gruffly.

"Not *exactly*," she continues with a small lift of her shoulder. "All entities are also required to both publicly register any assets, as well as disclose details of ownership and incorporation. Everything from the shareholders to the board of directors down to their janitorial staff."

"So what's the issue?" Apollo asks. His fingers lace together on the tabletop as he unconsciously leans toward her.

"The problem is LERNA's not just a simple umbrella corp, it's more like multiple ghost subsidiaries in a trench coat, masquerading as a multinational conglomerate."

"The beast with many heads," I murmur and she nods.

"And not knowing exactly *who*'s behind LERNA would rankle the Arbiter to no end," Zeus supplies, knowingly.

"Exactly," Sabine agrees. "I know from personal experience that following the trail on any of their public-facing companies only leads to a shell company. Which leads to another dead end of a registry notice and so forth."

"It says last known location: Themis," Apollo muses. "Do we have listings for all Underworld businesses operating in Themis?"

I shake my head, and my best friend shoots me a

quizzical look. "They were at the Symposium," I say pointedly.

"Most likely," Zeus agrees, giving me an encouraging smile. It's warm and my spine pulls straight.

"*That's* why it says Themis," Sabine repeats, nodding again. "It's technically No Man's Land, so they *could* technically operate there, but I doubt the Arbiter would allow them to do so from right under her nose like that."

"Of course, that would be too fucking easy," Dionysus quips, beginning to dismantle the same exact handgun for the third time today.

"I *hate* riddles," Hermes whines loudly.

"What happened to *Team Discovery?*" Sabine teases him.

"Give me something tangible to find or a virtual barrier to breach. Just don't ask me to think logically," he grouses, and I can't help the soft smile that pulls at my cheek.

Because I fucking *love* riddles.

"AND *DÜRERCA, Inc*'s a bust as well," Hermes announces, slamming his chair back.

He stalks off towards the kitchen.

He's not the only one who's frustrated. We're all starting to fray at the seams.

We sent the Enforcers out of the apartment at about the four hour mark, unable to stand their frustrated energy any longer.

Eight hours of slamming our heads against a wall made of LERNA's non-existent boards of directors and forged stakeholder meeting minutes, and we're no closer to *discovering* anything.

Eight hours of me surreptitiously watching every blink and every muscle twitch that Sabine makes. I've given her a wide berth. Keeping her as far from my personal space as possible. I need to conserve my focus for the task at hand and her proximity is a focus drain at best.

I don't want to be the reason we forfeit a second Labor.

Flexing my fingers, I flip the tablet back over, hoping that taking a break from staring down the same nine words for hours might grant me a much-needed fresh perspective.

It's the same jumble of words.

The beast with many heads rises with new growth.

The beast. Many heads. Rises.

The beast rises.

Many heads rise.

Rises with new growth.

The beast rises with new growth.

New growth.

"What would you consider 'new growth'?" I throw at the room, voice tired. My chords aren't used to the constant stretch of use but I was determined that if I could speak up during discovery I would.

"Expansion? Evolution?" Apollo replies from his new

spot on the couch. Both he and Zeus had migrated there shortly after Dionysus, Ares, and Morales had left.

"Inflation?" Zeus adds, without any real conviction.

"What about...*literal* growth?" I ask, running a finger along my brow.

"Like, a seed? Sapling? Sprout?" Apollo starts listing.

I blink. Then blink again. "And what does all new growth have in common?"

"Dirt?" Hermes asks helpfully, his blond curls flying as he skips back in from the kitchen, a red popsicle between his lips.

"No, it's usually what?"

"*Green*," Sabine suddenly calls from across the room. My eyes instantly jump to hers. There's always a magnet pull that has me finding her no matter where she is in the room.

"Green," I agree, locking my gaze on hers. "*The Green Knight*," she mouths, and I nod.

A nauseous bubble of relief pops.

"You think the Green Knight was behind LERNA?" asks Zeus, rising from his seat.

"Not necessarily," Sabine replies, staring straight ahead as she no doubt turns over what she knows of the fallen Sovereign.

"Rises *with new growth*," Apollo blurts, emphasizing *rises*.

I nod, excitement growing that he's picked up on my line of thought.

"Rises?" Zeus questions.

"As in rising from the ashes." I clear my throat before

I continue. "LERNA's setting up shop in Maker's Bay. Moving into the void left by the Green Knight."

Zeus spins in place at my words, a finger pointed directly at Hermes, where he's practically bouncing in his seat, waiting for instructions.

"Hermes, pull up a property search for the city of Maker's Bay. I want a list of all recent real estate purchases, including any still in escrow. Line it up against utilities and zoning permits for commercial properties," Zeus commands. "Hades, go through business registrations, focusing on the newly incorporated."

"Going back how far?" Hermes asks for us both.

"At least four months, anything that's been listed since the Green Knight's death."

The only sounds then are the sounds of fingers flying across keyboards and the tapping of my stylus.

"Okay," Hermes announces, finally. He swivels his monitor so that we can all get a visual comparison between our two sets of search results.

"There've only been four properties with commercial ordinances purchased inside the city limits in Maker's Bay, inside of the last sixteen weeks."

"And the companies?" Zeus prompts.

I turn my own screen around, pinching to zoom in on the table of data for them. "One of the properties was bought and then leased by an established property management outfit, but the other three are all new entities. There's *Hagden & Sons, Ltd*, a *Finis, Inc.* and a *Red Brick Co.*"

"Who's on the paperwork?"

"*Hagden & Sons* is registered to a Bill Hagden, Snr. *Finis, Inc,* to an Agnes Day, and *Red Brick* belongs to a Peter Farrow," I read out.

Sabine frowns, staring straight through us all while scratching at her temples like the words are itching at the back of her skull.

"Can you repeat those?" she asks, and Hermes reads them out once more.

"Flick them through, please. I need to *look* at the list of words. Something about the sound is throwing me off."

Her screen lights up with the attached email and her eyes fly back and forth across the screen. Over and over, until I see the moment the light goes off for her. "*Finis, Inc,*" she exclaims.

I look back down at my screen, reading the business registration information again.

FINIS, INC.
61 New Circle Way, Maker's Bay, GA
30000.
Agnes Day.

Something in the sound is throwing me off.
That's when I see it. Or rather *hear* it.
"Not 'Agnes Day'," I groan. "*Agnus Dei.*"
Zeus straightens in his seat. "*Agnus Dei?*"
"*Lamb of God,*" Apollo murmurs.
"61 New Circle," Sabine emphasizes. "61. Six. One."
"What's the significance of the numbers?" Zeus asks urgently as he stands, voice rising with the movement.

"*And I saw when the Lamb opened one of the seals, and I heard, as it were the noise of thunder, one of the four beasts saying, 'Come and see',*" Sabine recites, "Revelation 6:1."

"Registered August first. It's a closed corporation, too. No board of directors," Hermes cuts into to confirm, eyes skimming his screen again.

"*Finis,*" I rasp, the final piece of the puzzle clicking into place. "The end. The end times. Book of Revelation."

"The Book of the Apocalypse," Apollo muses with his brows raised.

"No wonder the Arbiter's pissed," Sabine says with a grin. "The answer to her question is *The Four Horsemen.*"

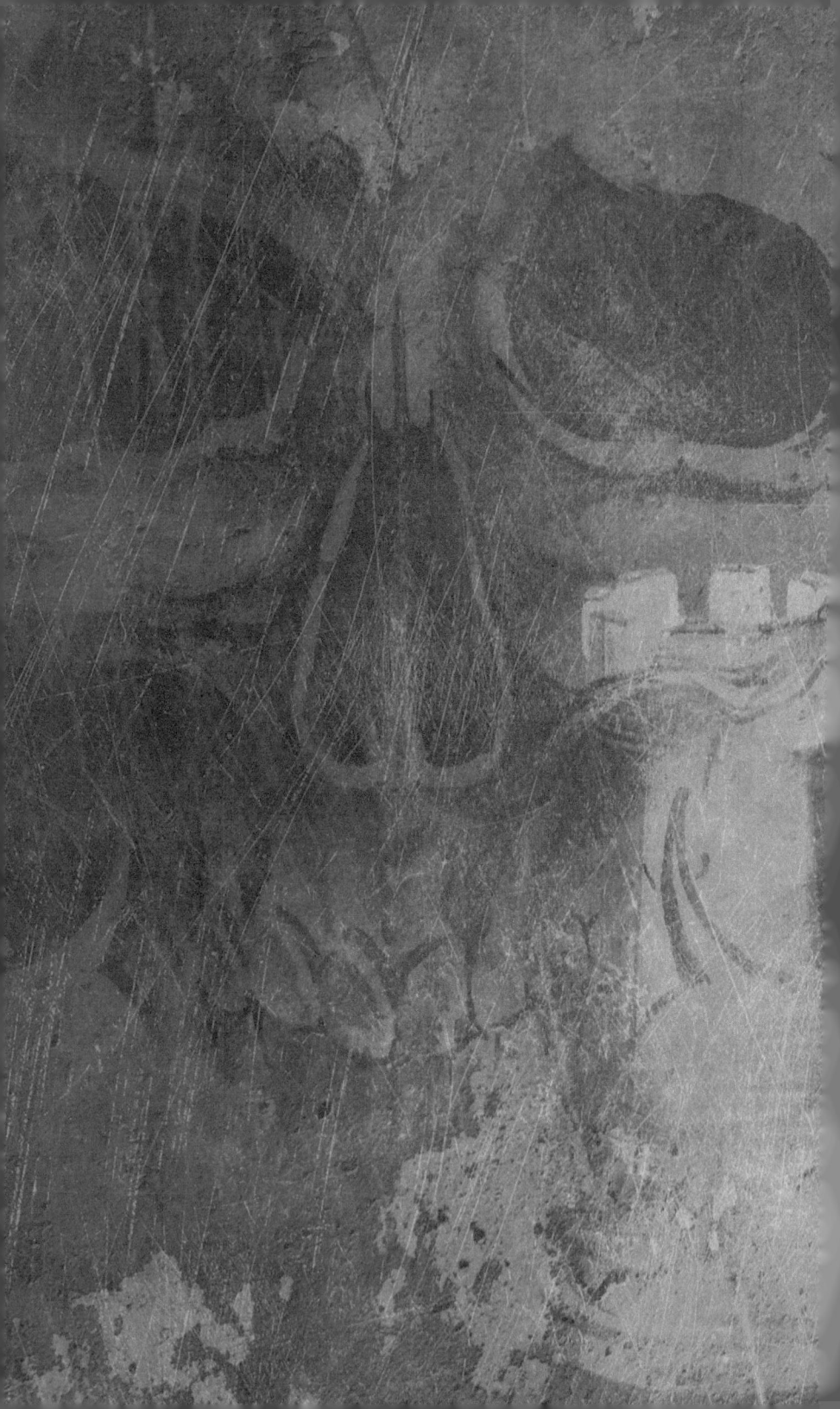

CHAPTER XXIV

SABINE

"ALEXANDER MORROW," I say in careful greeting to the man now haunting the doorway of my Roxborough dorm room at one o'clock in the morning. "How can I help you?"

Despite having cracked the small but cleverly hidden series of Horsemen's codes, the sum total of information I have on this man and his three colleagues would barely fill a single sheet of foolscap paper.

Each.

If I'm lucky.

"No, Little Bo-Peep," he says, a dark smirk carving across his pale, marble features, "the question is how might my brothers and I help *you*?"

My eyes dip to where his fingers dance silently against his thigh, tapping out an unknown rhythm. Across the back of four of his knuckles are the letters M-O-R-S.

Mors.

Death.

My throat bobs as I swallow.

"Is it?" I clarify, as evenly as I can, because the first lesson any *Imperium* fledgling learns is that nothing in this world comes for free.

Knowing that it will cost me *something*, I suppose then, the question I should be asking myself is: *Am I willing to pay that cost?*

"You found our lost sheep."

I blink, internally cursing how sluggishly my sleep-logged brain is moving.

Their lost sheep?

Sheep.

Lamb of God.

Right.

The victory broadcast had rolled in the moment we had contacted the Herald via secure line with our findings, two nights ago.

⟩ ⟩ ⟩ ⟩ **START OF ENCRYPTED MESSAGE**
⟩ ⟩ ⟩ **THE TWELVE LABORS OF SUCCESSION**
⟩ ⟩ **TRIAL II**
⟩ **NOTICE OF LABOR TASK STATUS UPDATE**
⊢ **STATUS: DISCOVERY COMPLETE**
⊢ **TARGET: THE LERNA CORPORATION**
⊢ **LOCATION: Maker's Bay**
⊢ **ACHIEVED: 08 hrs, 47 min from digital receipt of message**
⊢ **VICTOR: THE GRAY MEN**

"Yes," I reply, eyeing him, and not for the first time,

wondering at the consequences of having brought to light the head of the LERNA serpent. Perhaps the Horsemen had wanted to remain in the shadows.

I clear my throat. "Had you, uh, *wanted* your lost sheep brought home?"

The only response Morrow gives me is more of that faint smirk. A disconcertingly handsome man, he towers over me, pitch black hair framing porcelain white skin.

"Right," I say awkwardly, before trying again. "So how can I help you, then?"

A pair of wireframe glasses glint gently against the low lighting of the hallway as he shifts his weight.

"I'm here to offer you and yours a single boon."

I blink again.

Perhaps I'm still asleep, and instead of happily dreaming about spit-roasting little blond fuckboys, I'm conjuring up this paralysis demon instead.

My fingers flex against the wooden edge of the door.

"You're not upset the cat's out of the bag?"

"Let's just say that change is on the wind. We might have found a lost lamb of our own."

Okay. Heaven help that lamb, then.

I bring my finger up to run along my scar while I think.

A single boon.

"Parameters?"

When he shifts again, the light reflects off the surface of his glasses, and for a moment I'm unable to see his eyes.

"A single question and a single answer," he intones.

My brain kicks off with a zap of uneasy electricity.

Fuck, I've *never* been good at political intrigue. It's why being sent here to be a Front Man for the Grey Men was such a fitting punishment.

I wish Zeus was here. Or even Apollo. Someone a hell of a lot better at war games and strategy than I.

"I saw you at the Symposium, speaking with Trick Mahoney," I hedge, deliberately trying to buy a little more time while I think through my options.

"That's not a question," Morrow states, shifting again. I can see his eyes now, and they're almost coal-black in color. Like two voids. "But if you must know—I spoke at length with Sebastian Grayson, as well."

It's good information to know. If he was striking deals in secret with the Strange Aces, it would be a major faux pas to be seen with such a direct rival.

But I also don't know if that knowledge makes me feel better or worse.

Having Sebastian *anywhere* near this was just as equally disconcerting.

My stomach squeezes as I realize he's still waiting on an answer while I'm busy tugging at the ball of tangled threads.

How do I even know this visit isn't Sebastian's doing in the first place? And I can't even ask him that outright —I don't want to accidentally waste my question.

"You should probably know that Sebastian isn't our biggest fan right now," I offer, hoping that might force him to steer this conversation in a clearer direction.

"There've been rumors," he only agrees, bemusedly.

Oh wow, fuck. Also good to know.

Nothing like having your dirty laundry aired for the entire Underworld to see.

"You still haven't asked your question," he prompts, and now his voice has lost some of its jovial tone.

"Okay," I say, trying to stall once more.

Think.

Something pertaining to the Labors, obviously.

A bone that we can throw to Sebastian to keep him off our backs for just a little bit longer.

A bone.

That's it.

"Why would we *not* go searching for bones in a lion's den?" I blurt.

"*Very* good, Bo-Peep," Morrow praises, a flash of satisfaction briefly lighting up his dark gaze.

He spreads his palms wide.

"Because they were hidden in the rook's nest all along."

I'M STARTING to think this locker room is cursed. Either that or my last cheque to Lady Karma must have bounced.

Just as I'm trying to slip my sweaty self into one of the shower bays, I'm rudely intercepted by the one person I've been wanting to see even less than Leo Baker.

Sloane's dipping out on the Symposium had been a happy fucking coincidence, especially since I'd not exactly been looking forward to dancing around her bullshit in such a risky setting. I'd also managed to avoid her during school hours by planning my movements around her Academy schedule.

With great care—*and maybe not a small amount of luck*— I'd made it over three weeks without running into the O'Sullivan princess again.

Surprisingly, she's not flanked by any of her Prefect posse, and while she's just as annoyingly gorgeous as ever, the skin beneath her eyes is just a tad too dark, despite the efforts of her otherwise flawless makeup.

In fact, I'd go so far as to say Sloane Walker looks *tired*.

"Guess I needed to use something stronger, after all," she greets me with a sharp smile that's all teeth. "What kind of pest control even works on a *Suit*?"

Ugh.

To be brutally honest, I've always hated the song-and-dance of identity subterfuge. I knew that eventually my figurative pointe shoes would wear thin the longer I tip-toed along the halls of Rox Academy.

But it's actually kind of a relief to let loose the laces and slip them off every once in a while.

"Missed you in Themis, *mo rós fiáin*," I say conversationally, and the dark scowl I get in return makes me feel marginally better about the migraine I can feel building behind my eye.

"I heard they were giving out charity invites this year," she scoffs, pushing her hair back over her shoulder.

The normally lustrous red strands appear dull under the locker room's harsh industrial lighting.

"Yep, they just let me walk right on in," I muse, spreading my hands like *can you believe that shit?* Before I drop my chin and step right into her space. "Even got a little glimpse of your future while I was there."

Sloane's smile doesn't lose any of its condescension, but there's something like bemusement there now. "I highly doubt it. You have *no idea* what my future looks like," she retorts with a low laugh.

I have to mirror her cold smirk with my own, though, knowing it's only a matter of time before an arranged marriage to some high-ranking Southern asshole grinds that backbone of hers right into the dirt.

She would've made a hell of an *imperatrix* and I'm almost sorry to see it.

Almost.

I sigh. "What do you want, Sloane?"

Because I know what I want: *to shower in fucking peace.*

An ice pick lobotomy for this headache.

For a Horseman not to answer my riddle with another fucking riddle.

"Looking to join your friend, Zoe?" I ask pointedly, glancing at the shower and channeling all of the cool disdain I've borne over the years as Sebastian's ward. "Because I'm happy to make that happen for you."

Sloane's answering look is just as icy.

"No? Just hoping to darken my doorstep one last time before Papa Smiley ships you off, then?" I prompt, hoping she'll get to the fucking point soon so I can get these clothes off my clammy skin.

"I'm not going anywhere," she snaps.

Ouch. Sore spot.

"Oh? He's decided to let you finish school after all? Thought for sure the moment the roster went out he'd have his baby girl dressed in bridal white faster than you can say *the Green Knight.*"

Something flickers behind her eyes. *Fear,* maybe. *Guilt?*

"Sloane Reilly really does have a nice ring to it, don't you think?" I ask her sweetly.

But then the hint of trepidation is gone and she's lifting her chin.

"He tried," she shoots with an acidic smirk.

"And I suppose you said—*no thanks, Daddy, I'll pass*—and he agreed, just like that?"

No way her father rolled over on this. The Reilly brothers already looked like the Irish mobsters who got the cream.

"I have *some fucking* standards. I'm not going to just settle for a Family who can't even secure a dead man's estate, let alone a Crown."

My eyebrows flick up at her outburst. Her composure's all over the place.

Her pretty cheeks do have the decency to pink up. "Besides, I'm already *spoken for,*" she states through gritted teeth.

The way she says that has my blood running cold.

"Spoken for how?"

But suddenly she can't hold my gaze, and my eyes instantly narrow. So much for that *imperatrix* spine I was just giving her so much credit for.

"Spoken for...*how*?" I repeat.

"I'm pregnant," she mutters, still not looking me in the eye.

Jesus, I think my eyelids might have slipped over the back of my eyes. I was expecting clandestine engagements with Northern barons or plans to join the Maenads and swear off marriage completely.

I guess that explains the drawn features and high mood.

Hormones.

"Right, because what Sovereign wants somebody else's bastard as his firstborn son?" I drawl, the shock of her confession still prickling my veins.

Her eyes finally flick back to mine then and they're full of venom.

Ah, there it is. There's that spine.

"*Not* a bastard—his father promised we'd be married before the birth," she snarls. But then again, her gaze slides off mine, and suddenly, I need answers more than I need to blink.

To breathe.

"Wait, *who* promised?" I bark.

So naive to think that I was deserving of such fairytales. But it is always the fate of glass to break.

"*Who is the baby's father, Sloane?*"

I never register the triumphant expression on her face.

Just try and forget us twice, I fucking dare you.

I don't notice when she leaves or when my phone vibrates against my caddy with a series of back-to-back texts.

Just try and forget us twice, I fucking dare you.

I don't flinch when the hot water runs out and the cascade at my back turns to ice.

Because *Tristan Sinclair Knocking Up Sloane Walker* was *not* on this year's Rox Academy bingo card.

The Pantheon will continue in
Might Die Young

Did you enjoy this book? Please consider leaving a review on Amazon and/or Goodreads!

ABOUT THE AUTHOR

E.J. Campbell is an Aussie who loves caffeine and books, and spends most of her time living in Romancelandia. She chiefly enjoys reading reverse harem romances, especially when they're dark and dirty, contemporary, or fantastical.

She's a firm believer that every kink is sacred, and that romance novels are a beautiful way to let the average reader explore them, safely and unfettered.

Forget Me Twice is her debut novel, the first in her new *Pantheon* series.

Visit
ejcampbellauthor.com/stalk-me
for social links & newsletter sign-up

FIND & JOIN MY FACEBOOK GROUP
THE PANTHEON: E.J. CAMPBELL READER'S GROUP

hello@ejcampbellauthor.com

instagram.com/ejcampbellauthor

facebook.com/ejcampbellauthor

tiktok.com/@ejcampbellauthor

goodreads.com/ejcampbell

amazon.com/author/ejcampbell

pinterest.com/ejcampbellauthor

BOOKS BY E.J.

Imperium in Imperio

A SHARED CRIMINAL UNDERWORLD UNIVERSE

THE PANTHEON

(Reverse Harem Series)

I. Forget Me Twice

II. Carry Your Debt

III. Might Die Young

Curious about the Whitechapel Four?

BLOODY LOVE NOTES

(Serial Killer Whychoose/Poly Duet)

Devil's Night In The White City (Prequel Short)

I. The Bodies Between Us (*Coming soon*)

II. TLWB (*Coming soon*)

www.ingramcontent.com/pod-product-compliance
Lightning Source LLC
Chambersburg PA
CBHW030513120726
47904CB00005B/1446